# STATE OF HORROR

## LOUISIANA

## VOLUME I

# State of Horror Anthology Series

State of Horror: New Jersey

State of Horror: Illinois

State of Horror: North Carolina

State of Horror: Louisiana Volume 1

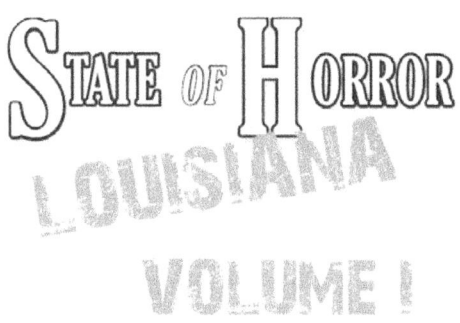

# STATE OF HORROR LOUISIANA VOLUME I

-Edited by-
Jerry E. Benns

CHARON COIN
PRESS

PO Box 478 High Ridge, Missouri 63049

**Charon Coin Press**
PO Box 478
High Ridge, MO 63049
www.charoncoinpress.com

Library of Congress Control Number: 2015935628
ISBN-13: 978-0692400401
ISBN-10: 0692400400

Printed in the United States of America

*"Men fear death as children fear to go in the dark; and as that natural fear in children is increased with tales, so is the other."*

Francis Bacon

# TABLE OF CONTENTS

❋ ❋ ❋ ❋ ❋ ❋

# ACKNOWLEDGMENTS

*State of Horror: Louisiana* has become such a forceful gathering, almost a force of nature in itself, rivaling even the best hurricane parties. What started out as a re-release received so much support from the authors who submitted, it was difficult to contain it in one book. What does one do with an overflow of great tales? This is what contributed to the book in your hands as *State of Horror: Louisiana Volume I.* As we put the book together, I reflected on the importance of the authors' support and talents. I hope you join us in thanking the authors from the previous release who had enough faith to continue with the series and the new authors whose appearances added greatly to the collection of stories. Our thanks go out to all the authors for submitting and making the project enjoyable.

When asked how I do everything, my answer is simple—I don't. Putting the books together is not an individual effort, but that of a team who comes together to create the product you now hold in your hands. I would like to take a moment to thank those who make this all possible. From the amazing cover illustration created once again by Natasha Alterici to the additional promotion assistance by Susan R., we are building a process to bring these projects to life. Thanks to Laura W. for doing what she loves to do, reading and lending her insight into the process.

I have mentioned before how important my dear friend and colleague, Margie C. is to me and this project, but it bears mentioning again how these books would not be possible without her help. Her enthusiasm is a driving force and her efforts can be seen throughout.

I asked myself how I could truly put in words how

much I appreciate all that the next person does to make things happen. Words cannot express fully the level of gratitude I have for my wife, Christine. I would like to thank her for her help with the book and with life in general. As we put this project together, her help kept my world moving forward throughout all the challenges. Thank you for all you do.

Last, but not least, all of us at Charon Coin Press, and the authors from this book, would like to thank you, the reader. Without your love for reading and choice of this book to read, we would not be able to make this happen. It is with our warmest gratitude that we present to you *State of Horror: Louisiana Volume I.*

Jerry E. Benns

# INTRODUCTION

The sun was creeping over the horizon, defining the trees in dark contrast to the lightening sky, all flowing past as the car continues heading south on Interstate 55. The sign ahead at mile marker 66 brings a smile to my weary face, "Bienvenue en Louisiane". After a night of driving, the destination is only a couple hours away, but it does not matter—I am in Louisiana. Soon, I will be driving along the elevated interstate as I cross Lake Maurepas and skirt around the edge of Lake Ponchartrain toward my destination—New Orleans. I have traveled this highway many times on my getaways. Maybe I will travel down Interstate 49 on the next trip and make some stops in Shreveport, Alexandria, and Baton Rouge. There are so many places to explore and history to absorb throughout Louisiana. Of all my travels across the Unites States, Louisiana is the state, outside my own, with which I am most closely connected. Each visit brings new wonder, appreciation, and respect for the uniqueness of the history of Louisiana. As the sun brightens the summer sky and the heat takes hold, I put on my sunglasses and relax in the driver's seat. Yes, "Welcome to Louisiana" is right. The decision to make Louisiana be the next visit on our State of Horror tour was an easy choice.

Before we explore this stop on the tour, let's look at the history that brought us here. *State of Horror: Louisiana*, was originally released in April 2011, and included eight stories. The overwhelming response by authors, as well as the quality stories submitted, left me in a dilemma—how to decide which to keep. The answer became simple—expand the book into two volumes. I went back through the stories with a new goal to seek out the stories that captured the culture, the history, and the feeling I so enjoy from Louisiana. The concept of a state having two volumes for the State of Horror series is the first. This book is just half of the journey on our tour of *State of Horror: Louisiana* with the updated stories from previous authors of the initial 2011 release: Pamela Troy, Sarah Glen, J. Jay Waller, and Henry P. Gravelle. Joining them are eight authors with new tales to tell and another visit to the *Dying Days* world by Armand Rosamilia. Overall, these thirteen stories are the launching point for our Louisiana tour.

As I have mentioned, I enjoy visiting the state of Louisiana. I may have lost count of the number of times I travelled down river from my home in St. Louis to the streets of New Orleans. Whether I arrive on a plane or explore the scenic routes down the interstates, each trip has been met with excitement. This trip is no different.

Recently, I explored a little culture outside the city streets, venturing out into the delta. My explorations took me to the traditional plantation homes as I learned more about the history and culture of centuries past. I spent hours hearing stories of the bayou from our guide, and exploring the Cajun culture and history. The bayous are full of mysteries, folklore, and danger.

While reading the stories selected for this book, I could feel some of the history and lore I had discovered resonating throughout. This is what we seek on our tours with *State of Horror*. The stories will visit the bayou, the parishes, cities, and the streets of New Orleans. Historical figures make appearances as well as historical sites. The stories are each unique in their tales, but connected through the pulse of the state of Louisiana. You can feel the culture and geography throughout. If you have not visited Louisiana, I suggest you do. Until then, explore it with us in these pages. It is time for you begin the tour—it is time to

explore *State of Horror: Louisiana Volume I.*
    "Laissez les bons temps rouler, my friend."

Jerry Benns
State of Horror; Editor

# GOODIE-GOODIE
by Chad McKee

Maxwell Tibbs gaped in surprise, unable to believe what his ears had heard:

"Mr. Tibbs…we're goin' to let you go. I'm sorry."

"What did you say?" Tibbs asked, though he heard the woman as clear as day.

"You're fired." She had her hands on her hips when she said it, as if to emphasize she meant it and the firm set of her lips – thin, rigid – brooked no arguments. But her eyes said different – uncertainty, darting up and down like and side to side like green pinballs.

It was unreal. He had worked for Lafayette's for forty-two years, scratch that bit in the Army. And that had been a short bit indeed. Bad eyes, they told him. And bad attitude. But who was perfect?

"Why…?" But he knew. After four decades, Justin was going to cut the fat from the prime meat. Dump the dregs. Times were hard in the Bayou just like everywhere else, and to be honest Lafayette's was never much more than gas and bait. Not even bait these days, as the Fish and Game people were putting more and more limitations on daily catches. Limits on catfish! They were the cockroaches of the Bayou, as far as Tibbs was concerned.

"He just can't justify having you on anymore, Max" the

woman went on. "With the high-tech equipment and all, we just don't need a handyman roundabout anymore. We've got service contracts on our coolers and for the gas pumps."

Out with Maxwell Tibbs, in with the service contracts. Well, Tibbs had known his days were numbered. Hell, he understood—but he didn't think it was a bunch of city pencil-pushers who would do him in. It seemed like Justin would keep him on just out of nostalgia after forty-two years.

His sentence was being delivered by Justin's daughter, Ruby. She was ringing her hands, just as she always had since she was a little girl and nervous about something. Max was astonished that Justin would send her to do this job. A nasty little part of his mind suspected she was illegitimate, although he couldn't prove it. It was more of an intuition. Her mother had been the catch of South Plaquemines Parrish before Justin tied her down in '64. Even Max had been with her once or twice, before the bottle had started to eat him up, just before Justin swooped in. A rare breed of woman then – *she weren't no catfish*, Tibbs might say.

"Well," he started with his blood coming to a simmer. "Maybe I have outstayed my welcome but you might think Justin himself would deliver the kick in the pants. So…you can just tell that *couillon* he can blow our friendship straight to hell!"

He spat to make his feelings completely clear but regretted it immediately. He had a soft spot for Ruby. Delicate glass, she was. Not a rotten bone in her. Pretty, too, but not in the tall, athletic way of her parents. She was a *petit four* – dainty and sweet. Another reason why he thought she was the product of someone else's loins.

Ruby was shocked. "Come on now, Mr. Tibbs. I know

you understand. This business doesn't make much money. You ain't got no *reason* to get all mad. Father has been good to you all these years."

Tibbs didn't answer, not able to put his anger into proper words around Ruby, and couldn't make himself spit again.

"I'm just going to ignore your anger and tell Father you took the news like a man."

"He didn't have the guts to do it himself, though," Max said, but mostly under his breath, not quite able to say it to her face. "I thought Justin was more of a man than that. You tell him so, too." And he pointed a knobby finger at Ruby's breast. "And that what comes around, goes around. Tell him to chew on that!"

Max's swamp shack redefined "humble" but he liked it just fine anyhow. He lived west of Murtle Grove, deep within a patch of swamp where the homesteads didn't significantly outnumber the amount of dollar bills he kept in his pocket in the best of times. The shack was little more than four tar boards leaning against each other. The roof was a fifth and he might have used a sixth for the entrance had he not found a perfectly usable screen door discarded in the Murtle Grove landfill. He built the floor himself from the wood of felled water tupelo.

Maxwell Tibbs didn't need creature comforts. He prided himself on that. A mattress, soiled from damp and age, was tucked to the corner of his one room apartment. Nudie magazines sat in untidy piles thoroughly read (or, rather, looked at very closely) by Max so many times they no longer had any staples to hold them together. Another corner of the room was a wasteland of empty sour mash bottles, and any other space along the walls not piled under with trash was occupied with his slim wardrobe of plaid shirts and overalls. A wood stove sat in the center of the room; tin piping snaked through to the roof to allow the smoke to escape.

No, wouldn't be in *Home and Gardening* magazine like the plantations in the surrounding county, but it was home all the same.

The first thing Max did when returning from Lafayette's was to grab a bottle of Southern Comfort, the last of his dwindling stock (he often bought whiskey on Friday – payday – and by the next Thursday the three bottles he could afford would mysteriously disappear). The liquor felt good as it smoldered down his gullet. To Max's credit, booze was his only indulgence. These days. Once, it might have been women, but only the nudies kept him company now. An aberrant thought of Ruby rested into his consciousness but he dislodged it with a shake of his head. She was not worthy of such thoughts. Her mother, perhaps, but not her. For some reason, any impure thought of the golden-haired teenager gave him a nauseous turn. From time to time he caught himself giving Ruby a closer eye than was gentlemanly. Just the other day he had given her a bundle of Irises, ashamed after looking at her with such interest.

There had always been something about Ruby. She was nice to him when others were impatient. She didn't comment on his odor, or his drinking, or his lack of education. She made his lunch sometimes—when she was a child, peanut butter and banana, crusts cut off and neatly folded up in those napkins with little floral patterns on them. It was about the only time he even held a fancy napkin in his hands. He knew Nora wouldn't have wasted those on him. Nora never talked to him with respect, even though they had shared a bed on occasion before Justin came along and made an honest woman out of her. A lot of men had their chances before, but that was a secret they all kept from Ruby.

His mind returned to Justin. Max brooded as he made steady progress on the SoCo, occasionally submitting a comment to the empty shack: "Not going to let that *couillon* push me out."

He talked on until he drained the last of the whiskey bottle and sleep threaded its way into his drunkenness. As he dreamt, he tossed restlessly, because those dreams were soaked blood-red with murder and death. When he woke up in the early hours of the morning, he couldn't remember everything that happened. But he knew enough – and the seed of an idea was sown into his subconscious.

◊ ◊ ◊ ◊

The walk to Lafayette's was not a long one, if he took a shortcut through the Deep Bayou, as the locals called it. That was where the soil made its final transformation from merely soggy to proper wetland: a labyrinth of water-embedded cypress with occasional muddy protrusions. Its border could be spied not far from the trail Max took to work on this occasion, though it was buffered with a stretch of woodland. Max took an uncertain path through this copse but after twenty minutes of bushwhacking, reached one of the spots where the earth became more water than soil. With a boat, one could thread between the cypress for a time and eventually obtain a distant view of the seedy collection of shacks and dinghies dotted along that desolate stretch of bayou. From Max's dim recollections – now going on forty years – the colony of hermit-like Cajuns was silent and gloomy. There was a colossal cypress which overlooked the swamp village like a protective mother; he remembered that clearly. Last night it was in his dreams. He fancied he could see its umbrella of hanging mosses from this great distance, just poking above the rest of the trees, but that was only the remnants of his dream playing tricks on him.

The inhabitants of the deep swamp were perceived as degenerate. By the reckoning of average townsfolk, these people were black magic and voodoo practitioners and all crazy as loons. Then again, the townspeople were crazy too, with their peculiar fire and brimstone Catholicism. Max never picked a side in the business of religion and carefully chose not to think about it too much. He was superstitious, of course – he didn't know about voodoo, but the regional tales he heard as a child still haunted him. The demons of a Cajun childhood tended to.

Max usually steered clear of the Deep Bayou, even in the daylight hours. Shady characters in there. He knew a few in passing, mainly because there had been moonshine in the vicinity for years. He was pretty sure the county had broken it up, but it was hard to deter a wetlander with a fat wallet. And moonshine had been good money for decades in these parts. For all he knew, the demons had been created to keep the curious out of the swamps.

Of course, he had also seen the Callers once, or thought he had. That's what Rawley had called them, and Maxwell had seen *something* through the dirty panes of glass of their shack all those years ago. There, on that mudbar, in a rickety pole house raised a few feet above the water, lived people who could call up things that had no place in the modern world of men and machines. They lived in the center of the swamp, apart even from the village that sheltered them. What they could do – if anything – was not completely known, but it was widely believed their magic was real. That's what his buddy Rawley Baker had thought.

But Max tried not to think about Rawley as he trudged on, leaving the Deep Bayou behind. Best not to ponder on such things.

When he emerged from the swamp, his nerves were a little on edge and the feeling of warm asphalt under his feet was more reassuring than usual – a prospect which shamed him. He was a local after all; the wetlands were his home. It didn't matter he had often slept on a mop room cot most nights of the week at Lafayette's – but only because his own home was three miles of walking both ways. Nonetheless, he kept his eyes on the road, which happened to be the only paved stretch of land until reaching the new highway fourteen miles to the north. Its construction was no doubt one reason why he no longer had a job.

*We'll see about that*, Max thought, picking up the gas and bait store as he rounded the county road. Hank Perney was pumping gas into his old International pick-up. As usual, he was sweating like ice in an oven, wiping some of it aside with his grimy bandana. The man was as round as a beet root, and almost as red on a hot summer day. When he saw Max walking up, he smiled good-naturedly.

"How ya' doing there, Max?" he asked.

"Not my best, Hank, if you want to know the truth."

"Sorry ta' hear that." He paused to remove the nozzle of the gas pump from his truck tank. "Any particular reason?"

"You ain't heard yet?"

Hank's brow creased in thought. "Heard what?"

"Justin fired me!"

Hank seemed shocked. "Nah! You been with him for forty years! When he first opened, even."

"Don't I know it! I reckon he finally tired of me. What do you think?"

"Can't ponder a reason. It's a damned shame, though. Where you goin' to go?"

"Don't know," Max said and realized he meant it. He really didn't know how he was going to make ends meet. "I'm fixin' to get that last pay check, you know."

"Hate to see you go."

"Well, Justin is going to be twice as sorry if I don't get some answers!"

He liked 'ol Hank but the man was a little dense. He didn't suspect that Max had been fired even though he was pumping his own gas for the first time in forty years!

The inside of Lafayette's was cool, as it usually was. This was always heaven to Max after stocking or sweeping or shoveling or whatever other piss-ant chore Justin had ready for him.

"Max?"

He wheeled. It was Nora, Justin's wife. She had a thin face, but it wasn't delicate like her daughter's. She was a tall woman, strong and flexible like a leather strap. Her face had only a touch of that old prettiness which made her desirable years ago, but not all was lost to the ravages of time. Max suspected though the grooves of age in her face might have smoothed if she didn't wear that permanent scowl. Always concerned, that Nora. *But only for herself*, thought Max.

"What are you doing here?" Her voice carried irritation, which rubbed off on Max.

"Is it a crime to visit the general store?" he asked acidly.

"No," she said with a measured voice. "But there's always a chance you might come back to cause trouble."

"Easy to imagine, the way I was treated."

"Don't be like that. You do your business and go on."

"I want to see Justin."

Nora's eyes disapproved. "I don't see what for."

"Do I have to spell it out? I want a man-to-man talk. A *powwow*. Where is he?"

Nora folded her arms and passed one of those sighs of exasperation he had heard over four decades. "'Round back." She wagged her finger at him. "But don't you start up trouble!"

Not bothering to answer, he made a direct path for the rear exit. He found Justin lifting crates out of the back of a Ford. He was dripping like a faucet, worse than Hank, maybe. Justin was in his late sixties – Max didn't know exactly – but knew very well he had been developing arthritis in his knees in the last few years. You could see the pain in Justin's stiff, robot-like motions. Max took a little mean pleasure in it, but after a time sympathy nudged it aside. *Dammit, Justin, I could be doing that for you*, he thought.

"How ya' doin,' Old Man?"

Justin didn't even pause. "Passable, I expect." He looked on the verge of fainting.

"Still getting along pretty good?" Max asked with a straight face.

"Oh, yeah, I s'pose."

Still his friend wouldn't look at him. It was enough to make a man angry.

"For Christ's sake, Justin! Would you stop and look at me?"

"Yes, Max? Speak up! How can I help you?" He rested on the tail-gate of the truck, panting. He used the wrist of his work glove as a sweat-sopper. He looked more exhausted than annoyed.

Max stood coolly. "You really don't know?"

"Well, I'm sure you're hot about me letting you go for a time."

"I knew it would come to ya."

"Look," Justin began as he went to sit in the shade for

a bit. Sharp pains were wracking his body. He had a mental image of someone out in the bayou putting pins through his effigy. He glanced over at one of his oldest acquaintances and already regretted firing him. Useless as the man was, he didn't have arthritis and that meant Justin wouldn't have to do all the heavy lifting he's doing now. "Look-y here, Max, it's a money thing. I just don't have the money to pay your wages. You could've kept working, but I couldn't have paid you. You're my friend."

Max considered the argument but rejected it. He would have worked for a bite of supper, a bottle, and a rest-up on the mop-closet cot. That wasn't a lot to ask.

"If that was the case, why'd you get Ruby to tell me instead of yourself? That was embarrassing. I've got pride. Forty years of time in this place gives me a right to respect."

"I was planning to but I was in Port Sulphur the last two days." Justin shook his head, wishing Nora would've handled that task instead of his daughter. There was a strange familiarity between Ruby and his broken-down old friend which he didn't want to encourage. And this business with Max giving her flowers. Ruby had seemed touched, but Justin was disturbed all the same. "Ruby likes you, Max. I think she feels…a sort of kinship with you. Simply put, she beat me to it." He stopped short of asking why. "I'm sure she meant well."

Max liked that. He might have let things rest, but the way Justin wouldn't meet his eye wound him up. It wasn't enough for Max. Not by a long shot. Forty-two years. What was next for him? He remembered his dream from that morning and decided to have a little fun with his longtime friend.

"That's all good and well but I've got my own surprise for you."

"What are you talkin' about now, Max?" Justin asked tiredly.

"I'm talkin' about what you deserve," Max said, then after a theatrical pause, popped it out like a jack-in-the-box: "The Goodie-Goodie. *The Goodie's gonna get ya.*" Max said it like the kids did, low and urgent, with an unpleasant hiss.

The man was startled, that much was obvious. Max enjoyed a highly satisfactory moment when Justin's eyes turned round with terror. The old Cajun even clutched at his chest for an instant. Max thought that look alone might have been revenge enough. But then Justin gave him an eye that would give Death himself pause.

"You can go to hell!"

It was Max's turn to be stunned. Forty years of faithful service and this man was cursing him. Cursing back-broken old Maxwell Tibbs. Suddenly, the dream took on a new urgency. Maybe it made sense after all.

"You'll get there first!" he said venomously and spat in the dirt at Justin's feet. Unlike with Ruby, he felt good about it this time.

He left quickly. He was so mad he didn't return Hank's cheery "Good day!" and in fact didn't really even register the man as he turned purposefully down the road. Yes, purposefully. Max didn't realize until halfway home what he was going to do.

◊ ◊ ◊ ◊

In the swamps of Southern Louisiana, legends were taken seriously. Any folk who lived in the swamp had a favorite devil. The Bayou Catholics had the *Rougarou.* The true wetlanders had the *Goodie-Goodie*—an avenging force for those who called it. You had to have a good reason, like its name implied. Max had a brush with that particular devil. Though he did not experience its dark work in person, he had seen its aftermath. The only real friend he ever had – Rawley Baker – used the forces of the Goodie-Goodie against his own wife. Looking back, it was a terrible deed. Myra was a pretty good woman and Rawley, despite their friendship, was a no good son of a bitch. They had both met a bad end, but for Myra's part the punishment possibly did not justify the means. Like any dangerous tool, the Goodie had to be used properly.

For people who *truly* had wronged you.

The thought rolled over in Max's mind. Did Justin deserve his fate? Did Max have enough justification? He might have still dropped the whole matter but another thing Bayou folk understood was the power of the sub-conscious. More than once in his life, Max had seen plans altered as the result of a dream—marriages called off because of a predicted infidelity, festivals moved to avoid prophesized hurricane floods. In an astonishing event, Rawley's teenage son was killed just a few days after Myra died. Rawley supposedly had dreamt it. The police called it a gator attack and nobody could really dispute it. A spooky coincidence, though. Rawley drank himself to death afterwards, a slow suicide (though many would say that he was just finishing off the job he had been working on for years). Yes, dreams were given a lot of credence in Plaquemines Parrish.

A dream was not always a warning, though. Sometimes it was a suggestion. Max had dreamt of the Goodie the previous night. He had seen the massive tree in the Deep Bayou pier. On the far side of the pier, on an uneven slope of earth, hardly more than a muddy sand bar, was a shack, not unlike his own. A family of people lived in it—he didn't know them by look, their faces were smooth in the dream, indistinct as if being viewed through gauze. He had seen them that one time so long ago. They knew how to call the Goodie-Goodie, that much was clear. They may have been calling Max, touching him through his anger. It was as if his frustration and the remnants of the dream had tied themselves into a rope and were leading him like the call of a siren song. Whatever alarms alive in his mind were being smothered by a new found purpose: revenge.

When he woke the next day, the Callers had him baited like a catfish. Max decided to visit them. Or the Callers had decided that Max would. He couldn't know for certain.

The Deep Bayou could only be reached by boat. Max dragged his dinghy over fifty feet of moist, spongy grass to the tributary that would allow him to access the region. Max, like any sensible local, didn't keep his boat on the side of the peninsula that shared its waters with the Deep. More than once people had found their skiffs sunk or gone altogether if left unattended for any length of time. The people on the Deep side liked isolation and few bothered to fish there, certainly not far in. Alligators prowled the shallows and occasionally took out foolhardy anglers. Rawley's son had found that out. Most preferred to fish in the pond close to Lafayette's.

To go where he needed, a day-lit excursion was the only way. Today the demon would be summoned. An unfounded urgency gripped him – he wasn't interested in having patience or waiting to strike at an unexpected time. When the supernatural was doing your bidding, having an alibi was easy to achieve; you just didn't want to be anywhere in the vicinity of the crime or you might share the victim's fate.

Max guided his boat gently through the marshland. The water was not particularly deep but it was absolutely still. Gators roamed the bottom or floated along like deadly driftwood. He kept eyes out for anything drifting his way but the only thing Max had to dodge were the cypress roots and occasional creeper. The Deep Bayou was more eerie for its odd lack of sound. The Bayou was alive with birds and frogs and other swamp critters. For some reason this stretch of wetland seemed only to produce snakes and alligators in great number. Perhaps all the animals had been eaten, or moved to other regions of the swamp. Max didn't know. It occurred to him suddenly that the Goodie must reside here as well. Nobody really knew what it looked like; a Bigfoot like creature had been rumored, but that was a lack of imagination on the part of the locals, Max thought. He had it on good account the Goodie was long and thin, so it could swim underwater like a snake, but with legs like cypress stalks allowing it to rise above the water to a terrifying height. Long, skeletal arms were used to scoop up its prey. Scissor-like claws were used to eviscerate its victims. Rawley's wife had been killed in such a manner—sliced open and cleaned out, like a fish filleted. No man can do that, the Sheriff had said.

Max began giving the trees a wider berth. Who knew where such creatures spent their time. Were they called from hell or did they reside in the real world, just hidden? He felt conflicting emotions of relief and dread as he coasted into the Deep Pier. No one greeted him. The Pier was a ghost town, completely silent. But not uninhabited, because he saw obscured faces in the shadow of every window of every shack.

There was only one shack he was interested in and it rested on that mudbar. Eventually, he could make out two pairs of eyes glaring at him from the recesses of the hovel: he could still only see their faces faintly, just as it was the first time he had visited. But now he would go inside, not just wait in the dinghy for Rawley to do his thing.

They waited for Max to push his skiff upon the sodden

soil and tie it off before they left the window. He knocked on the flimsy door. A man and a woman of indeterminate age met him. Dour expressions were impressed upon their faces, perhaps permanently. They wore plain dress—worn and colorless blouses and trousers, no shoes. They were expecting him, and nodded a greeting. He returned it, not knowing what else to do. A quick glance around the room revealed little more than tables and wooden chairs arranged in a roughly circular jumble. As if the inhabitants spent much of their time staring into each other's dark visages, perhaps linking hands together to send out their mind control. Max got a chill at the image and tried to blank his mind; he could stay calmer that way.

"Name," the man said in a thick monotone.

Max licked his lips. His throat tightened as if to prevent the words from leaving his tongue. He felt profound dread – *wrongness* – here. Why hadn't he just jumped back into his boat and gone back to his home? He didn't need Justin or Lafayette's. He would get another job, or some sort of assistance. He was an old man. Certainly that counted for something in this country.

But he might as well have been frozen in place. His legs could barely carry his weight, much less pivot and run. A great weight seemed to drape over his shoulders the moment the door had opened.

"Maxwell Tibbs," he managed finally.

Max noticed for the first time implements of destruction leaning in a corner: long knives, machetes, and an axe. One wrong word and he was done for. These were degenerates, the townspeople were right. Absolutely right. He regretted coming, but all was in place now. Soon enough hands were beckoning him deeper into the shack, where shadows dominated. Max went cold, and it wasn't only because the door shut out the bit of feeble sun shining on his back.

Their grimy feet shuffled over the damp wooden floor. Max's work boots made a thudding sound as he followed them. His guides lead him to the back of the shack, which boasted the sole window. Here two more people sat perfectly still at a table without a lamp; indirect sunlight from the windows cast the forms in a hazy illumination. He guessed they were the actual Callers, the ones invading his mind. Max could not easily tell their sex in the weak light or from the androgynous white blouse/dark trouser ensembles they wore. Their eyes were sunken. Two cups and a kettle sat between them. They looked like a pair of propped up corpses pantomiming a domestic scene. *Tea with the Dead,* he thought. Max could had have used a Cajun Tea himself then, the type loaded with spiced rum. That would calm his nerves, which jumped like plucked guitar strings.

When he got close enough, he realized why their eyes looked so deep set—they had no eyes. He didn't know if this was part of the legend or just genetics gone wild. The Deep Swamp was known for inbreeding. His nerve snapped then and he back-peddled, about to politely excuse himself. However, not only was there no light in the tiny cabin, but no way out, either. Arms grabbed him gently but firmly and pulled him closer to the eyeless corpses. Max did not really resist; his two guides could obviously see and were using their eyes to spear him like fish just under the water. They must be the ones who took care of the Callers. Max thought of them as the Keepers.

They almost shoved him into the single chair in front of the unstable table. He could see from a bit of stubble that one, at least, was a man. They were breathing, which was a relief to Max. At least they used oxygen like normal people—they could die like everybody else, too. Both were clearly ancient—so old they were *dry*, and that was something in the Bayou – and sat in waiting for him to say his piece. There was a certain hypnotic quality to the scene. Maybe the corpses were working their mind trick on him again. Gradually, his mind stopped racing and he relaxed. Max's anger suddenly came back in a flash and the clarity of the dream also returned. Words filled his mouth and his grievances were aired. By the time he finished, Max felt almost at home with these Deep Bayou witches. They did not ask what required –it was understood, Max thought. But to make it official, he croaked out: Goodie-Goodie."

There. Done. It was a relief, in a way. Now he could leave, or…

"Blood," said one of the corpses, the one who looked like a woman. Her voice was surprisingly strong, if cold, and heavy. Immovable. She surprised him by moving, and pointed at his arm.

"Blood," Max repeated stupidly. Of course, he would have to make a sacrifice. Like cutting a chicken open on an altar. Cutting your wrist into a cup for a demon to drink. Using all his will power, Max spared a quick glance at the Keepers. They returned his gaze with bug-eyed intensity. He offered his arm out tentatively, hoping they wouldn't simply chop it off with one of those rusty looking axes…

"No," the woman said. "Later."

What did that mean? Jesus, would he have to see them again? Oh, God, oh Lord, he didn't think he could do that.

The Callers were silent though.

One of the Keepers did come over to him. "It's done, Maxwell," he said in a Bayou accent that was at least familiar to his ears. "You can go."

◇ ◇ ◇ ◇

Max could see the ambulance. He could also see there were a half dozen or so locals milling about as well. There was a body bag being lifted onto a stretcher—but he couldn't see who was in it. Just a formless bag, not unlike a black rain slicker. Max had a sudden strong urge to unzip that bag and see for himself.

He watched his hand shake in the early morning sun. Its light was not strong; fall was coming upon the Bayou. It wouldn't affect the temperature much, but a little sun would be lost every day. Long nights in the Bayou were lonely. It struck Max suddenly that he might not be able to show his face much. He didn't think he could be tied to Justin's death, not without evidence, and he had an alibi. Without thinking he clutched at the cut on his leg. He'd done that with own hatchet, just outside of town. There were stitches where the pretty nurse had sewn up the wound, but the painkillers they had given him were long gone.

Max felt a pang—maybe guilt, he didn't know. It made a funny feeling in his gut, hollow somehow, like his actions had removed something vital from the blood. He did his best to shake it off and his stare didn't waiver to the path which led into the Deep Bayou. An appointment with his beloved Southern Comfort was in order. That would fill any holes he might have.

By that evening he was deep into the bottle. The feeling of guilt or resentment or whatever it was had passed, at least for a time. He felt content.

His reverie was disturbed by sounds in the night. Not a rustling brush from an animal or someone passing on the trail. This was several individuals—perhaps an entire group—moving through the Bayou, making good time. Max sat up, unaccustomed to visitors, friendly or otherwise. And the resolute thud of boots somehow did not seem friendly, quite the opposite.

He had barely arisen to peak through a crack in the wall when there was pounding on the flimsy screen door. The thin wood buckled under the blow, heavy and angry.

"Who is it?" he asked.

"Max, open the door," a voice commanded.

It was familiar, that voice – drawled but tight and hoarse.

"Hank," he said hesitantly. "That you?"

"Yeah, it's me. Now open her up or we aim to do it for you."

"We? Who's with you Hank?"

"Open up!"

"No," Max said, but it was more to himself than to Hank. There would be little use in denying them if they really meant to get in. Hank could probably push the door through by simply leaning on it. His only hope was the reluctance of Bayou folks to enter another man's house without permission.

His hopes were dashed when Hank and another town fellow, Luke Burgundy, popped the door in with a fresh crack. Max was so startled he dropped the SoCo bottle he was about to drink from. It didn't break though, only hitting the ground with a hollow thump. More angry faces followed, flashlights playing on Max's eyes like spotlights. He was a captured criminal but he didn't know how he had been caught.

"What's this all about Hank?" he asked the fat man, who was mopping his brow while cradling a shotgun in the other arm. There was no friendliness there.

"Justin was killed," he said. "And don't play dumb on me, Max. He told us you sent the Goodie."

"Oh, Hank, you don't believe that old wives tale! You're a grown man!"

"We know Justin is dead."

"I was at the hospital! Look at my leg, that tells the story. Gator nearly took it off!"

"You were in the Deep Bayou then," said Luke and the others—maybe a half dozen locals—gave half nods as if the facts were plain as day. "Those gators hardly come up this way and your boat's on the wrong side!"

Max uttered a curse under his breath. Had he had not switched the boat over to the dry side? He had been too bewildered by the whole episode at the mudbar. With the booze and the pain pills, his recollections of actions yesterday were a blur.

"You can't deny it. You called the Goodie and it left its mark."

Max told a half-truth: "I don't even know what happened."

"I'll tell you," said another voice. A woman. Oh, Jesus, oh God. It was Nora, looking as tall and lean and intimidating as ever. "He was torn limb from limb. I found his head in the back of the pick-up. You killed him. He told me you was going to call the Goodie!"

"But that's nonsense. I was just funning. Everybody knows it's just a legend. What's the proof?"

Hank put a reassuring hand on Nora's shoulder. The woman had begun to cry, quick, haltering sobs. "The proof is that the Goodie always takes your own blood along with the victim. That's why only a fool would call it."

Max pointed to his leg absently, forgetting his defiance momentarily.

"No," Nora said. "Not your blood. Your kin's blood. You took your own daughter down with Justin."

"What?"

"Ruby's dead, you bastard! Ruby's dead. It ripped her apart, too! We couldn't even find all of her!"

Max sat back down on the bed, dazed. The whiskey in his stomach was churning—he thought it would be up his throat and out onto Hank's shoes if he didn't get a grip of himself.

"That would mean…"

"That's right. Ruby was yours. We all suspected, even Justin, but nothing was said about it. But you always did give that girl queer looks. That's why Justin was rid of you. Thought you might do something to her one day. And you did!"

"I would never…never," Max said but his speech faltered under the eyes of the lynch mob. He made his best defiant face. "You're all wrong. And you're going get yours if you try to lay this on me. I really *will* call the Goodie!"

"No you won't," said Luke, who raised a rope. "You're not going anywhere but up that cypress out front."

"No," Max strangled out. "This is just a dream. Part of my dream!"

Hank shook his head "No dream, Max. You don't play with things you don't understand."

As he was dragged out of his house to the tree, Max was reminded that the people of the Bayou took dreams seriously and often weighed legends as truth. As the rope was fitted around his throat and he was hoisted into the air by the enraged mob, Max thought he could see a demonic shape in the Deep Bayou. The image was brief—spots were filling his vision—but was it the Goodie just beyond the trees, laughing? Or just the witches in the Deep Bayou? As the rope mercilessly lifted higher and higher, he thought he could see two bodies in a dinghy, watching. A younger man and just maybe, a woman. Plain clothes and no shoes. Neither of them moved, but one of them held something across its lap.

An axe. And probably from a certain old pole house in

the Deep Bayou.

In his dying breathes, Max realized maybe he had things all wrong, after all. The Callers were actually the Keepers. And that the Bayou folks had the wrong idea about what the Goodie-Goodie looked like. He didn't know what Rawley Baker's son had seen when it was all over. Maybe it was gators. Maybe there was a monster which could lift itself above the trees to take its victims.

Or maybe the Goodie could look like a man or a woman. Hiding in plain sight. Biding its time, sitting in that little circle of chairs in the parlor of the shack on the lonely mudbar, waiting for the next victim pass under its window…

# RISEN
by Pamela Troy

There is a picture of it in a book I found recently about plantation houses. The text doesn't mention any ghosts, though in the photo taken in 1935, the place certainly looks haunted—a gray derelict with peeling Corinthian columns and shattered or boarded up windows. According to the book, a wrecking ball brought it down the year after the picture was taken. Almost all that's left, more than seven decades later, are the foundation and the name –"Risen." I can't say for sure any ghosts remain, but I think it likely. In the south, there are dead who won't rest until the soil they tilled is sown with salt.

In 1965 I was only eight, an age when the preparations for a journey are mysterious, off-stage, and unimportant, so the memory for me begins with us turning off the broad highway onto a two lane road. The road narrowed, became a single-lane truck track filled with shell-gravel, and my father slowed the car to a crawl, while Mother winced at every bump. I sat in the back seat, my comic book forgotten, and watched wet vines slap the windows, listened to the sound of gravel hitting the bottom of the car.

This was, my mother had told me as we loaded the car that morning, an adventure, which was her way of selling us leaving our brick ranch-house in Slidell for three weeks while the workmen finished up on the remodeling. Tank Caskey had been kind enough to lend us his family's summer house so Dad could finish the last draft of his latest book without being distracted. "It's no trouble," Tank had told my parents while they sipped Old Fashioneds on our back patio. "We never stay there this time of year anyway."

He was one of my parents' set, young, clever, and successful, a liberal, a Bridge player and an athlete. I remember Tank as a slender man in tennis whites, so dark-haired and hirsute that his arms and legs looked slightly blue. We would be staying where Tank and his family used to live year-round oh, about a hundred years ago, in a real plantation house! But the big house was all gone, and what was left was a summer cottage built on its foundations, so I mustn't be disappointed, mustn't expect anything like Tara in *Gone with the Wind*.

Still, I sat up and strained for a glimpse of columns and balconies over the treetops when Dad slowed the car to a stop, got out, and swung open a low metal gate next to a hand painted sign that read simply, "Risen."

What we saw a few minutes later when the trees suddenly fell away was a broad clearing of long blowing grass and, across it, a modern looking two-storied wooden building painted a pale green and accented with dark brown shutters. Behind it was a bulging cloudbank of trees gloomy with Spanish moss. As the car moved along the road that curved around the clearing, I noticed that the house seemed to be sitting on a table of land, an irregular, flat-topped rise that was probably the outline of the old foundation.

"So here we are," Dad said, as we pulled up into the patch of gravel next to the little brick patio that fronted the house. And he turned to smile at me. "This is our home for the next three weeks. How do you like it?"

"Thank God we picked up some groceries," was all Mother would say.

"It's in a jungle," I said, looking around at the trees that surrounded the clearing, and Dad laughed.

The inside of the house was like most weekend places – slightly musty and filled with gray daylight and frayed, second-best furniture. The kitchen smelled faintly of cooking gas, there was a living room/den with a TV and sofa, and the upstairs, where the bedrooms were, had a dark interior hallway with an ashen out-door wall-to-wall carpet. My bedroom was empty of everything but a narrow bed, a baby's crib pushed up against one wall, a chest of drawers, and a throw rug the size of a bath towel that was more of a hazard than a decoration on the slick linoleum floor. What thrilled me was the window over my bed. "I can see everything!" I called to my parents as I stood on the bed and looked out, my elbows on the sill. "I can see the whole world!"

"That's nice!" my mother called back from the kitchen, where she was loading cans into cabinets.

My father, who was setting suitcases down in the room next to mine, came in behind me. He set his hand on my shoulder, looked out the window, and let out a long whistle. "Carol!" he called. "Come up here. She's right!"

There are valleys even in the Mississippi Delta, where the land slopes gently down towards where water has cut its way through the soft, shallow landscape. From where we stood, we could see that we were on what passes for high ground in Louisiana. There was the clearing, and beyond that, the trees, so thick they might have been a single mass of leaves, with no sign of the road that cut through them to the highway. They diminished, growing smaller with the downward curve of the land, and visible far beyond them was a treeless expanse of pale grass, dark stumps, solitary bushes and the black cockeyed skeleton of an occasional dead tree. This ended with the levee, rising sharply like swollen skin around a scar, curving across the horizon to mark the path of the river beyond it.

We'd arrived late on a damp afternoon, so I didn't go outside. I spent that first afternoon and evening trying the reception on the TV, which was snowy but serviceable, and making some houses out of a deck of sticky playing cards I found in the cabinet under the TV. Dinner that night was boiled shrimp we'd picked up at some little highway market on our way in, and afterwards my parents played gin rummy behind me on the sofa, while I lay on my stomach and watched TV. It was to be like most of the nights we would spend at Risen, closed in by the sound of crickets and frogs and the occasional long burp of a distant gator.

The next morning, Saturday, I awoke to a blaze of sunlight and riot of chirping birds. I stood up on my bed and looked out the window to blink at a sky so clear and blue it hurt my eyes, the leaves glittering like coins beneath it. "You'll have to stay close to the house until Laura gets here," my mother told me while I ate cereal in the kitchen. "You're not to put one foot outside the front yard by yourself, do you hear me?"

It was while I was upstairs tying my shoes that I heard a sound that made me stop and listen. The dull thud of galloping horse's hooves was drawing closer and closer to the house. They slowed to a walk, then a stop, and I heard voices just beneath my window. As soon as my shoe was tied, I leapt onto the bed and looked outside to see a black girl astride a red horse. She was talking to my mother, while

Mother patted the horse's nose. I leapt off of the bed and ran downstairs.

From my first glimpse of Laura Renfro smiling down at me from that mare I was smitten. She was probably no more than fifteen, very slender, and blacker than anyone I'd ever seen before in my life, so black I thought she looked like a shadow. Laura wore a faded pink T-shirt and jeans cut off just above the knee. Her long legs looked as shiny and hairless as onyx and her sockless feet were shod in dirty but elegant narrow-toed Keds. Her head was very round, her hair done up in three short, tight, kinky braids. "Want a ride?" she asked.

"But there's no saddle!" my mother said. It was true. Laura was riding bareback, and the bridle looked like little more than a creatively tied hank of rope.

"We won't go fast. I promise." She said, and she reached down to offer me a hand with a tender looking pink palm.

"Well, what are you waiting for?" Mother asked me. I took the hand, was lifted easily up onto the horse's broad back and plunked behind Laura.

"Now you hang on," she said, and I clung tightly to her waist. She clucked her tongue and the horse turned and began to walk slowly about the yard, while Laura kept up a line of chatter that soon caused me to relax and look around and occasionally giggle. The horse's name, I learned was Obliging Dolly, and she was a sweet old gal. Laura's favorite comic book was Wonder Woman. The small piles of clay visible in the grass were crawdad holes, and it was very dumb for little girls like me to stick their fingers in them.

After Laura got tired of riding, she slid off Obliging Dolly and lifted me down and we walked about on foot, the horse following us and cropping the grass nearby.

There was a tire swing in the side-yard and when we grew bored with swinging on that, Laura showed me a honeysuckle bush and taught me how to suck the nectar from the flowers. We sat on the back porch and I learned some clapping games, Ol Mary Mac, Three-Six-Nine, and Doctor Kildare. My mother sat nearby and read, and my father's typewriter tapped away in an upstairs room. At lunchtime, Laura said her good-byes, swung herself onto the mare's back, and cantered away while I stood and waved until she'd vanished down the road into the trees.

"So, how do you like Laura?" Mother asked.

"She's wonderful!" I exclaimed, as I listened to the sound of Obliging Dolly's hoofs fading.

On weekday mornings at Risen, I would get up even earlier than usual and eat breakfast in the cramped kitchen while it was still dark outside. Once I was fed, dressed, and combed, I would be led, still drowsy, out to the car and mother would drive me through that windshield-slapping tunnel of trees, and down the two lane road back to the highway. By the time I was awake and the sun was up, we would be turning off into some white bedroom community that had a school bus stop to Slidell Grammar, where we would wait together for my ride into town.

It seemed odd to me that my days were perfectly normal, the same old desk at school, the same old teachers, the same old friends at the playground, while my evenings were spent in a house that had a name and sat smack in the middle of a jungle. Returning to Risen in the late afternoon was like walking slowly into the deep end of a pool, the strangeness steadily rising from the suburb where I got off the bus, to the long drive with Mother to a place which had no sidewalks, no 7-11s, no sliding glass doors. Instead, there were just trees and water and Spanish moss. Round, silent Ruby, Laura's mother, was always waiting with Kool-Aid and cookies set out for me, just as she did at home in Slidell, but I was in her neighborhood now. I ate with my head down, unbearably shy, listening to the soft patter of rain which always began in the afternoons and continued into a night so thick with bugs that the legs of our beds rested in saucers filled with poison. The rainfall seemed to make my father slightly anxious, and once he went upstairs to the bedrooms to look out the windows with his binoculars, frowning as he peered through the failing light to the levee far in the distance.

One Friday night the TV died, blinking out in the middle of a movie my father was watching, and failing to respond to his thumps and curses.

The next day, Laura rode over on Obliging Dolly at a little before noon, and after trying vainly to get the TV to work for several minutes, flopped back onto the sofa, crossed her arms and stared at the blank screen, obviously thinking. I sat next to her, watching and trusting and then disappointed she'd been unable to work her magic on the TV so we could watch the morning cartoons. Laura seemed to make a decision. She looked at me and tweaked one of my long braids. "How'd you like to meet my brothers and sisters?" she asked.

Mother looked skeptical when we went into the kitchen to ask her permission, but she'd been impressed with Laura, and had an admiration for Ruby which bordered on awe. "You won't be scared?" she asked me. I shook my head. Mother crouched so that her face was level with mine and looked deep into my eyes. "And you'll be polite? You'll be very, very, very, very, very, very, *very* polite?"

Laura laughed, and I nodded, looking as grave and

sincere as I could. "She'll be good," said Laura. "I'll see to that."

"All right," Mother said. "But she needs to be back by 4:00. She's going out to dinner tonight with us." She gave Laura some money, telling her to treat herself and her siblings and me to some lunch.

When I realized I would be going back with Laura on Obliging Dolly, I had second thoughts. Riding the horse while she walked around the front yard had been one thing, but galloping off at the speeds I'd seen Laura reach when she rode into the yard was another. Much to my relief, Laura set me not behind her, but in front this time, her arms on either side of me. "If you get scared," she said, "you hold onto the mane, you hear? I'm not going to let you fall."

For much of that ride, which probably never rose above a canter, I kept my eyes firmly closed, convinced that Laura was going to be leaping the horse over fences and other hurdles like riders did in cowboy movies. In spite of this, I never felt the urge to grab hold of the mane, and never even came close to tumbling off. There was much swishing of grass and clopping over firm ground. Occasionally we would slow to a walk. The horse never jumped, to my mingled disappointment and relief, and when Laura said, "Here we are!" I opened my eyes.

The house was wooden and huge and innocent of paint, dark gray and set high off the ground with concrete blocks. It had a porch, two stories, and a chimney. There was a cleared dirt area in front of it where a pickup truck was parked, and I could see black people on the front porch, older and younger, taller and shorter, watching us as we approached. The younger ones let out a whoop and ran up to us. When Obliging Dolly stopped and Laura slid off, she lifted me down into a crowd of children. "She's visiting with us today," she said, after introducing me.

I wish I could say that I could remember all of their names, but I can't. There was Tommy and Lucrece, and Petite, and Franko, and Feef, but they all blend together in my mind. As we walked to the house, they asked so many questions that I forgot to be self-conscious, preoccupied as I was with just trying to get a word in so I could answer. Occasionally one of them would reach out to lightly touch my hair, something I took as a compliment. The house itself was, I now saw, not quite as remote as Risen. It was surrounded by the woods on three sides, but on the fourth was a two-lane highway.

Ruby was standing on the front porch, along with three tall, unsmiling young black men, Laura's older brothers. As we approached I realized, with shock, that Ruby was smoking a man's pipe.

I suppose there are people who would have called Ruby fat, though that term never occurred to me in connection with her. Fat to me meant soft, and there was nothing soft about her. She was broad and tall and solid and she always looked angry. This did not change as she gazed down at me from that front porch, flanked by her slender but equally grim-looking sons. She removed the pipe from her mouth and said something to Laura in a liquid, rapid language that I couldn't understand. Laura responded in the same language, resting one hand on my shoulder.

"You be good," Ruby said to me. I nodded, as I always did when Ruby said this. "We're going to town to get hot-dogs," Laura said, and the children around me cheered.

"What I said," Ruby snapped down at me, before putting the pipe back in her mouth.

"I will!" I squeaked.

"Town" was not far down the highway. We walked alongside it, Laura in the forefront, the rest of us frisking behind her in a babbling, skipping, crowd.

They called town "La Place," after the name of the general store that seemed to be its center. We didn't stay long, but I remember a narrow, dusty main street and covered sidewalks. The buildings were wooden, and what paint was left was white and flaking. There were rusty signs for 7-Up and RC Cola, and the dark interior of a shop that smelled of salt meat and onions. The old black woman who handed Laura the hot dogs and sodas stared hard at me and erupted into that same bubbling language I'd heard Ruby use. Laura responded with a word or two in the same tongue and a pert toss of her head that made the other children laugh and pat me on the shoulders. We walked back to the house in that same skipping parade and settled down on its front steps to enjoy our lunch. Ruby and her older sons were nowhere in sight.

Laura held court on that front porch. She decided what clapping games we would play after we ate, what songs we would sing, and she refereed the game of tag I played with her younger brothers and sisters. At some point, after we'd collapsed dusty and exhausted on the steps to rest, one of the little boys leaned forward to jab me gently on the shoulder with one finger. "You're in the old white man's house, ain't you?" he asked.

"The *wicked* old white man!" corrected a little girl.

I must have looked blank because suddenly they all began crowing with amazement, "You don't *know*? You've never heard of the *wicked old white man*? Laura, tell her! Tell her about the house and the wicked old man!" They then fell silent, and Laura rose from her seat on the front steps and stepped down into the dirt yard.

"There once…" She spoke in a hushed voice, one finger raised her eyes very serious and on me. "There once was a wicked old white man who lived in the big house high, high up on the ground," she said. "He was a greedy old man, a rich old man who had a roomful of gold coins and he would go there and run his hands through them and laugh because he had taken it away from poor people who lived low to the ground. He was a *wicked* old white man…" ("Wicked, wicked!" cried the other children.) "and he carried a whip and a gun and if you talked back to him he whup-whup-whupped you until you were bloody and if you talked back to him *again* he'd shoot you dead!"

"One day it began to rain. It rained, and it rained and it rained, and the water got higher, and higher and higher. And the wicked old white man thought, 'That water's going to drown me! What will I do?' So what did he do? He walked down to the levee and then looked at it and the thought and he thought and he pulled out his whip and his gun. And he went walking. And every poor man he met he would point his gun and say, 'Come with me.'"

"And soon he had a whole mess of poor men marching in front of that gun. And he walked them to the levee and he said, 'Get to work.' Now, the poor men, they knew that it was no use. The water was getting higher and higher and they could work and work and it would still get higher. 'Mister,' they cried, 'let us go home carry our children to high ground.' He shook his head and cracked his whip. 'Mister,' they cried, 'let us go home and tell our families to run to high ground.' He shook his head and he shot his gun. And they got to work. But the water got higher and higher."

"'Lay down.' the wicked old white man said. 'Lay your bodies down on top of the levee or the water will take everything.' And he shot his gun in the air and they lay down one on top of the other. But the water kept rising. And when the old white man saw that, he up and run as fast as he could. And before anyone could stand up and chase him and catch him the water rolled over all those poor men and they drowned."

The old white man ran and ran and ran and got to his house and slammed the door.

But all those poor people who lived low to the ground, they saw the water rising too late because the wicked old white man wouldn't stop to warn them. And that water, it was all full of dead men and fish and snappers and snakes and gators. And the people had to try to run in the water that was rising and some of them got et up by the alligators, and some of them got bit by the snakes. And when the water hit an ant-heap, those ants, they would all hang onto each other in a ball, and the first thing they touched in that water, living or dead, they'd boil over and bite, bite, *bite* and they'd run right up the arms of the women who held their babies high out of the water, and they got bit and et up, and the little children whose heads were too low, they got drowned, and they were all trying, trying to get to that house, that house set high to the ground…"

We didn't see Laura's oldest brother come out to the porch. We just heard him behind us say her name and let loose with a long, angry string of foreign-sounding words which silenced Laura in mid-sentence, her arms still over her head to demonstrate a desperate woman holding an infant in high water. The young man stood on the porch with his hands in his pockets, his narrow, handsome face set with the cold rage that seemed to be his and his mother's normal expression. He concluded whatever he was saying with a statement in English that was apparently addressed to Laura though he was now looking at me. "She is a guest," he said.

There was a moment of silence. Laura slowly lowered her arms. Then she giggled, and the children tittered and nudged each other. Her brother still stood, his eyes on her, and she sighed and flopped her arms in a helpless gesture. "Well, then the story's over!" she said.

I glanced back at her brother. He was looking at me again. "It's time to get you back to your folks, I think," he said. "I'll ride you in the truck. Laura will come with us."

◊ ◊ ◊ ◊

Honey Devereaux was a small, husky-voiced, Shetland pony of a woman with long dark-blonde hair tumbling over her shoulders, beautiful, heavy-lidded green eyes, and a slow drawl that always sounded slightly sarcastic. She worked at the university in my Father's department, doing historical research, I believe. We met her that night in Slidell at the Broussard House, a fancy place where I had to wear a dress and "be a little lady," as my mother said. Over dessert, Mother observed affectionately that I was being very quiet and good. "But then," she said, smiling at me, "I think our Amy's a bit tired. She spent the whole day running around with Ruby's children."

"They came to Risen?" Honey seemed surprised.

"She went to visit them."

Honey went from being surprised to amazed and stared at me with widened eyes. "You went to Caskeyville?" she asked.

"No, I went to a town called La Place," I said.

"Same thing, though if you're smart, you'll never call it Caskeyville in front of Ruby or her family, or anyone else from there." She shook her head in wonder. "If you were invited, I hope you understand what a compliment that is."

"What do you mean," asked my father.

"White people don't go there. White people aren't welcome." Honey sat back and looked at my father. "You can't blame them."

"Well, all those troubles last year in Mississippi…"

"Nuh *uh*, Henry, nuh *uh*. Worse than that. Don't you know?"

"I guess not," Dad said. "What's the story?"

"Oh it was a terrible scandal!"

"Honey," my mother laughed, "get to the point. Tell us what happened!"

Honey stubbed out the cigarette she'd been smoking and folded her arms on the table with the air of someone who planned to be talking for awhile. "The Easter Flood of 1925," she said. "A bad, year for rain. The river got higher and higher and it began to be pretty plain that the levee wasn't going to hold, and so the Red Cross decided they needed to get everyone out – everyone being the coloreds who lived there. Problem was, it was Caskey's property, and Caskey wouldn't let the Red Cross in. It was all about labor, you see, all about the folks who picked his cotton. Caskey knew that if they were taken away, they might never come back to farm his land, and then where would he be? So he blocked the way, literally, I mean, he had the sheriff and his deputies with guns guarding the area so nobody could get in. And of course, the poor coloreds couldn't get out past those guns any more than anyone could get in."

"It's not really clear exactly what happened next because, of course, he and the other whites wouldn't say afterwards, but the Red Cross never got there, the levee busted on the night before Easter Day, and scads of the coloreds died, drowned like rats. Of course, the world being what it is, Caskey himself didn't get washed away, but I understand almost a whole Negro town disappeared. Caskeyville is what's left of the survivors. The story is that there's a mass grave now where the old town was. The new one is on higher ground. And let's just say it's not a place where Caucasians are appreciated."

"Tank never mentioned it," said Mother.

My father shook his head. "That's not surprising. It's a Hell of a thing to live down."

"Poor Tank," Mother said. (Honey clicked her tongue with contempt.) "Now, he can't help what his Granddaddy did, can he?" Mother's voice was gently reproving. "And I think it was very nice for him to let us stay there. Over a holiday, too."

"They never spend Easter there," said Honey.

"What do you mean?" asked Dad.

"Tank and Doreen Caskey. They never spend Easter at Risen. Nor did Tank's parents. Ever."

My Mother glanced at me, and then laughed. "Well of course not," she said. "It's a *summer* place."

◊ ◊ ◊ ◊

The rain began again on Wednesday afternoon and showed no sign of stopping for the next three days. This time it was not a gentle pattering fall that came only during the evening, but a steady downpour which would sometimes stop for a couple of hours, then resume. The ride to and from school became a slow, sloshing ordeal, and while Ruby was there every afternoon, I never did see Laura again. Mother began to get worried about the levee, but Dad told us, at dinner one night, we had nothing to worry about. He'd telephoned the Caskeys and been assured that the Risen property had withstood far worse storms and even a bad break in the levee. "I didn't tell him we knew that," he said, smiling. Still, he seemed relieved when Friday morning was clear and sunny. "Looks like we'll have a pretty Easter," he told me.

On Saturday morning, the rain was back, very light and intermittent, but with an ominous rustling of the treetops and an angrier, darker cast to the sky. "Oh well," Dad sighed. "Looks like the Easter Bunny will have to stay inside."

The weather got steadily worse. I spent the day playing double solitaire with Mother and drawing pictures with her in her sketchpad. The wind did not pick up, but the rain sometimes came down in sheets, and there were distant rumbles of thunder. At nightfall I heard my parents talking very quietly and seriously in the kitchen. Their conversation stopped when I came in, and they both seemed to make an effort to be unconcerned afterwards. They needn't have bothered, because I wasn't scared. I was used to storms, had even been through a hurricane and regarded it as an adventure.

So we spent the evening playing board games and dyeing eggs and had a dinner of Irish stew on the little table in the kitchen. I went to bed excited about the eggs and sweets I knew my parents were hiding downstairs, and about the bigger egg hunt later when we would drive out for an Easter brunch with some friends. Occasionally there would be a gust of wind which rattled the windows. For a while I lay awake, my heart thumping in anticipation of tomorrow's holiday, but I eventually dropped off to sleep.

I'm not sure what time it was when I was awakened by a flash and a peal of thunder which shook the house. I lay with my eyes opened, exhilarated by the roar of the storm. After a moment, I stood up, hefted my blankets around my shoulders, and gazed out the window.

At first I could hardly see anything because of the water running down the glass, but then a flash of lightening that revealed for an instant the pitching treetops, the silhouette of the levee off in the distance. I drew in my breath, delighted, and rested my elbows on the sill. Thunder roared, shaking the house again.

Another flash and I looked harder, waiting for another bolt. Something was different about the stretch of clear land between levee and the trees. Something moved on it. The next flash bewildered me. What I'd seen rolling and shining there in the wasteland had made no sense to me, and I shifted my gaze to the treetops, to our yard. Another bolt of lightning revealed something which almost made me shout in surprise and I let the blanket drop from my shoulders as I gripped the windowsill.

What I glimpsed in those two instants were, people, black people. They were staggering out of the woods, struggling through the storm towards our house. In one flash I saw a white-haired man, his arms around a hunched woman, in another, a figure with a fringed shawl which blew and glowed bright red in the lightening, and all around them were many more than that, people moving, falling, some carrying burdens that they clutched close to their chests, some with empty arms outstretched as the rain and wind pelted them and water rushed around their legs. I heard a steady rumble beneath the thunder. I heard voices, snatched by the wind, wails, screams...

I don't remember jumping from my bed and running from the room. All I know was I pounded downstairs and hurled myself towards the kitchen door, ready to throw it open. My father grabbed me just before I reached it and jerked me back with a roughness which shocked me.

I shouted, "There are people out there."

He shook me and yelled, his voice cracking with fury, "There is nobody out there!" But I felt his arm reach around me and heard him lock the kitchen door.

"Oh my God, oh my God," my mother was saying somewhere in the darkness.

"The windows," my father said in a voice that was only slightly above normal. He stood up now, holding me tightly in his arms, the same way I'd seen the people outside holding their burdens.

"They are closed," my mother said breathlessly, "They are locked."

"The levee is breached." He looked at me and shook me slightly, "Do you understand? There has been a flood. It may come in here. We need to go upstairs." I expected him to put me down, but he didn't. Instead, he carried me upstairs, Mother following close behind us.

We sat huddled in the darkness on the bed in my parents' bedroom, Mother and Dad on either side of me. I don't believe we even tried to switch on the bedside lamp. As we listened to the storm, we began to hear something else, something that made my mother tighten her grip on me. It was a rattling, a beating against the sides of the house downstairs, the sound of the door being shaken, the windows and walls being pounded.

"The water," my father murmured. My mother made only a faint sound in response.

There were the flashes and the thunder and the wind, and that low, steady roar, and the pounding, but worse than any of that was what I knew my parents would never admit. Worst of all were the voices. There were a few instances when frightened wails, angry shouts, words I couldn't understand in that same bubbling language I'd heard in La Place, drifted up to us over the storm, as brief and lucid as the lightning which showed how white my father's face had gone. After a while, I buried my face and covered my ears. I pressed my cheek against my mother's chest and thought of the filthy water filling the rooms downstairs, dyed eggs bobbing as snakes wriggled past and ants swarmed up the walls. Surely we were safe here; surely the water wouldn't rise so high, but what of the things which lived in it? Would there be alligators and snakes on the floor around our bed?

Would spiders and ants come seeking a dry warm place? I waited, and eventually the storm seemed to merge into one long cacophony, punctuated by thunder. All I could do was listen and keep my eyes closed.

◊ ◊ ◊ ◊

When I opened my eyes to the morning light, I was lying alone in the center of the bed, the blankets tucked firmly around me. Downstairs, I could hear my parents' voices.

Cautiously, I raised my head and looked around. Everything seemed normal. The floor was apparently dry and there was no sign of wildlife. With some effort, I disentangled myself from the blankets and stood up on the bed to look out the window at what Easter morning had brought us.

There was the sun and the blue sky and a landscape reflecting it, and it made me blink. From the levee to the woods was water, and in the forest a silvery mirror flashed beneath the branches. The clearing around our house was unflooded except for the usual road puddles when it rained, but it did not look normal. Scattered from the tree-line right up to the house was a strange litter, bits of cloth, dark, tangled looking objects, a few long, pale, smooth rods in the glittering grass, one or two things that looked like water smoothed rocks.

After a couple of experimental taps with one foot, I stepped onto the floor. I heard the sound of footsteps coming up the stairs, and after a moment my mother came into the room. Her face was white and haggard, her eyes set in deep hollows, and she pulled her lips back in an attempt at a smile. "Aren't you ready to go look to see what the Easter Bunny brought?" she asked.

I followed her downstairs. The first floor was exactly as I'd seen it before we'd gone to bed the night before. With one difference – a beautifully decorated Easter basket rested on the coffee table, filled with a huge chocolate bunny and some malted milk eggs.

"Where's Daddy?" I asked.

"He's gone outside to look around," Mother said. "Let's just stay inside for now and hunt for Easter eggs."

It was the strangest, most silent and solemn Easter egg hunt I ever undertook. Mother sat on the sofa and smoked a cigarette while I searched, and every now and then I would come over and show her one of the eggs. The sun was streaming in, but when I walked towards one of the windows my mother very sharply called me back.

"Why can't I look out?" I asked.

"Because it's a mess," she said.

I'd found all the eggs and had settled down at the kitchen table to eat a couple of malt balls and examine my takings when Dad came in. He seemed tired, but less shaken than my mother. After pausing for a moment to wish me good morning and exclaim over my Easter basket, he went over to my mother and spoke quietly with her. "I cleared away what was closest to the house," he said, "I'm not touching anything else if I can help it. Did you call the Sheppards about the brunch?"

"The phone doesn't work."

"Oh well."

It was Laura's brother who rescued us. We heard tires and a motor and ran out to the kitchen porch, only to realize that the sound was coming from behind the house. As we watched, the truck emerged from the back, moving with agonizing slowness. He did not pull all the way into the yard, but stopped the truck and walked over to us, carefully edging around the litter.

"We were worried about you folks," he said. He wasn't smiling, but he didn't seem angry anymore. "You need a ride away from here?"

"The car's working fine," Dad said. "I tried it an hour ago and the motor turned over without any trouble. But if you could show us a way out that's not under water, I'd appreciate it."

So we packed up our things and loaded them into the car one week earlier than we originally planned. Dad and Laura's brother kept talking quietly and then stopping every time I came near. After almost everything was in the car, I said I'd forgotten something in my room and ran upstairs. Once in my bedroom, I carefully cracked the window and sat on the bed for a moment, listening to the conversation outside.

"...the burial ground," Laura's brother was saying. "It's happened before. The water table's so high here."

"Well, I've heard about that kind of thing, no doubt about it," Dad said. "Maybe you should move them so those poor souls can rest in peace."

"Maybe so," Laura's brother said, "maybe so. Once you folks have cleared out, we'll come in and clean up. It's a pity your wife and little one had to go through this."

"I moved some of them this morning. They'd washed right up to the door. I hope that's all right."

I stood on the bed and slowly straightened up so I could look over the sill. Just below I could see Dad talking to the black man next to our car. They were too engrossed in their conversation to notice me. I swept my eyes beyond them, at the yard.

The objects were still scattered across the clearing, though this time I noticed that there were several piles I hadn't noticed when I first woke up, carefully arranged in a row just beyond the marks of the old foundation. This was,

I suspect, what my father had moved that morning while I was searching for Easter eggs. They looked to me like bundles of sticks wrapped in rags. On one of them, I could make out a bright red pattern and what remained of a fringe.

We drove away from Risen slowly in our car, following the truck through a dirt road in the back we'd not noticed before, the road to higher ground and Caskeyville. Once we reached the highway, Laura's brother raised one arm out of his truck window and my father sped up and passed him, raising his own hand in farewell and thanks. On our way home, my mother pointed out to me a car being towed. It was caked with brown from the top of the wheels down. "See?" she said, "It got caught in the flood. That's how high the water was." I didn't ask her why our own car did not have a similar waterline.

The Caskeys were never invited to our house after that Easter, though I did sometimes hear their names and see them at other people's parties. My parents were cordial and correct with them, but there was always the faint sense of forgiveness withheld. I don't think it was the Caskey's past they resented so much as the conviction that Tank had placed us in harm's way.

Only once did I ever hear either of my parents refer to Risen again, and that was in a conversation my father had some years later with a friend who worked at Tank Caskey's Real Estate firm. It had been another bad year for rain, and Andy was worried about the levee breaking. He was afraid some files Tank was storing for him at Risen might get ruined.

My father shook his head, his lips compressed. "I

wouldn't worry about the files," he said, in a voice that had only a faint edge to it. "No matter how bad it gets, Risen never floods. Come Hell or high water, that place stays as dry as a bone."

# STEALING SIGHT
by Tommy B. Smith

For most people, it was just another Saturday night. The woman in the gray hat and dark trench coat sat in the Old Absinthe House on the tourist-clogged stretch of Bourbon Street and kept her head down while she watched the green fairy dance in her glass.

It wasn't every day that she wandered back to the streets of the French Quarter, but it inevitably drew her back as it did many others who were curious for a taste of its dark heart, though her visits were of another nature altogether. She had tasted that darkness, but what she sought here was rather the light of illumination.

Few, if any, recognized her. None here knew her born name. Entranced by the fluid murmurs of the spirits of the river, she had surrendered her past for the sake of enlightenment. She had become *Tarantula*.

She took another sip of her drink. Though she kept her eyes on her glass, she noticed the girl who stood near the entrance. She was a dark-haired girl likely in her late teens, and she was alone. Not many noticed her, aside from Tarantula, who sat by herself.

The girl looked in her direction. It was just a momentary glance, but those slight motions never escaped Tarantula's perception.

The blue eye was cool against the upper curve of Tarantula's chest. It hung from a wire around her neck.

Below the eye, on her right breast, was the tattoo of a cobalt blue tarantula

The teenage girl looked around, not missing another opportunity to glance again toward the woman in the gray hat. Tarantula didn't look back at her, not yet, but she watched.

The girl's stance and eyes betrayed her uncertainty. She was another stranger in a strange place among legions of tourists from afar. She was curious, but an apprehension stayed her against the fountains of indulgence which surrounded her at every turn.

The girl was special, even if she didn't realize it. Before Tarantula could venture any further rumination, the girl made an abrupt turn to leave.

Tarantula stood and paid for her drink. She slipped into position to watch the girl from inside the doorway, but ducked away as the girl turned again, but saw nothing aside from the standard throng.

The girl moved on. Tarantula stepped onto the street and followed. She concealed herself behind each passing body while working her way closer. The liquor burned a hot breath of intoxication through her footsteps along Bourbon Street, past countless establishments on both sides where drinks ran freely and hot passions fueled desire's fires.

An aimless stumbling drunk wandered into her path. She halted to avoid collision, but kept her eyes ahead, on the form of the slender, swift-moving girl.

The crowd thinned and the girl walked faster. She emerged onto the wider stretch of Canal Street and turned left. Tarantula stepped to the corner, paused at the streetside, and backed against the nearest building. She stood to one side of its window display and leaned against the wall.

The girl walked past the trees which sprang overhead at the corner. She neared the front of a souvenir shop and came to a halt.

She turned around to stare. Tarantula didn't move. Even if the girl couldn't see Tarantula's exact position, she could see beyond the murk of the human facade and she *knew* someone was there.

This gift was the gem Tarantula sought. It was also her greatest obstacle. She could not hide herself from this girl's clearest blue eyes.

"Why are you following me?" the girl asked.

Tarantula crossed Canal Street in plain sight. She raised her head. "Are you talking to me?" she asked the girl, who took a step back. She started as she bumped into the wall behind her, and Tarantula almost laughed.

"Why do you think I'm following you?" Tarantula asked, walking past the girl at a generous distance. "Do you think it's all about you? Please. I have better things to do than follow random people around."

The girl paused. She watched Tarantula pass and continue walking away. "Sorry," she muttered, though she remained wary. After a moment of thought, she turned and started in the opposite direction, back along Canal Street in the direction from which she had come. A hard grip squeezed her arm. She gasped. The sharp point of a narrow blade pressed into her side.

"Then again," Tarantula spoke quietly, "there is nothing random about this."

The girl looked at her, wide-eyed. "Just keep walking," Tarantula added. She stood close so that no others on the street tonight could see the blade in her hand.

The girl's eyes began to fill with tears. She fought to draw a breath against her anxiety.

"Walk," Tarantula ordered. "I won't tell you again."

She pressed the knife's tip deeper.

The girl swallowed. Helplessness welled in her eyes, but she began walking. Tarantula remained close.

The girl stumbled. Tarantula yanked her upright and pushed her along.

"Keep walking," Tarantula advised, "and don't do that again."

"Please, don't do this," the girl choked between emerging sobs. "I don't have much money but I'll give you whatever I have."

Tarantula didn't answer. She continued to guide the girl along, and they turned onto St. Charles Avenue. The girl cast her head around, her eyes wide. The other passersby were oblivious.

"What is your name?" Tarantula asked her.

"Jocelyn." The name emerged as a whisper.

"Listen to me, Jocelyn," Tarantula said in a very low voice, "I could kill you right now. Do you realize that?"

The girl swallowed again. Her eyes never left Tarantula's as she managed a nod.

"Do you want to get out of this alive?" Tarantula asked.

The fear never left the girl's large, watery eyes, but she had discovered a trace of hope. She forced another faint nod.

"Then stay quiet and keep walking and I'll see what I can do for you."

Jocelyn turned her gaze ahead. A tear slid down her pale cheek. Tarantula nudged her along and into another turn, this time down Common Street. A distance farther, she redirected the girl toward a dark, narrow opening to their left.

Jocelyn drew in a sudden breath. Their walk, she sensed, was coming to an end. They stepped into darkness. Tarantula's gloved hand dug into Jocelyn's ribs and jerked her to a stop by the fabric of her clothing. Jocelyn stifled a cry.

Tarantula stepped in close. She scrutinized Jocelyn's fearful blue eyes for several seconds.

"Hold still," Tarantula instructed.

She moved behind the girl and pressed the knife's point against her back. Jocelyn bit her lip, but couldn't suppress a sob when Tarantula's arm encircled her throat.

Tarantula paused. Jocelyn could feel the warm breath on the back of her neck for a long moment, until a sudden pressure on her throat startled her. Everything spun when Tarantula flung her to the ground. Hard ground bashed into the teenage girl. Without hesitation, Tarantula kicked her once, twice, and again a few more times until Jocelyn's senses scurried away in the flood of pain.

Tarantula looked back out to the street, but there was no one within sight. The altercation had been quick and silent. Good, she thought.

She knelt down beside the dark-haired girl. She pressed a gloved thumb against one of the girl's eyelids and pulled it up. She peered into the blue eye. After studying the left eye, she proceeded to examine the right.

The left, Tarantula decided. The left was the clearest and the purest.

She regarded the girl for a quiet moment. "You don't understand it, do you? Your gift. Like with so many others, it's lost on you, and you don't understand it — but I do."

Tarantula lifted the knife, pointed the steel blade downward, and lowered the blade toward the unconscious girl's face. Before she could press its tip into the corner of the girl's eye, Jocelyn awoke and screamed.

Startled, Tarantula lost a second's focus and Jocelyn swung. Her open hand struck Tarantula in the face and knocked the hat from her head. Her dark-brown hair spilled down. Tarantula almost fired a string of obscenities, but instead gasped and clenched her jaw when the girl's fingernails raked across the side of her face.

Tarantula's agitation became fury. She belted Jocelyn in the side of the head and the girl's body went limp.

Tarantula pulled back a sleeve and raised her wrist to her face. She felt blood, but it was just a scratch. She had scars far worse. Such was the price of the truth, Tarantula reasoned with herself against her anger. She resisted the compulsion to slice the blade across Jocelyn's throat; the eye must not be clouded by death. While the sight was still within the girl, the blue eye must be freed. Tarantula went for it.

She again opened the left eye and moved the thin silver blade into position, but another distraction came, the sound of movement behind her. Tarantula moved to pull herself to her feet, but not quickly enough. A heavy weight slammed into the side of her head and she toppled over. Her mind whirled.

Through her daze, Tarantula looked up from the ground to absorb the sight of a dark, bearded, bald-headed man with a wiry frame beneath a greasy tank-top — and one icy blue eye. She didn't miss the sight of the cudgel in his hand, a leather strap dangling from its handle.

Tarantula scrambled to her feet, wiped more blood from the side of her face, and addressed the man. "You?"

It was the man from the shop. She remembered him, though it had been — how long *had* it been? She couldn't recall, but she certainly remembered the day she stepped through his open door into his incensed world of dangling necklaces, crucifixes, dolls, and glass blue eyes.

In contrast to the lifeless glass eyes, "evil" eyes as they were called, the sentience in the man's blue eyes, the intensity and clarity in them, did not escape Tarantula's notice.

*Only through the clearest eyes will you find the truth of a soul.*
This was the conundrum the spirits of the water had
delivered to her. It was this discovery of purpose which
first brought her to transformation. The clearest eyes,
Tarantula found, were blue, and there was one blue clearer
than the rest.

The shopkeeper's single remaining blue eye stared
through Tarantula with a hatred sharper than any she had
ever seen. She hid herself well, but she could not hide from
him. He knew what she was. She had cut him deep last
time, but he had survived, and she knew what he wanted
now more than anything else—revenge.

"Would you like this back?" Tarantula asked him. She
reached beneath her clothing and pulled out the blue eye
attached to the wire.

The man faltered. He wasn't prepared for the sight of
his own eye.

Tarantula seized the man's break in focus. She flung
herself at him. The shopkeeper raised his arms in defense
but too late. She crashed into him and rammed the knife
into his face as they went down. The blade punched
through his cheek. He half-shouted, half-gurgled while his
mouth filled with blood.

The back of his head collided with the ground. To
Tarantula's surprise, his struggles weren't over. He batted at
her with the club but couldn't gain the angle for a proper
blow. She thrust the knife deep into his chest and twisted it
around. The man's final breath came in a shuddering gasp.

He went still. Tarantula slid the blade out and cleaned it
against the shopkeeper's pants with a sigh. She reached for
his eyelid and lifted it. His eye was not young like Jocelyn's,
but its iris was the same color of clearest blue. It would
suffice as the first had, would it not?

She inserted the knife into the edge of his ocular opening and slid its flat side alongside his eye. She pushed the knife beneath the eye and with a delicate motion, began to pry the eye outward. With a quick cut, she severed the attachments at the back of the eye and it came free. She extracted the orb from its socket and held it up.

She studied it. It was almost as good as the first one. She pulled the old eye, now becoming rancid, from its wire necklace and threw it into the darkness.

She unwound the intertwined tips of the wire and skewered the new eyeball through one side. She pushed the wire through until its end poked from the opposite side and rebound the ends of the wire together. She wiped away the stray fluid that glistened from it. She replaced the wire around her neck and tucked the fresh blue eye beneath her clothing. The eye was wet against her flesh.

She looked down to the empty sockets of the shopkeeper's face. He had been searching for her since their last meeting, it seemed. She considered herself lucky he hadn't warned the police, but what about the girl? The next time, Tarantula might not be as fortunate. She had a brief thought of finishing the girl as well, but a shout caught her attention.

She lifted her head to see a couple roaming near, a drunken young woman with a young man trying to support her wavering steps. Tarantula remained still and kept her eyes on them. To her misfortune, they moved right for the dark enclosure where she hid herself.

The girl vomited onto the ground. The young man held her hair back. Tarantula slipped past them and fled to the street. She didn't know whether they had seen her or spotted the bodies lying there, and didn't care to know. She had to get away from here *fast*. She hastened ahead to move around the next corner, pushed her hands into her pockets, and slipped away.

Once alone and secure from sight, she abandoned the trench coat and hat in favor of the outfit she still wore beneath. With the sharp blade of her knife, she cut her length of hair, working at it until it was close-shorn. She applied a cherry-red lipstick and a lighter makeup to her features. She hoped this was enough for now, because it was her best effort given the hurried situation.

Tarantula walked back toward the noise of Bourbon Street where she could vanish again into the crowds and revelry. Right now she needed another drink — badly.

Jocelyn awoke to the sound of vomiting. She tried to stand but about halfway up, she almost collapsed again.

"Someone's here!" exclaimed a female voice.

Jocelyn hurt everywhere, and everything was wobbling.

"Oh, no!" a young woman exclaimed. "Are you okay?"

"Do you want us to call an ambulance?" a male voice asked.

Jocelyn put her hands to her head. "Call the police," she said. "I've been attacked. I —"

She froze at seeing the body some distance away. Her mouth fell open at the sight of the eyeless black holes in its face. She quickly shut her eyes against it and clasped her hands to her mouth. After a moment, she lowered her hands, trembling, and found her voice again.

"Call the police," she repeated. "There has been a murder."

Before either of them could respond or register what was happening, Jocelyn stumbled away from them, toward the edge of the street.

With the fresh blue eye nestled against her and hidden

beneath her black top, Tarantula watched several faces in passing. Her stare penetrated them. She looked into the truths of their souls, the blemishes, the imperfections, the gray areas. It was peace, in a way, but each time she looked deep into the others with renewed sight, she wondered of herself.

*We all have evil in our souls,* she reflected, *and some far more than others.* Those who looked upon Tarantula with the clearest blue eyes must see in her the monstrosity which was the blackest black. On some level, hadn't Jocelyn? Hadn't the shopkeeper? Hadn't the others?

Farther along the street, she chose a spot for her drink, another glass of absinthe but in an altogether different spot from last time.

"So this is what I have become," she mused into her glass.

Would it ever end? To live without the sight was unthinkable now. It was blindness. It was madness. The world was wrong to her and she could not endure it without the pure blue eye which could see in ways her own impure vision could not.

With it, she never dared to look into a mirror. Misanthropy was easier this way, and it thereby made it easier for her to do what must be done.

She hadn't the precision of her early efforts, she acknowledged, when the secrets of the river spirits were fresh in her mind and the desire for truth powerful. It hadn't helped that she had waited so long to renew the sight this time. Her growing carelessness might one day be her downfall.

At least, with her desire for the clearest sight appeased, she could again begin to appreciate the simple pleasures. She swirled the final bit of absinthe around in the bottom of her glass and drank it down.

She felt a bit better, but not by much. She stood, paid, and left.

She didn't plan to linger here any longer. The night hadn't gone as planned, but the sight was hers again for however much longer it would last, and it was the best she could do.

Two police officers caught up to a bleeding, battered girl across the crowded street. "You need to come with us," one of them said.

"No," the girl breathed, and on the brink of collapse, she turned. "That's her."

The officers looked to where she pointed.

"That's her!" Jocelyn shouted.

Surprised, Tarantula looked up. Dark uniforms and badges set fires of warning ablaze through her senses.

Looking into Jocelyn, she saw fear overcome by determination. In the two police officers, one each side of her, Tarantula saw steel, a sense of duty.

Before either of the officers could reach for a gun, Tarantula bolted away.

"Stop!" one officer shouted. "Police!"

Tarantula didn't look back. She smashed her way through the crowds and ran.

"*Stop!*"

Tarantula's mind raced. If Jocelyn had warned the police, this meant they had found the body of the shopkeeper. If caught, she would be arrested for murder. The best case scenario would be death. The worst case scenario would be rotting in a cell for the rest of her life, suffering an endless madness of clouded sight.

She *had* to escape or die fighting. She ran and dodged the obstacles of moving bodies all around her.

Once in the open, she would be more vulnerable. She had to use the crowd to her advantage.

She twisted through the openings she saw and darted around a corner. The way was open, but they were still in pursuit. The police had her description, at the very least, of what she was now wearing. If only she could find a place to elude their view for just a minute, she could do something, change her appearance again, perhaps, but could she hide from Jocelyn's blue eyes?

No. Apparently not.

She had broken away from the crowds but the footsteps of pursuit were still strong behind her. She couldn't seem to get out of their sight. When she ran across the next street, she heard the siren of a police vehicle and saw flashing lights farther down the street to her left. They were coming this way!

She turned right and kept running. Her heavy boots were good for kicking the lights out of someone but not so much for running. She clenched her jaw and did her best to defy the heaviness of every pounding step and force a greater distance between herself and the pursuing officers.

Her muscles were straining, hurting. She heaved hard for breath and her lungs burned, but still she ran.

She had made some deadly mistakes, she couldn't argue against that, but among her rush of thoughts there existed a reasoning to her path. Well before she had gotten careless, Tarantula's methodical approach had ensured her survival on many occasions. She didn't know if her calculations would save her tonight, but what was left?

*The spirits of the river.* They were her only hope. With Tarantula's world collapsing around her, there was one place left to run. She had to reach the water.

She ran left and then right. She never turned to see whether her pursuers were gaining. She could barely breathe and her head was light, but she couldn't afford to stop. Across Decatur Street, the world flashed by her in a strange black-and-white.

She ran into the parking lot ahead and darted between cars. She heard another siren screaming and a screeching of tires from the same direction. She cut across the railroad tracks and her feet found soft grass.

She could see dark water ahead. Moonlight gleamed from its rippling surface. She raced for the waters of the Mississippi.

In the last seconds, her senses registered the railing ahead and she leaped. She hurtled over it and down to the ground below, where her boots struck with a shock throughout her body.

She swayed and steadied herself. Shouts carried in the night. Rapid footsteps were coming closer. She looked to the water.

"Spirits of the river," she managed to gasp. "Help me!"

She imagined the police running for her location, guns drawn. Desperate, Tarantula began to call the names of the river spirits, almost stumbling over the strange pronunciations in her near-panic.

During the chase, Tarantula had forgotten the blue eye altogether, but now, as she saw the forces which misted from the waters of the river, she remembered the eye and knew it was the reason she could see their forms at last, rising and coiling upward, clashing wills in and of the darkness. She could hear their voices, but could make no sense of them. They were a mass of chaos.

"I don't understand you!" she almost shouted. The swirling mists continued to murmur and wail.

"What can I do?" Tarantula called. "What sacrifice must I make?"

The voices quieted, and one rose above the rest.

"Come to us," it spoke.

"Stop! Police! Put your hands up!"

Tarantula vaulted into the water. The shouting which followed seemed distant to her senses. The world became dreamlike.

The fatigue was overwhelming, but she fought against it to swim for her freedom.

She couldn't see much of anything now but the darkness and the gentle water which surrounded her. Around her neck remained the blue eye of clearest sight.

She struggled to keep swimming, but her strength was failing. She mustered every last trace of energy from within to push on, but try as she might, she began to sink.

Her attempts to battle for the surface were useless. She wasn't only sinking; something was *pulling her down*.

She heard again the voices of the river spirits below her, deep into the depths. One voice sifted through, a whisper into her ear.

"There is but one escape," it said. "One true path to freedom."

*Downward.*

She screamed, or would have, but water rushed into her open mouth. She thrashed in panic. Water seeped into her lungs. With the blue eye around her neck, she could see in full the nature of what awaited her just before the depths drank her down.

◊ ◊ ◊ ◊

On the Sunday evening news, reports of another murder and another victim met the public eye. From the small television, a familiar face stared at Jocelyn. A name appeared on the screen above her picture. *Tara Araignée*. It was the name of the drowned woman pulled from the dark water.

Lying among the sheets of a hospital bed, Jocelyn

shuddered and pulled the blankets closer around herself. Her friends moved near and clung to her.

"It's her," Jocelyn whispered. "The woman who tried to kill me."

Her appearance was different yet again in this image, but there was no mistaking it. To Jocelyn's clearest blue eyes, it was the face of a monster.

# THE PEA FARM
by Amanda Hard

*June 1936*

"As you can see, there ain't no fences on this farm," the deputy Sam shouted, fingering the trigger guard on his rifle. "Well, 'cept for one. Ain't nowhere to run to but woods and more woods."

Black Eyes, remembering he was once called Pierre, shifted his weight to the shovel buried in the dirt between his feet and tried not to think of the penal farm's only fence; a wrought iron perimeter around a single rectangle of unattended soil. The bright sunlight in the humid air was piercing and intense. If he kept his head bowed low enough he could shield his eyes, sacrificing the thick skin on the back of his neck instead. A mosquito buzzed in his ear, but he didn't have the extra energy to reach up and brush it away.

"You make any kind of trouble, I will shoot you dead. If you try to run, I will shoot you dead. If you run off in the middle of the night, either the cats or 'gators out there in them woods will kill you dead sure as I will." The other four deputies smirked. They nudged each other and nodded.

Pierre—he still thought of himself as Pierre, he couldn't help it—glanced up to see a half dozen similarly bowed black heads. In the fields behind them were dozens more, and even a few white ones. Heavily muscled arms held hoes and shovels; weary eyes evaluated the new convicts being introduced to the farm.

"Ain't no mess hall on this farm. You will eat what you grow yourselves. You will cook what you grow, serve yourselves what you cook, and clean up your trash after. If you don't work, you don't eat. Carrot-Man here will show you to your ground and get you some tools. If y'all want to eat dinner, you best get started now." The deputy shouldered his rifle and ambled off, as the other farm inmates distributed shovels and directed the new arrivals to their plots of land.

Carrot-Man was ancient, his paper-thin skin eroded by sweat and hard labor. He was the oldest and inarguably wisest inmate on the farm back when Pierre had arrived and been assigned a plot of cow peas. When the white beans with single black eyes looked up at Pierre, the first eyes he'd seen in a long time which hadn't been accusatory and fearful, his shaking hands had dropped them all over the ground. "It don't matter if you innocent," Carrot-Man had told him. "You colored, so you guilty. Just tend to your land and you be home one day."

A thin stream of sweat dripped down through Pierre's lashes and when he tried to wipe it away, a fragment of dirt lodged in the corner of his eye. As he rubbed it, tears blended with the sweat and dripped to the ground below. Pierre quickly turned away, both to hide his shame and to prevent the salt tears from falling and poisoning the little patch of earth that had been his land now for the last ten years—and would be for the next ten to fifteen.

Beside him, Tomato Joe dragged a rake through scraggly looking plants. "Gonna be some good times tonight," he told his neighboring farmers. "Gonna meet my lady and trade me some love apples for some lovin'.'" Pierre kept silent, but the others snickered.

"You oughta take old Black Eyes there with you tonight," one of them said, motioning towards Pierre. "He looks like he need some cheering up. Been a few weeks since he seen his Hannah-Honey." Pierre looked around in alarm, but none of the deputies were listening. They sat on the back of the truck, rifles slung over their shoulders, talking and laughing. One of them took a long drink out of a glass jug. The sight of it made the back of Pierre's throat burn. The heat was almost unbearable during the day, only made worse by the tiny rations of water they were allowed every four hours. He wiped his eyes with his sleeve, but even in the humidity, his sweat had already evaporated.

"I don't want no trouble," he said quietly and slammed the shovel back down in the soil, again and again. A small cloud of dust arose and slowly dissipated into the damp air. He felt the palms of his hands prickle and warm as fresh blisters began to form. "No trouble," he repeated.

*June 2013*

"The website says there's a hole in the fence on the north side," Jason told the others. "We'll have to park back off the road and hike in, so we don't alert the security guard. They don't have video surveillance, just one guy up at the front gate." He rummaged in the camera bag for a lens. "I'd like to get some infrared shots if I can, before the sun goes down."

"Uh, I don't know what you all think, but I plan on being long gone and out of here before the sun goes down," his girlfriend Diana said emphatically. "It's creepy enough in the daylight."

"Are you sure it's not electrified?" Meredith asked. Without taking his eyes off the road, Chad elbowed her in the ribs the way he always did when she embarrassed him. She glared at him but said nothing.

"Jason's not an idiot; he did his homework. Why you always gotta be doubting people?" Chad turned his head to look at her as they slowed to a stop on the side of the road, a dense cluster of kudzu hiding the car and its occupants from view. His blue eyes met hers, the skin around the eyes crinkling as he gave the kind of toothy smile which usually allowed him back in her good graces. He snorted a laugh as Meredith looked out at the woods and shuddered. "What's the matter? Is the big bad ghost-buster afraid?" He grinned at her, one side of his lip curled up in a slight sneer. It was a recent affectation, and one she hated. In their four years together, he had adopted a number of offensive and piggish behaviors, but his condescension was the most troubling. He always knew better. Always had to get his way. He disregarded her concerns as meaningless. She'd considered calling it off ages ago, but that was before she'd taken the test.

"Well, she should be afraid," Jason said. "I read they prosecute trespassers. We need to be careful. Di, grab the video cam and Chad, here take this," he said, handing him a lunch box full of electronics.

"You got the EM meter and the recorder?" Chad asked.

"In there. With some other stuff. Just in case."

"Just in case of what? I thought we were just taking pictures?" Diana asked, sliding out of the car. "Dammit Jason, I thought you were done with the ghost hunting?" She frowned at him, then looked at Meredith who shook her head. "How many times have I told you I'm not comfortable with this, at all?" The men ignored her and began the long trek to the fence.

"Boys will be boys," Meredith offered, falling in behind them.

"As long as women make excuses for them, yes they will," Diana replied. She took Meredith's arm and pulled the girl closer. "Don't lie to me; something's up. Are you going to tell me what's going on, or will I have to beat it out of you?" she asked.

"Later," Meredith said with a sigh. "Let's just do this and get out of here. I don't want any trouble today."

◊ ◊ ◊ ◊

"You ain't gonna cause me no trouble, are you girl?" Deputy Sam swatted another mosquito on his neck and raised an eyebrow. Hannah stood motionless in front of him as he picked up one of her long braids and wound it around his finger. "You ain't the trouble-making type, are you?" She shook her head, releasing her hair from his hand.

"No sir," she said. The kitchen was hot, but her face burned hotter. Her dark skin could only conceal so much of the blush.

"So you ain't gonna tell nobody about the bacon. You just gonna make me a pot of my own Hoppin' John and you can keep a quarter of that pork for yourself. And you ain't gonna say a word to nobody, am I right?"

"No sir, not a word."

"You a good girl, Hannah. And the best cook I ever know, save for my own momma. I've a mind to bring you to my house once your sentence is up, let you cook for me every night. You think you might like that?" She just smiled. She knew he enjoyed thinking of her as an innocent girl rather than a grown woman, and if it kept him from touching her in that way, he could think what he wanted.

Hannah's doe eyes and slight overbite gave her a schoolgirl appearance which belied a ferocity underneath. He'd have his slow-stewed black-eyed peas and one day she might even spice them up with some of the hemlock her friend Hattie had been secretly cultivating.

From outside the kitchen came loud yelling and cursing. The deputy gave Hannah's shoulder a squeeze and left. She peeked out the window of the kitchen and saw two of the greens girls engaged in a tight bear hug, their faces scrunched and teeth bared. Turnip Greens craned her neck and bit Spinach girl on the shoulder. She howled in pain, but the deputy's fist ended her cry and sent her sprawling to the ground, blood pouring out of her mouth. The other fell to her knees after a punch to her stomach, and guards led both women away, gasping and still cursing at one another. Hannah, the Cow Pea girl, felt her good mood dissipate. She was really going to miss that spinach.

Nobody on the farm actually called her the Cow Pea girl, as was the custom, or even the Black-Eyed Pea Girl. Most everybody just called her "Girl," except for Hattie, the Green Pepper woman who called Hannah by her Christian name, and Pierre, who just called her "my love."

The Black-Eyed Pea Girl hid her secret store of salted bacon in the back of a cabinet and returned to the stove where she stirred a large pot of beans and sang softly to herself, a lullaby she remembered her Nana singing to her so many years ago. Her left hand strayed to the tiny swell of her lower belly. When she became aware of her hand's movement, she quickly removed it, reminding herself to be careful. She couldn't afford any trouble.

"It's been abandoned since the '50s," Jason told them

as they hiked across a field of wild chicory and smacked away mosquitoes. "Every kid who grew up in Caddo Parish knows the story of the P Farm. Hell, half us had relatives incarcerated there. The city sold the land a while back but I heard they can't build on it because every place they want to set a foundation they dig up bones."

Diana kicked at the flowers and slapped at her arms. "I heard they can't build on it because the mosquitoes keep carrying people off," she muttered under her breath. Meredith giggled.

"I'm serious, Di," Jason said.

"Leave it to the Yankee to make fun of the hicks in the sticks," Chad added, grabbing a twig from off the ground and tossing it back at her. "Ain't there dead people walking around Boston? Like a bunch of Paul Reveres and shit?" He quickly slapped a hand against his neck, leaving behind a tiny blood trail of dead mosquito. He wore short sleeves, but Meredith noticed insects seemed to prefer the soft warm flesh below his ears.

"Did they export a bunch of peas or something?" Diana asked, ignoring Chad.

"Oh, they didn't actually grow peas here. It's P, not like the food but like the letter P. Short for penal. It was kind of an alternative to prison. The inmates had to raise their own crops for food and they sold off the rest at a farmer's market kind of thing," Jason explained.

"So why is it haunted?" Diana asked. Chad turned around and stuck his tongue out and flapped his hands, bent at the wrists, under his chin. It was his impression of a mentally-challenged person, and it never failed to get a laugh from everyone—except Meredith.

"Duh, uh, because people died here? Duh?" He dropped the imbecilic look and rolled his eyes. He shook his head at Jason, who gave a little smile, before continuing to stomp through the field.

Diana looked over at Meredith, who lowered her head.

"You ever consider killing him in his sleep?"

"Quit," she whispered. "You shouldn't say stuff like that." Her friend shrugged.

"I'm just saying what we're all thinking. What you see in him is beyond me."

"He can be an idiot, I know, but it's because he's trying to be funny. Overcompensating, I guess. When you're the youngest of eight, you don't get a lot of attention."

"He's a bully."

"He's redeemable, Di. I —"

"I see the fence," shouted Jason. He began running towards it, with Chad right behind him. Even Diana's interest was piqued, and she quickened her pace to catch up with the men. Meredith continued with her slow, even strides. The others were struggling with the ragged fence when she came up behind them.

"— but the only way I know is to piss on it, see if you get fried," Chad was explaining.

"Yeah, you can try that somewhere I'm not standing," Jason said. "It's not electrified, but the edges are ragged so be careful." He got down on all fours and carefully crawled through the small opening. "Chad, come on, then we can pull the girls through."

When it was Meredith's turn, she caught Chad's eye and silently willed him to be kind for once, and not allow the raw edges to scrape against her arms. He smiled at her, the kind of smile which had won her heart when they first met—the kind worn by a happy child sharing a delight with a friend. He pursed his lips and, for once, complied, pulling her clear of the fence and up onto her feet. He left her to Diana's grooming ministrations and ran to catch up with Jason, who was already treading through the tall grass.

"You don't really believe in ghosts, do you?" Diana asked, pulling a stray leaf out of her friend's long auburn curls. "I mean, with Jason it's kind of a religious thing, but with you—you're a nurse, a scientist. You just went along with the whole paranormal investigative thing because Chad was into it, right?"

Meredith shrugged and started after the others. "I couldn't see that it was doing any harm," she explained. "But we never actually broke into any place before. We always had the owner's permission. This is different. It's wrong."

Diana nodded, but Meredith could tell from the tense silence she hadn't answered the question.

"No, I don't believe in ghosts," she admitted.

"But all the EVPs and the pictures and the weird electromagnetic readings Jason's always talking about? How do you explain all that?"

Meredith shook her head slowly. "I think we expected to see things, so we saw things. We expected to hear ghosts talking, so we did. Seriously, if I played the recordings for you and didn't tell you what they were saying, you'd swear you were hearing 'my sweet Satan,' or 'Paul's dead,' or something. It's not about science. It's more about wish-fulfillment." She felt her hand straying to that place just below the waistband of her jeans—the place where she rested her fingers in anticipation. Quickly she removed it and shoved it in her pocket. She caught a glimpse of Diana watching her with narrowed eyes and a furrowed brow.

"Ultimately, people see what they want to see," Meredith said with a shrug. Walking ahead of them, Chad picked up a small handful of rocks and lobbed them over his shoulder.

"That they do," said Diana, ducking the rocks, her eyes still narrowed. In the sky, the rumble of thunder grew closer.

◊ ◊ ◊ ◊

Pierre knew it was Tuesday, even without his tally stick, because it was two nights after the deputy came out to the fields to read the Psalms. Every third Tuesday was his night to sneak through the woods to the women's camp, with Tomato Joe and Turnip and More Potatoes. It had been awkward at first, with the other men so close, but they'd all quickly learned to turn a blind eye to the other black figures in the darkness, and all had the sense of decency to pretend to look away while the others undressed.

Walking in between the aisles of the tree branches he'd converted into a large trellis for the beans, he reached out a hand to brush against the long pods of black-eyed peas, now ripe almost to bursting. He pulled one pod down, snapped it off the vine, and ran a jagged thumbnail down the center split. Shiny yellow beans with their characteristic black spots glittered in the moonlight and threatened to spill out. He raised his hand up and let them fall instead into his open mouth. He imagined them boiled with ham, imagined the smile on Hannah's face as she served him up a big slice of cornbread, buttery and warm, from the kitchen of their own house, miles and miles from the P Farm. He would eat in that kitchen soon, he told himself.

Curling vines reached into his own tight curls as he passed underneath them, clinging to him as if trying to pull him back. He stepped as lightly as he could through the rows, gently brushing the vines aside. He could hear the others coming up behind him and quickened his pace. Together, they made enough noise to scare off snakes and four-legged predators, but caution and silence were their only defense against being caught by a guard out for a midnight piss in the woods.

There was no path. Faint markings in the bark of the live oaks which defined the perimeter of the farm were the only directional signs. As the group plunged into the woods, curly tendrils of moss formed a curtain that parted and brushed against their shoulders. What small moonlight had illuminated their way was extinguished by the heavy canopy of leaves. They moved faster, guided by memory and symbols in the stripped bark, until they emerged in a small clearing, where they were met by white smiles, brown eyes, and soft hands. Pierre took Hannah into his arms and kissed her, the green taste of the raw peas vanishing under the sweetness of her tongue.

◊ ◊ ◊ ◊

There was a path, clear and well-trod, nestled in between rows of tall, thin trees and cane. Meredith ran her hand over the tops of the cane, letting them brush against her palm. Last autumn's leaves crunched underfoot as they walked the path, stopping together to slap at mosquitoes and finally to stand in awe of a massive structure that appeared to be in the process of being reclaimed by the forest. A gaping black maw in the center of a dense curtain of ivy and vines revealed itself to be a doorway, flanked on either side by square gaps which had once been windows. The overall visual effect was of a waxy green skull, buried up to the nasal opening in dry grayish dirt, slightly tilted backwards, and screaming.

"Whoa," said Chad.

"Goddamn," said Diana, her voice barely over a whisper. "That is amazing."

"This is the main building," said Jason. "Pretty impressive, yeah?" The rest just nodded, speechless, stunned by both the age and the enormity of it.

"Grab a flashlight, and let's get set up," he told Chad. "We're losing our daylight."

"It's too quiet out here," Diana finally said. "You can't even hear any birds. What's with that?"

Meredith just motioned to the trees, their tops swaying back and forth slowly in the wind, leaves flipped upside down and hanging limp. "The storm; they know it's coming. Look at the leaves. The birds have already found shelter." She gave her friend's shoulder a squeeze. "Let's go humor them so we can get this over with."

The open entryway in the giant wall reminded Meredith of a tiny keyhole for a much larger door, in a house whose topmost eaves reached up into clouds. She stepped over the threshold and into darkness, shivering at the abrupt temperature change and the air's dank sour taste of mildewed stone. Flashlight beams illuminated several decades' worth of graffiti and vandalism. The interior was empty save for the scattered bits of trash and spray painted warnings of "death ahead" left by previous trespassers. They passed through the main room into a larger room with metal pipes overhead.

"Man, this place is messed up," Chad said, staring in awe at the spray-painted and overgrown interior. "Check out the window." He swung his light up to highlight it, the rusty iron bars still intact. "Shit, maybe the electric chair's still here, you think?"

"Doubtful," said Jason, as he scanned the area with an electromagnetic field meter. "I'm not getting anything out of the ordinary here. Let's take a look around and then come back here and set up for photos. This is the best light we're gonna get."

"I don't really feel like going exploring, Jason." Diana brushed imaginary cobwebs away from her face. "I'm going outside. It smells weird in here. Smells like..."

"I know, red beans and rice, right?" Chad volunteered, looking at Diana without a trace of his usual sarcasm. "That's kind of weird."

"I think this might have been the kitchen," Jason said. "The plumbing looks right and bars on the windows make sense. The barracks must be in the other wing. Mer, can you set up the audio? I want to get a sample reading here, just in case." Meredith sighed and nodded. Chad handed her the lunch box, the confused look still on his face.

"You don't smell that?" he asked. She shook her head. He frowned and followed Jason down an even darker hallway.

"Can you imagine being sent to a place like this?" Diana asked, flashing her light across the debris-covered floor. She sidled up to her friend and shivered.

"Chad's grandpa was here in the '30s." Meredith said. She took Diana's hand and trained the flashlight on the interior of the lunch box. Diana took the hint and held the light steady.

"So he comes by his not-exactly-juvenile delinquency honestly, then?"

Meredith smiled and shook her head. "No, he was on the Sheriff's department. At least, that's what Chad said. He claims the old guy told him all this horrible stuff about what went on here, how many people died, that kind of thing. He's wanted to do a proper ghost investigation on this place for ages." She tested the voice recorder and addressed the darkness in a loud voice, "My name is Meredith."

"Are you—" Meredith put a finger over her friend's lips to prevent her speaking. In her mind she counted slowly to ten.

"Is there anyone here who would like to speak to us?"

Again, a slow count to ten. "Can you make a sound to let us know that you're here?" Silence.

*One. Two. Three.*

Silence.

*Eight. Nine. Ten.*

Nothing. She clicked off the recorder and took the flashlight back from Diana, who shivered again.

"God you're all a bunch of ghouls. What happened here, anyway? Plague? Zombies?"

Meredith packed up the box of electronics and led the way through the debris to the main room with the open doorway.

"I don't think it was anything like that. More like your typical prison abuse: inmates killing each other, guards killing inmates. Probably a lot of sexual abuse too. Chad said the farmers weren't locked up; they lived in big tents out on the fields. Most of the records went missing before they shut it down, so nobody even knows what prisoners were here or what happened to them." She looked out over the expanse of vine-covered ground in front of them. "I wonder how many mothers went to their graves wondering what became of their baby boys." Her hand drifted to just below her waist band, and Diana grabbed it before she had a chance to pretend it wasn't an unconscious gesture.

"How far along?" she demanded.

Meredith looked at her feet. "Thirteen weeks on Tuesday." Suddenly she felt an uncomfortable warmth spreading in her belly. The dank air was choking her; she needed to step outside in the fresh—

A thick stream of vomit erupted from her mouth. She angled her head just in time to avoid splashing it on her friend's feet, then hugged herself tightly as sequential waves of nausea elicited a series of dry heaves. Diana helped her walk out to a patch of moss-covered ground isolated from the thin trees. She dropped to her knees and tried to breathe slowly, through her mouth, to avoid the smell of rotten vegetation that drifted in from the woods.

"Does dipshit know?" Meredith nodded. "And?"

"He offered to pay half and drive me to the clinic."

"How gallant."

"He's afraid. We both are. It's not like either one of us had great role models for being good parents." She sighed and squeezed her head between her hands. "I couldn't just *not* tell him, you know? I mean it's his flesh and blood too. He didn't get mad; he just … well, he's right. This is a terrible time for both of us." she said.

"Meredith? You can't! You want this baby; don't try to tell me otherwise. You've always been all about kids and--"

"I can't do this right now, not with him still…" she trailed off. Meredith looked up and exhaled slowly. Her eyes met Diana's. She wanted to explain, wanted her best friend to understand why she couldn't raise a child with Chad. It took all of her energy and focus, her best efforts, just to keep him from self-destructing, and even those were starting to fail. She wanted to tell her about the escalating abuse, the humiliation, the tantrums and violent fits which left bruises on her wrists and arms. She opened her mouth to ask forgiveness for her hubris, to be absolved of the sin of thinking she could change someone who didn't want to change, but no words came out. Only a loud and extended belch which broke through the uncanny quiet in the woods and surprised both of them.

"Gassy much?" her friend laughed.

"It tasted like peas," Meredith said, hot tears forming in the corners of her eyes.

◊ ◊ ◊ ◊

"Tuesdays is gonna be special meal night," Hannah told Pierre. "When we get away from here, Tuesdays gonna be like our anniversary day, and I'll cook something nice, every week." She knew from the way he sighed he liked that suggestion. She was naked, resting on her side, with her head on his chest. One hand stroked his curly hair; the other was buried in the patch of curls hidden under his trousers. "We gonna have our own farm, with as many tomatoes as we want. And we ain't gonna be growing no damn black-eyed peas," she laughed. "That's for sure."

"Soon, my love," he said.

"We best be running off sooner than soon," she told him. "I won't be able to hide it too much longer." Her hand moved up to brush his belly and he moaned. She brought her hand back to her side and draped it over her navel.

"We having a girl," she said suddenly. "Hattie done told me already. She made this for her." She reached into her sock and pulled out a tiny doll, no bigger than her thumb, made of red and white gingham with black yarn hair. "It's got beans in it—some of yours and some of mine, just like this baby. Hattie says this is good juju for unborn souls." She toyed with the doll for a moment before holding it out to Pierre. He reached out and Hannah placed it gently in his palm, closing his fingers around it before kissing them.

"I gonna call her Alice. After my Nana."

"That's a fine name," he said quietly.

Moonlight that had been in the shadow of clouds all night broke free and illuminated the clearing. Naked bodies slid back into pants and dresses, and all around them dozens of pairs of eyes peered down from the tree branches. Hanging moss in the lower limbs made a curtain surrounding them, hiding the other pairs of eyes which now watched, narrowed and cold, as the lovers kissed their goodbyes. Hannah thought she heard something in the trees and stood up, squinting into the darkness. She took a step towards the tree line and dropped to the ground just as the sound of a rifle shot tore through the air.

Screaming all around her and the sounds of feet pounding the ground surrounded her. She crouched in the grass, eyes closed and still naked, as barking dogs and yelling and more gunshots filled the air. A hand around her wrist roughly jerked her to her feet, and she felt a thick wad of spit hit her forehead. She opened her eyes and saw hate in the blue eyes of the deputy who'd given her the bacon. He looked at her with disgust.

"Nowhere to run to, you little whore," Sam said as his fist slammed into her face. As she fell to the ground her fingers clenched and grasped at her empty palm.

"Shit, did you see that?" Diana pointed off into the distance. "Lightning. We need to get out of here before it storms and we find the car floating in a mud puddle." Chad put down the video camera and cocked his head, listening.

"The storm's miles away, we're fine." He walked farther out in the woods and panned the camera across a wide stretch of land where the trees were less densely packed. "Let's get some audio here," he yelled. "I think this might have been part of the actual farm." Jason slung his camera over his shoulder and moved to follow, but Diana caught his arm.

"We need to be getting out of here soon," she whispered. "Meredith is feeling really sick."

Jason peered over Diana's shoulder at Meredith sitting in the grass, her head bowed as she toyed with a piece of vine, wrapping and unwrapping it around her finger.

"I just want to get a few more shots, I swear. Then we'll go."

"This place is gross," Diana said loudly as Jason started to walk away.

"Do you hear that?" Meredith asked, looking up suddenly. "It sounded like a cat. There, just now. Did you hear it?" Diana and Jason looked at each other and shook their heads. Jason hurried to catch up with Chad.

Meredith stood up. She wrapped the trailing ends of the vine around her wrist into a series of bracelets. She looped another curling vine around her neck like a string of green pearls and began walking into the woods.

"I want to see the farms," she said flatly.

Chad and Jason were not far ahead, and Meredith could see Jason fiddling with something in the lunch box. She came up behind him and put a hand on his shoulder, startling him and making him drop the audio recorder. She picked it up and activated it, walking slowly over the soft grass. A pale sliver of crescent moon hung in the late afternoon sky.

"This is Meredith," she said loudly. "If you can hear me and want to talk with me, please give me a sign." She waited and counted.

*One. Two.*

A sudden breeze blew a small white flower past her face. She reached out to grab it.

*Three. Four. Five.*

The two petals were silky and reminded her of pursed lips.

*Six. Seven.*

She brought the flower to her open mouth, resting it on her tongue.

*Eight. Nine.*

It had a sweet but earthy taste, with a salty finish when

she bit into it.

*Ten.*

She spit the pieces out and spoke again. "Is there something you want to tell me?" She waited, her breathing stopped. She heard the same sound as before, closer now, more desperate. It wasn't a cat, she realized. It was more familiar than that. More human. A child, maybe. A baby. A crying baby.

"Are you crying?"

Meredith jumped and her friend reached out to take her hand. She looked down and saw she was still holding the recorder, which she clicked off. Diana asked again, "Are you crying?"

"No, I'm just—" But she was crying, and the tears spilled off her cheeks and onto dozens of shredded pieces of tiny white flowers that littered the ground.

"I was just recording…" she began, then shook her head. "I'm in my own world, I guess. Really, I'm fine." She brushed at her eyes with the back of her hand and saw Chad and Jason making their way towards them. Jason was beaming; Chad wore his usual frown, deepened and lengthened by the hardness in his eyes.

"I got some amazing infrared shots of the outbuildings," Jason practically exploded with enthusiasm. "And we got some really weird shit on film. You gotta see this." He tried to hand the video camera to Meredith, but she ignored him. A flash of light in the trees caught her attention. It was too low to be lightning. Chad grabbed the camera.

"There's something out there," Meredith said softly, pointing past the tree line. "Something metal, maybe. You can see the light hitting it."

Rows of cane grew tall with kudzu vines and moss curled thickly in between the stalks, forming a dark curtain between the clearing and the deeper woods in front of them.

"I don't see shit," said Chad.

"I thought you said they didn't grow peas here?" Diana asked casually, kicking at the ground.

"They didn't," Chad said. "My Grandpa Sam said they can kill you if you don't cook 'em right. They grew vegetables, like turnips and tomatoes and stuff." He slapped at a mosquito on his neck, leaving another tiny splotch of blood.

"Then what do you call these?" she asked, nudging a vine with her foot. In between the green leaves, thin grayish brown stalks poked out. They were shriveled and dried, but their contents were still recognizable.

"Green beans? Who cares," he said, picking at the remains of a pod.

"Cow peas," Meredith said. "My grandmother used to grow them." She bent down and gathered a handful of the desiccated shells. Taking one in her hand, she split the pod with her thumbnail and tipped it upside down. "Some people call them black-eyed peas," she said, as a dozen tiny yellowish marbles with their characteristic black spots spilled out onto the ground. "And they're also known as Crowder peas, because they grow so close together."

"Well thanks for the fascinating horticulture lesson, Meredith. Really, we all learned a lot." His sarcasm was icy, his voice cold. "But can we get on with this shit sometime soon?" Chad demanded. In the sky over the woods, lightning flashed again.

"You need to see this, Mer," Jason said, his voice concerned but insistent. "You gotta check out this video we shot. I think we actually got something this time." He took the camera from Chad and ran the video backward.

"You can see something moving through the cane if

you look…" he stuck his finger on the lower left side of the screen. "Right here, see it?" Meredith squinted. She played and rewound the clip several times before pausing it and studying the still image.

"Is that a dog's tail?" she asked.

"Are you serious?" Jason asked, grabbing the camera. "God dammit, how did—"

"Dammit, I told you I heard barking," Chad said. He kicked out at the vines curling on the ground. "At least we know it's not a guard dog, or it wouldn't have run off. Might mean somebody else is out here, though."

"Great," said Diana sarcastically. "You got your pictures and great video of a dog's ass. Can we please go now?"

"Jesus Christ, shut that pie hole for five minutes!" Chad yelled. "You've been bitching since we got here. Give it a rest." He punctuated his last request by shoving Diana sideways. She shoved him in return and he leveled a back-handed slap at her face, which she neatly avoided by stepping back towards Meredith.

"Don't you touch me, you asshole," Diana hissed. Jason grabbed Chad's arm.

"Dude, what the hell is wrong with you? You need to chill out. Now."

Chad lifted his hands in mock defeat. Jason released him and gathered Diana in his arms. The couple walked quickly back towards the main yard as a rumble of thunder rippled through the suddenly tense quiet.

Meredith's fingers clenched into fists. The vine bracelets around her wrist loosened and dropped in a loop to the ground. She stepped in front of Chad and met his cold blue eyes with her own soft brown ones.

"You are a bully," she said quietly. Saying it aloud felt good; she found strength in the truth of it. "You don't deserve to be a father." At that, Chad smacked her across the face with one hand; with the other he grabbed the vine necklace around her throat, pulling her to him.

"And I ain't gonna be, now am I?" he asked her as his lips twisted into a snarl. "It's probably not even mine to begin with, ya little whore." His face was inches from hers, their bodies nearly touching. His rage was palpable; she could taste it on her tongue. She smiled at him, leaned in as if to kiss him, then kicked her foot, slamming her boot forward just under his knee. He dropped like a sack of flour, his hands clutching his shin, and screamed as pieces of tiny white flowers blew by in the wind.

◊ ◊ ◊ ◊

Pierre ran like a deer chased by a mountain lion, thinking only of getting himself and Hannah to the banks of the Red River, where they could finally enact, prematurely, the escape they'd planned for months. Panting and gasping heavily, he couldn't draw enough breath to call out to her. Instead he tightly squeezed the little poppet she'd placed in his hand just minutes before. He tucked it in his shirt, near his heart, as he ran. He thought of praying to God for safe passage, but couldn't remember any of the Psalms and not much from the Lord's Prayer. In his mind, he settled on making a deal of sorts: God would let them escape and they would bring the baby to church every Sunday.

Intense and bright light flashed in his eyes, blinding and disorienting him, and he tumbled over a root and onto the ground. He scrambled to his feet, and looked behind him for Hannah or one of the others, but saw only guards holding flashlights and rifles surrounding him. Hands took his arms and forced them behind him. A foot slammed into his shin. White-hot pain shot through his leg and he fell to his knees on the ground, a penitent whispering to God to spare Hannah and their unborn child. Men with barking dogs on chains joined them, and a big man Pierre recognized as the penal farm superintendent walked into the circle. He kicked at a baying dog and reached up to catch a length of rope thrown to him by one of the deputies. He studied Pierre with cold but exhausted eyes.

"Take this one back the farm," the superintendent said. "Hang him over his own crops, and let the others eat what grows under him when he shits himself. Dump him over the fence when you're done. I'm gonna see to the women."

Pierre tried to lash out, tried to scream a warning, but guards held him fast. He saw the butt of the rifle coming at him, heard the crack as it met his skull. He fell forward and felt his face scrape the ground as they dragged him back to the camp. One arm managed to reach up to his shirt. His hand felt the bulge that was the poppet doll, and he felt Hannah's warm fingers in his, squeezing one last time. The fingers fell away and his own hand went to his neck as he felt the rough fibers of a rope wrapping around his throat.

A bolt of lightning flashed above him, illuminating the terrified eyes of the other prisoners, as Pierre was hoisted up over the makeshift cross. Pea pods brushed his hair and face like soft fingers, and tiny tendrils with delicate white flowers curled around his neck and thrashing body, embracing him as his vision dimmed. His fingers curled around the vine-clotted rope, scratching and clawing, before his body shuddered one last time and the fingers relaxed. In the darkness, crushed white pea flowers dropped to the ground in silence.

◊ ◊ ◊ ◊

Barking was the first thing Hannah heard when she regained consciousness, intense and desperate barking and howling. When she opened her eyes she saw white blossoms above her she at first mistook for angel wings. Long green fingers stuck out at right angles, wagging and poking her face. "Shame on you," they said. Only it wasn't the peas, it was the deputy, Sam. The bacon man.

"You're nothing but a whore," he said again. Her hair was wrapped around his fist and he yanked her head towards him. "I trusted you. Treated you right. And here I find you acting like nothing but a common whore." She was still naked, with her hands tied above her head on a makeshift trellis overrun by white pea flowers. Curling vines hung down next to her own curly hair, reaching for her, clinging: her cow peas; her crop.

The superintendent's voice was unfamiliar to her, and the voice read her sentence with no small amount of joy. Fifty lashes. She could take that. She could take whatever they gave her, knowing Pierre was waiting for her. Bacon Sam showed her the chain.

"My Grand-daddy kept slaves on his farm," he said. "This here was one of the chains he kept them on. I thought you'd appreciate knowing that," he whispered to her before drawing back his arm and letting the chain fly forward, where each link fell in an agonizing sequence across the delicate black skin of her back. Her scream instantly silenced the crickets and cicadas, even the wind in the branches. After ten lashes, those screams died in her throat and the other women in the barracks stuffed their fingers in their ears to drown out the horrible silence. At 20 lashes, she choked and coughed on blood and bile, her salt tears and saltier blood pouring to the ground beneath her peas. At 25 lashes, the raw skin around the column of her spine finally split and peeled away, and small chunks of meat fell from the connected links of chain which now rained down on her buttocks and the backs of her legs. That tender flesh survived only a few strokes before flaying away in neat, almost parallel rows. By 50 lashes she was unmoving and covered in dark blood so thick that nobody noticed the bright trickle on her inner thigh. Before they finished cutting her down, it was a river pouring out of her, thick red clots falling to the ground as her uterus contracted, spilling pieces of her baby to the ground the way a freshly picked cow pea spilled its beans from the shell.

Hannah didn't feel the blood. She felt Pierre's lips on her cheek, his voice in her ear.

"My love," she heard him whisper from behind the hanging moss curtain in the trees, the amorphous boundary between the men's section of the farm and the women's. She could barely crawl, but she went to him, following his voice through the woods and between the iron bars of the farm's only fence, the barrier between the tilled land and the field of unmarked graves within. He whispered for her and she spread herself next to him. She took the poppet from his calloused hands and cradled it in her bloody ones. When the guards found her stiffening body behind the fence, she was still singing, but if they heard her song, they took no notice of it, although Sam shivered when they threw lime on the ground. When the iron gate clanged shut, nobody noticed the tiny, blood-covered poppet doll that seemed to be sprouting.

Meredith ran, following the sound of crying while fleeing the smell of old peas and rot. She ran away from the voices which yelled to her, and toward the soft whispering of vines and white flowers blowing in the breeze. A series of lightning bolts illuminated the woods, flashing on metal in the thick tangle of trees. Beyond the leaves was a fence. Beyond the fence, freedom. Safety.

She ran harder when she felt the first drops of warm rain in her eyes, faster now as her stride lengthened and her vision blurred. A shower of tiny pea flowers splashed against her face as she sprinted past a curtain of vines through the rust-covered iron gate. Green leaves and swirling tendrils wrapped themselves around what was left of a wrought iron fence. The pea pods themselves reached out for her, beckoning, while brown and dried beans spilled out along the ground, wordless tears that contained and curtailed the crying voices. She could hear her own pulse in her ears, intertwined with a more rapid heartbeat which grew stronger with the thudding of her feet on the ground.

Meredith stopped suddenly when she saw the flash of red fabric. Kneeling on the ground she reached into the overgrown and unruly vines and retrieved a tiny doll, faded and filthy. She brought it to her lips, inhaling the scent of blood and rich black Louisiana soil, and felt a flutter in her lower belly, just below the waistband of her jeans. She brought her hand to it, feeling the life inside. It felt like a second chance, and she smiled.

"Little whore," Meredith heard above her. The field of flowers around her became stinking mud and a lightning flash revealed Chad's furious eyes, his hair dripping and his mouth twisted into a snarl. His weight shifted to one leg as he moved to kick her, but she dodged him and he slipped in the mud, falling backwards. She stood, still clenching the doll in her fingers, and tried to run past him to the fence in front of her. He reached out an arm and grabbed at her jeans, and she tripped, falling forward into the mud and losing her grip on the poppet. She watched it sail out of her hands, tracing a slow arc in the air, before landing between two bars of the wrought-iron fence just above her head. It hung there, clinging to the vines as the rain washed over it. She extended her tongue and tasted the drops of decades-old blood that dripped down, baptizing her with renewed strength and purpose.

She wrenched herself up out of the mud and saw them, all of them, gathering themselves up from forgotten bones and standing between her and Chad, their black faces smiling, black eyes kindly in the flashes of lightning.

Chad struggled to his feet. Wiping his sleeve across his forehead, he saw Meredith and smiled again. "Nowhere to run, bitch." He took a step toward her. Her back against the fence, she scooted sideways, but he grabbed her arm before she could run away.

"Shame on you," he said and brought his hand to her throat, trying to wrap his fingers around it. She tried to keep her chin mashed against her chest so he couldn't get a grip on her windpipe, but his hand blocked the flow of blood from her carotid artery and already her vision was dimming. She kicked her feet behind her against the fence, which she began to climb, backwards, as her boots found purchase in the dense iron curls and tangled vines. Up she stepped, up again, buoyed by the foliage and the dark hands which lifted her. Chad held her with one hand, the other pulling his weight up the fence underneath her. She could hear him panting and swearing under his breath as he climbed, and then she was at the top, hanging for the briefest of moments between the pain of consciousness and a black void, suspended on the barrier between worlds, weighed in the balance.

With her last bit of strength she threw herself backward, falling for years, generations even, before the back of her head hit the ground and she saw stars. No, not stars, she realized, but white teeth which smiled to her from the other side of the iron fence. The smiles belonged to the faces and hands that were busy pulling a thick rope of vines tighter around the neck of a man hanging suspended from the iron fence, his fingers clawing at theirs and legs kicking against a sudden rain of white pea flowers.

Meredith closed her eyes and lay back on the ground, feeling raindrops on her lips and soft green pods stroking her cheeks. In the distance she heard someone calling her name. The combined sounds of footfalls, shouting, and a muffled scream tore through the air, and then someone was shaking her and telling her to wake up, telling her "It's going to be okay," as if she didn't already know.

"It's gonna be okay, Mer," Diana repeated. "But we have to get you out of here, right now. We need to get you to a hospital, okay? You had a bad fall and you need to go to the hospital." Her friend's voice was tearful, and when she opened her eyes, Meredith could see Diana's were red and puffy. "Don't look, okay?" she warned. "Just don't look. You don't need to see that."

Meredith didn't look. She knew what she would see hanging on the fence, and she knew it wasn't the doll, which she also knew had been washed away, disintegrated by the rain. She let her friend lead her out of the clearing while Jason stood near, stammering into his cell phone for an ambulance.

"It's gonna be okay," Diana repeated again. "We're gonna get you to a doctor and you and the baby are going to be fine, okay?" Diana tried to smile. Meredith could hear sirens in the distance. She squeezed her friend's hand and inhaled the fresh green scent of ripe black-eyed peas. Her other hand drifted to the familiar spot just below her waistband, and this time she didn't move to hide it. A tiny white flower floated down from vines woven through the branches and landed in her hair. She patted her lower belly. "I'm going to call her Alice," she said, smiling.

# FIRST, MAKE A ROUX

by Allie Marini Batts

Blanche started her lessons in the kitchen with her grandmother when she was still so young the top of her head barely reached the waistband of Grandmother Evangeline's apron. Blanche studied the pattern of the fabric—half wedges of happy citrus fruits with stick feet, marching down the rows of her *granmere*'s apron together, and listened carefully to every word, which came from Grandmother Evangeline's lips. Her first lesson was in scrambled eggs. Once mastered, they moved on to the proper methods of cutting vegetables, and when Blanche was finally tall enough to see over the top of the stove and stir, they began learning main courses, soups, and stews. It was when Blanche was not old enough to really understand what true fury felt like, that Grandmother Evangeline explained patiently that everything had its own place and flavor in the pot. Anger, she said, had a taste and a smell; it was like chopped onions cast into a hot iron skillet. They sizzled and perfumed the air with steam, three parts bitter to one part spicy. Like anything, if left unwatched over the heat, it would burn and blacken, ruining the balance of the other ingredients. Tended to, with the heat lowered, the rage of the onions would mellow, caramelize, and eventually disappear into the dish, leaving behind only the tang of their outburst as a reminder of their power. Though at the time Blanche thought she understood, she did not, but Evangeline's lesson was like a seed. Once planted, it sprouted roots and grew, regardless of whether or not Blanche noticed it in the garden.

Blanche had lost her Crock Pot when she and Renault divorced; though why he had taken it, she couldn't say, since he was never much of a cook. The slow cooker was on a long list of things to replace. Blanche didn't need it as much as she needed a bed to sleep in or a table to sit at, so it took a few months of settling into her new apartment before she really felt its absence. She had three basic pots to cook with, a good knife, a cutting board and her grandmother Evangeline's rolling pin, so it wasn't as though she wasn't able to make dinner for herself—it was also true slow cookers weren't generally looked on by Cajuns as an authentic way of cooking gumbo or *etoufeé*. But she worked as a clerk in the county office, and was away from the house during the daytime, so the traditional method of cooking those dishes, hours spent stirring the pot over low heat, was impossible. Blanche, like many other good Cajun girls of her age, cut corners a bit and used a Crock Pot. After all, as long as she had good filé powder and took care when making the roux, it tasted every bit as good as Grandmother Evangeline's.

For the first six months she spent on her own, she did no real cooking at all, bringing home grocery bags full of frozen dinners, instant coffee and canned fruit. One evening, spooning mandarin oranges straight from the tin, she realized how much of a caricature of herself she had become. *Good God, girl*, she thought, *Cook a real dinner for yourself, already. You're pathetic.* And so on an ordinary Wednesday, after leaving work, Blanche went to the grocery store to collect the ingredients to make herself a simple chicken and rice dish. She decided to start small, afraid she'd lost the knack for cooking. The rice was a little crunchy, but inside of two weeks, she'd settled back into the rhythm of shopping, slicing, peeling, chopping, stirring and tasting. It was only then she started to have a hankering for gumbo, jambalaya, and crawfish *etoufeé*. She started to miss her old kitchen and its fancy tools, most of which had been wedding gifts or hand-me-downs from Mother Gaspard, and thus, things Renault had taken with him when he moved out of their home and back in with his mother.

Weekends were still lonely for Blanche, who didn't much care for the other clerks in her office. Her friends seemed to be one of the many things divided up in the divorce. Like the kitchenware and the furniture, Blanche did not get an equal share of those, either. One Friday afternoon, she bought coffee and a newspaper on her lunch break, sitting outside at a picnic table to enjoy the sunshine. She flipped through the pages, looking for the crossword puzzle and only briefly glancing at the horoscopes, before she came to the classified ads. She skimmed them, though she wasn't looking for a new job and was just barely beginning to settle into her new apartment. Under the *Community News* header, she read: "Estate Sale, Saturday, 8 a.m. Follow signs from Magazine and Jackson. No earlybirds. Housewares, books, art, clothing, miscellaneous. Fair prices, mixed lot." Blanche circled the ad, and when she got home that evening, she set her alarm clock for 7:30.

The next morning, she followed the signs from the intersection to the estate sale, finding a place to park just a block away. She felt proud of herself for getting out of the house instead of staying in all weekend watching reruns of shows that weren't good the first time they aired, like she had almost every weekend since Renault left. The lucky parking spot close by, on a Saturday morning no less, seemed to confirm to her fortune was with her, and that her luck might be on the upswing. The mansion next door to the estate sale was imposing; one of the historic majesties of the district, a 19th century revival manor whose garden was still well-maintained and gave off the heady smell of honeysuckle and magnolia blossoms. The sale itself was at the smaller home adjacent to the big estate, one of the many houses erected when the mansion's original plot of land was subdivided and the city became more urban. The Victorian flourishes made it look like a gingerbread house at Christmastime. Blanche was happy the estate sale was not at the mansion. If it had been, even at a sale, there wouldn't have been anything she could afford.

She felt odd, walking up the steps of an unfamiliar house, crossing the threshold and realizing that room by room, the home was almost exactly as its last owner had arranged it. The only thing that indicated Blanche had not mistakenly walked into a stranger's living room was the crowd of people picking up items throughout the house and the bright orange price tags on the things they considered. At the door, a bent-over woman, with silvery-white hair carefully pinned in a bun on top of her head, stood collecting money, handing buyers plastic shopping bags to carry their purchases, answering their questions and haggling over the prices.

Blanche went to the kitchen first. Though she fully planned to explore every room and its contents, she knew she was looking for cooking tools first and foremost, and wanted to make sure if there was anything on her list at the sale, she would snap it up first. The kitchen was gaily accented with lemon-printed curtains that reminded Blanche of Grandmother Evangeline's favorite apron, immediately making her feel at home in the stranger's kitchen. It seemed once again, Lady Luck was with her. On the counter, priced at ten dollars, was a Crock Pot that Blanche guessed was as old as she was—which was perfect, because older appliances were built for durability. It was one of the reasons she had not simply gone to the department store and purchased a new one. She remembered the brown pattern print and tough ceramic liner of her grandmother's Crock Pot, and though Evangeline did not often use it for gumbos or traditional dishes, she had been proud of the appliance and kept it on the kitchen counter at all times. The model on the counter in front of Blanche was the exact same style, color and size as the one in Grandmother's kitchen. Blanche was almost embarrassed for herself when she lunged for it, pulling it tight to her chest, so that no one else could claim it. She walked toward the silver-haired woman at the door.

"May I have a box to put this in, and can I leave it with you, so I can keep looking?" she asked.

The woman took the Crock Pot from Blanche, and set it in a box under the table where she was collecting tags off the sold items and affixing them into the pages of a notebook, with prices written next to the tags.

"Write down your name, *beb*. If you want to put anything else in your box, you just bring it on back up to me, here," she said. "That cooker belonged to my sister Marigny. She was a very good cook, very handy in her kitchen. I think you will like the cooker—go on, now, keep looking; I will keep it safe for you."

She smiled at Blanche and shooed her back towards the kitchen. Blanche spent hours poring over the contents of each room. She had no impatient husband tapping his foot, pointing at his watch or making her feel guilty about wanting to explore each room and its collections of furniture, clothing, nick-knacks and heirlooms, all of which painted a very clear picture of the woman who Marigny must have been. By the time the estate sale was over and the final inventories taken, sales tallied and buyers wished a fine afternoon, Blanche felt as though she'd spent the day out on the front porch with Marigny, rocking in the hanging glider with a glass of iced tea, listening to her stories about the eccentric life she'd lived. In the drawing room, Blanche had learned that Marigny was fairly accomplished in watercolors, and throughout all the rooms, she noticed the display of delicate washes of moonlight over still waters, native mushroom varieties, and assorted wildflowers. Marigny had travelled, taking photographs that documented her adventures from Brazil to Alaska. By Blanche's count, Marigny had also wed no less than three husbands.

Blanche imagined what the house must have looked like at Christmastime from the boxes of decorations, lovingly wrapped in labeled boxes, and could see the conviviality of Marigny's welcome to her Mardi Gras guests. The library of her home was impressive, with everything from antique editions of *Gray's Anatomy* to modern novels, a variety of cookbooks from all the places she had ever visited, and exquisite collections of art, proudly displayed on the coffee tables. Blanche searched out one small item from each room: a Christmas ornament, fashioned from a blown eggshell and hand-painted by Marigny; a handkerchief, with a hand-tatted lace edging; a wrought-iron letter opener; and a hand-bound print of Colette's *Sido*. There were the things, which when Blanche laid her hands upon them, buzzed and sang with the energy of the woman who had made, owned and loved them. By mid-afternoon, she was the last of the shoppers, and took her time walking towards the front door to settle up with Marigny's sister. Blanche didn't want to leave, but she knew it was time. She laid out her choices in front of the silver-bunned woman, who nodded approvingly over the items and said.

"Twenty dollars for all. These are good things. You will take care of them, yes, *beb*?"

"I will. Your sister…um, she was quite a woman, wasn't she?"

Marigny's sister looked at Blanche with eyes, though watery with age and crinkled around the corners, remained clear as the moon over the surface of the water in one of Marigny's watercolors. She took the twenty dollar bill from Blanche's outstretched hand, holding it in her own for a moment. There was symmetry in the exchange of the bill, from Blanche's smooth, youthful fingers to the older woman's knobby knuckles, which had begun to gnarl and twist with the onset of arthritis.

"She was. You wait here, now. Put these things in a box. I must find something for you. That cooker you bought, it was my sister's favorite, for special occasions, like. Your Grand'Meré, she too, had one just like this one. You remember it? I must give you the recipe that comes with it. You will appreciate it like no one else who could have bought it today. I will find it for you. Only a moment or two, *beb*."

Grandmother Evangeline was gone before Blanche had married Renault. Blanche had often reminded herself what a blessing it was, that her *granmeré* had never lived to see Blanche divorced. Evangeline had herself been married for over sixty years before Peré Remy passed on—to have seen her favorite granddaughter cast aside would have made grandmother's heart heavy. In a way, by spending her Saturday at the estate sale, Blanche had been paid back twofold. Not only had she gotten to vicariously live Marigny's well-traveled life through the objects in her

home, but Blanche also felt closer to the presence of
Grandmother Evangeline—who she thought would have
enjoyed Marigny's colorful personality greatly, though she
herself had not lived as adventurously. Marigny's sister
returned, with a recipe card, tinted with age and speckled
with the stains of dinners past, tucked between the hooked
fingers of her hand. Blanche set her box down for a
moment, as the old sister reached out to press the precious
recipe into the warmth of Blanche's waiting palm.

"This recipe, it is only one to make in the slow cooker.
It is special, you understand?"

The skin of the old sister's hand was thin and cool, but
not unpleasant, reminding Blanche of Grandmother
Evangeline's hands, which though twisted with arthritis,
were always capable in the kitchen by rolling out dough,
then cutting, slicing and dropping beignets into sizzling hot
oil for Sunday afternoon brunch. She held onto the
woman's hand longer than she needed to, remembering.
Marigny's sister seemed to sense this, and she didn't seem
to mind.

"You must make this tonight, for yourself. Please,
promise. Go to the market when you leave. You have
much time still to make a bill. You must heal your heart in
the kitchen, tonight. Follow the recipe. Marigny will help
you, you see. There is magic in her cooker. It kept her
happy with many husbands. It will do your heart good to
eat this meal. It will break your *mal pris*; no more *en d'oeuille*.
Promise this. You will make Defan Evangeline, Defan
Marigny proud when you set down at your table tonight,
*chèr*. Go now, make a bill. Get your ingredients, and follow
sister's recipe. Eat tonight, eat well."

Blanche paused. "How do you know my *granmeré*'s
name?" The old sister smiled, and patted Blanche's hands,
curled protectively around the recipe.

"No matter, that. Tonight you use your new cooker. It will bring you much happiness, from my family into yours. Much luck, *beb*, Marigny is happy you have her pot. Off, now, you."

In truth, it was not all that odd to Blanche. Grandmother Evangeline often knew who was buzzing at the doorbell before she opened it. When Peré Remy's heart failed down at the docks, Grandmother Evangeline had dropped the cast iron skillet of cornbread she was taking out of the oven, and sat down to cry at the table, while the dog gulped down hot hunks of cornbread from the kitchen's clean linoleum floor. To be touched was a blessing. It was nothing Blanche had not seen before and nothing, she knew, to fear. Many Cajun women had the gift, and to have one share a family's recipe was not a compliment to be taken lightly. Blanche looked to the recipe as she walked to her car to stow her box of treasures. Though she had come to the estate sale that morning because of something she had lost, leaving it, she did not feel the same weakness she had felt over the long months since Renault left. Perhaps Marigny's sister was right, the cooker was magic, and it would heal her heart. She could use a good meal.

At the market, Blanche collected each item into her grocery buggy, feeling both bold and eager to get home and begin cooking. It was only yet late afternoon. Supper would be late tonight, she thought, but no matter. She bought fresh bread, cheese, and grapes to snack on. She wished she had something nicer to serve with than the collection of thrift-store dishes she'd bought to tide her over while getting settled again. When she got back to her little apartment, she took the box from the estate sale up first, placing the Crock Pot up on the counter with the precious recipe beside it. She unpacked the eggshell ornament, the handkerchief, the letter opener, and the book, placing them on the table to put away after supper. Once she'd unpacked the box, she took it back downstairs to load her grocery bags into. Though she still fumbled to balance her groceries when unlocking the door again, for once, the key didn't stick in the lock, and the door opened easily, without Blanche having to thump her shoulder against the frame to unstick it. She unpacked her groceries and arranged them on the kitchen's sideboard, taking out her cutting board, her one good knife, and a colander to rinse the grapes and vegetables. She removed the ceramic liner from the Crock Pot, ran a sink full of warm suds, and carefully washed the dust from the glass lid and pot lining. She read over the recipe's instructions and set to work.

As with all Louisiana recipes, it began with the words, *First, make a roux.* Feeling joyful and free in the kitchen again, Blanche was patient as she stirred the flour, and when the color of her roux changed into the deep, velvety color of chocolate, she removed it from the heat. When the garlic tipped from bitter to sweet and the onions turned translucent, she found herself suddenly ravenous. When the meat was browned, she turned the ingredients into the Crock Pot and sat down to the table. She took the handkerchief to her bedroom and placed it in her delicates drawer. From the top shelf of her closet, she took down a shoebox, filled with the only ornaments she'd managed to take with her when she moved out of the home she had shared with Renault. She found a sheet of tissue paper and carefully wrapped Marigny's eggshell ornament. When she put the box back on the shelf, she caught herself daydreaming about decorating a Christmas tree, and realized she wasn't sad about the prospect of spending the holidays on her own anymore.

When she returned to the kitchen, she took the letter

opener to the small wood box hanging on her wall where she kept the mail. All she'd received that day was her utility bill. Nevertheless, opening it with Marigny's opener made it feel special. She didn't hold her breath when she unfolded the bill to look, and was pleasantly surprised to find that the bill had gone down twenty dollars since last month. She chalked the happy coincidence up to the day's good fortune and put the bill on the top of the stack, arranging the opener in its proper place at the letter box. The ornate loop of the iron handle slid over the peg as though it had been meant to hang there. Finally, she set the kitchen timer to remind her when it was time to add the last of the ingredients, and sat down to read *Sido.* The kitchen filled with the rich smells of dinner cooking, of home and hearth, the aroma of everything Blanche had felt she'd lost when Renault had left her.

It was half-past ten when the timer sounded. Blanche tested the meat with a fork; it was tender and shredded beneath the tines. She added in the last of the ingredients and replaced the glass lid. Inside the slow cooker, she heard the comforting bubble of her meal cooking, and measured out the rice. At a quarter after eleven, Blanche sat down to supper. She poured herself a glass of wine in one of her mismatched glasses. Though the glass wasn't any fancier than the wine she poured into it, that night, with her late dinner, it tasted better than the finest claret Mother Gaspard used to serve at Sunday dinner. The smell of gumbo tickled her nose, teasing her tongue to indulge in what she'd created, with the spirit of Grandmother Evangeline in the kitchen and Marigny's good fortune in the recipe.

Each bite set her taste buds to dancing, and Blanche remembered how joyful eating could be. Her bowl emptied quickly. As she savored the final bite of her meal, Blanche felt something hard crack against her back teeth, and spat into her napkin. *A splinter of bone, or a bit of shell I missed*, she thought, *I must be more careful in the kitchen*. Looking into her cupped palm, she saw a button. She checked her cuffs, and finding none missing, checked the sweater she'd slung over the kitchen chair. No buttons were missing. *Odd. How did I miss that?* She thought, before taking it to her sewing basket to add to the button box. She put away the leftovers and washed the dishes before she went to bed. The Crock Pot, clean again, stood proudly on the countertop, just as Grandmother Evangeline's had. Blanche patted the lid before cutting off the kitchen lights. She slept well that night, never once troubled by the fitful sleep, which had plagued her for months. *Yes*, she thought, drifting off, *I guess I just needed to eat a proper meal.*

As promised by Marigny's recipe, the leftovers were equally delicious cold, the day after, when all of the unique flavors had married together into a bold pastiche for the palate. On Wednesday afternoon, Blanche stood at the break room sink at work, scrubbing the empty Tupperware from the last serving of her good fortune gumbo, when her supervisor Margeaux came in.

"Blanche, someone's here for you downstairs at check-in. I know you're at the end of your break, but he says it can't wait. I'll stay at the desk until you get back, all right? Try to hurry up, ok? I haven't gone to lunch yet and I'm starving."

Blanche nodded and thanked her. When she reached the bottom of the stairs, she was surprised to see Renault's lawyer, James Fahy, waiting on a bench in the atrium.

The visit came as a surprise. Her divorce from Renault had been finalized months earlier. Surely she had nothing left that Renault or his mother could possibly want to take. There was no way for her to disguise her confusion. Mr.

Fahy gestured towards the guard and secretary at the front desk. "Let's take a walk, Blanche." He smiled and patted her shoulder. Despite the fact that Mr. Fahy usually brought her bad news, Blanche had never held it against him. He always seemed to deliver Renault's and his family's terse communications to Blanche with a heavy heart. When they walked outside, the sun was warm on Blanche's office-chilled skin, though her stomach had begun to churn and tighten in fear, knotting up the last serving of gumbo. They walked for a minute or two in silence, before reaching the picnic table where Blanche sometimes spent her lunch break reading the newspaper. Fahy sat down and invited Blanche to join him. In keeping with his manner, he quietly told her the news that only later, she would realize, had been part of the change in her fortune.

Months before, when Renault had left Blanche, he had told her it was because he had fallen in love with another woman. "It's not that I don't love you," he'd said, "It's just... I love her *more*." It was clear he had thought himself kind—generous, even—in telling Blanche this. Whenever she had occasion to think about that moment, she would remember Grandmother Evangeline's cooking lessons, and would pinpoint *that* moment, sitting across the table from Renault in a crowded restaurant, as the moment when the lessons finally made sense. The memory had a flavor--onions, like heartburn, creeping up her throat, burning a path from her stomach to her mouth. Sitting next to Mr. Fahy, with her fists clenched into a prim ball resting on her lap, she could taste the rage and bitterness of that moment on her tongue again. Onions.

During the bitter months during which the divorce dragged on, Blanche had often wished she was a widow. Once the divorce was finalized, on nights she felt the most alone and unloved, she would find herself comforted by imagining misery and misfortune coming into Renault's new happiness without her, ruining the meal for him and his mistress. Who could say whether or not Blanche should have been more careful in her wishes. The fact of the matter was that Renault had been as unfaithful to his new mistress as he had been to Blanche, and his actions had fulfilled the blackest wishes of a scorned woman. Blanche tried to practice the deep breathing technique of a yoga class she'd gone to once, during the divorce, to see if it helped ease the stress. *Inhale, hold.* She listened as Mr. Fahy explained the history of mood disorders and poor impulse control, which checkered the past of Renault's mistress. *Exhale.* Mr. Fahy's voice broke into her breathing: *Renault and his mother are gone.* Blanche blinked. *Inhale, hold.* She concentrated on her hands, as Mr. Fahy's voice drifted back out of her breathing. *The girl committed suicide upstairs. She left a note.* Blanche concentrated on unballing her fists and re-weaving her fingers together, while listening to the legal terms Mr. Fahy was trying to explain. *Exhale.* Blanche tried to wrap her head around how neglecting to change a will during the divorce could mean that she inherited everything, even if she wasn't his wife anymore.

James Fahy reached into the interior pocket of his blazer, and pulled out a handkerchief. Though it was not nearly as hot as it would get in the dead of summertime, it was warm outside the office building, and delivering bad news always made him sweat, especially when he was dressed for business. He wiped away the glisten from his forehead and the shiny bald patch at the top of his head, carefully re-folding the handkerchief before putting it back into the same pocket he'd taken it out of. He sighed, and patted the top of Blanche's hand, as he carefully explained what her change in fortune meant. Renault and his mother were the last living Gaspards—no aunts, no cousins, no one to contest a will which had been changed to include Blanche when she'd married into the family. A will that had not been changed during the divorce, or after. Blanche Gaspard, who had not petitioned to change her name during the divorce, was the sole beneficiary. All those dark wishes, granted. The smell of burnt onions filled the back of her throat.

"So you're my lawyer now?"

"If you want me to be."

"Do I have to sign anything?"

Mr. Fahy pulled a slim stack of papers from his briefcase, and flipped to the pages where he indicated her signature was required. She signed, and stood up to go back into the office.

"I've got to get back up, Mr. Fahy."

"I know. Thank you. I'll send over the rest tomorrow."

"The arrangements? If I'm the only one left..."

"It'll be handled. If you want to do it, I'll tell you who to contact. If not, my office will handle it for you."

"I think that'd be best. Thank you."

"You're welcome. And Blanche, for what it's worth, I'm sorry."

She shrugged. When Renault had taken her out for dinner on the night he left her, she had managed to maintain her composure, and had even finished her meal, though Renault had left before his entrée arrived, right after he told her about the other woman. Etiquette and civility had been lessons that had gone hand-in-hand with cooking, in Grandmother Evangeline's kitchen. *Never make a scene, there will be time enough for dirty laundry in private, later.* So Blanche had asked the waiter to box up her husband's meal. *He's been called away for a work emergency, no, it's fine, I'll stay here and eat while it's hot. No, there's no sense in spoiling it, is there?* Though she could not remember what she'd ordered that night, she remembered the task of eating. To save face, she had even ordered dessert. Every forkful of her meal had been the same flavor: onions, onions, onions.

As Blanche walked back to the building, leaving Mr. Fahy to go about the business of settling what was left to be settled, she knew she should feel grief, pity, remorse. She knew she should cry, having once loved her husband. But instead, all she could remember was her nauseous belly, sitting alone in an expensive restaurant, a plateful of food that only tasted of onion, and gorging on Renault's dinner later, in the darkness of their empty house. She remembered hunching over the toilet, the sickness and tears of that night and so many which followed, and could not muster up even one more tear for him; every sorrow Blanche had felt had already been grieved. All that was left was the sulphur taste of onions. The bitter tang of it backed off, retreating back down her throat, and subsided into the quiet knot of her stomach. Blanche felt faint, and took the elevator back upstairs.

She found Margaeux, asked for the rest of the week off and drove home with her heart pounding and her head spinning, as though she'd had too much to drink, her armpits slick with sweat that did not even have the good sense to be hot. Blanche sat down at the kitchen table, head in her hands—the shock of irony only tempered by the unexpected violence of it all. It was late afternoon, and suddenly the apartment felt oppressive. She stared across the table at the countertop, where the Crock Pot sat, quiet and still. She remembered the button. *Saturday,* he'd said. *Near midnight.* Blanche ran to the bathroom. In the watery pit of the toilet bowl, shreds of meat and roux the color of the heart's darkest blood sank to the bottom. She flushed the last swallow of the weekend's gumbo into the coils of piping snaking beneath the floors and landings of the apartment. She needed to get out of the house, so she got back into her Honda Civic, and drove to the corner of Jackson and Magazine. Blanche circled the streets for nearly an hour before finding a place to park, the words *dental records*, and *toxicology report* blurring the names of the streets together like ink beneath a spill, until she could read nothing. She desperately tried to retrace the corners and avenues to the gingerbread house where she'd bought the Crock Pot. *Was it the same girl?* She had never known the girl's name, and there had always been another girl, so there was no way to be sure. When she finally parked, she turned the key in the lock of her Civic, her reliable, nondescript Civic that got great gas mileage, and for once, wished that she drove something just a little bit flashier.

Blanche had always been a careful, methodical cook. It was the one thing Grandmother Evangeline could not seem to pass along to her, the carefree element to cooking. Blanche always followed the recipe, always measured, and her meals always turned out exactly as the recipe intended. Blanche took this trait to her marriage as well, following the measurements and ingredients to the letter. Unfortunately, her husband had a taste for adventure and often stayed away past suppertime. Remembering a marriage full of cold suppers eaten alone, Blanche walked back and forth, crossing the streets in a systematic grid. She even managed to feel pity for a girl, whose name she had never known until today, recalling all too well the humiliation of betrayal and the taste of jealousy. Grandmother Evangeline had said that its taste was like too much salt in the stew. A pinch enhances the flavor. More than a teaspoon makes a meal no one cares to eat. Blanche rolled the memory of that flavor over her tongue, and considered how the taste had set Renault's new cook to a different kind of work in his kitchen. How much it was like a clove of garlic, or the angry onions her *granmeré* had described to her, when she first began learning to cook. On one hand, these ingredients were spicy and tantalizing. With heat and butter in a pan, they mellow, caramelize and turn into something sweet. But with too much heat or a careless cook, they burn, becoming black and bitter, ruining the whole meal.

Blanche walked the streets which should have been familiar, recognizing nothing, turned around when there was no reason to lose her sense of direction. Finally, she recognized a tree on the corner—where she'd found the lucky parking space, the morning of the estate sale. She was only a block away. Though she expected the house to be empty, she thought perhaps the neighbors could at least tell her where to find the old sister who had sold her the cooker. It was near dusk; the streetlights came on with a gentle *pop*. From the sidewalk, Blanche recognized the looming silhouette of the mansion next door. She hurried up to the next house's gate, and stopped dead in her tracks when she reached the front yard.

Though, it was the same house, it was not the house where the estate sale had been. That house had looked as though the owner had only recently passed on, with each room arranged exactly as it had been when Marigny lived there. This house was completely empty, too empty for a house which only one week ago, held an estate sale. This house was abandoned. The windows were shuttered and the gutters were full of decaying leaves, suggesting no one had lived there for quite a while. The walkway to the front steps was strewn with yard debris. The grass was tall, as though it had not been mowed since before winter, and now, with the advent of spring, the weeds grew rampant, tangling and choking the remainder of what had once been a garden. The Victorian flourishes Blanche remembered as looking like the ornate icing work of a gingerbread house were old, with white paint peeling back over the gums of the house to reveal a mouthful of rusty teeth. It smelled of sitting water, rotting leaves and the stray cats who sprayed the home's siding in the absence of an owner to chase them away. She risked the treachery of the lawn to wipe away the grime on a window and peek inside. Inside, the humidity of the closed-up house had caused a long strip of wallpaper to come unglued, revealing the stark wall beneath. The wallpaper sat mostly crumpled on the bare floor, clinging to the bottom of the wall it had fallen from like a forgotten Sunday-morning ribbon. Blanche wiped the dirt against the backside of her jeans and sat down on the front step to quiet the dizzy sickness she felt in the deepest pit of her stomach.

"Who did I buy the cooker from, then?" she whispered to the garden.

To its credit, the garden did not insult her by reminding her of what she should have already known, having lived here for her whole life. These things happen, sometimes, when a person is not strong enough to carry the weight of the lot they have been dealt. That weight divorces itself and takes substance, it takes form. With the touch of moonlight over swamp water, sometimes a simple appliance seizes a spirit, making a meal of a scorned woman's sorrow and the rage she has been holding beneath her tongue like a sliver of raw onion. *Surely it must be a coincidence*, Blanche hoped. Once again, to its great credit, the garden did not contradict her, and held its silence. Once Blanche felt steady on her feet enough to walk back to her car and take herself home, she stood up and headed in the direction she'd come from. No longer disoriented, she realized she had parked not even four blocks from the abandoned house, yet it had taken the better part of two hours to find it.

On her way home, she stopped at the grocery store.

Tonight she would cook a simple supper. Bitter greens: dandelion, turnip, collards and mustard. Bacon, fried salty and crisp. With the grease, she'd pour cornmeal batter into Grandmother Evangeline's cast iron skillet and make cornbread. Lenten meals, for a while. Just to make sure there was nothing left clinging to the cooker. No reason to rid herself of it, she thought, sitting down to the table—no matter how it came to rest on her kitchen counter, it was the very same make and model her grandmother had owned. And no matter who it had come from, she did not doubt that Sister Marigny had, in fact, kept several husbands happy with the meals she cooked in it. It would also seem that the cooker and its special recipe had provided assistance in clearing the way for better husbands to replace *bon riens* who did not appreciate good and wholesome home cooking, and instead sought mutton on the outside. Though her sudden fortune would make replacing it an easy thing, she would not dream of it, nor would she put it onto a high shelf away from view, or close it into darkness behind a cupboard door. It would stay there, on the counter, just as it always had in Grandmother Evangeline's kitchen.

Mr. Fahy had been right; no one came forth to contest the will. In two months' time, the Gaspard home and its assets belonged to Blanche, free and clear. She put the house on the market and hired an estate services specialist to sell off its contents. Despite the market being soft, it sold in just over a month's time. With that detail dispatched, there was nothing left for Blanche to take care of. In the months that followed, though she could afford a nicer apartment than the one she'd moved into after the divorce, Blanche stayed on there. She kept her Honda Civic, because it was reliable and fuel-efficient, but she spent more money than she would have ordinarily on the luxury of having it repainted—a shimmery, metallic purple, like moonlight over swamp water, a shade of purple which magically changed beneath the play of light bouncing off the paint. Instead of moving, she chose to use up some of the vacation time she'd accrued over the year and travel. She visited Brazil and Alaska. She bought an old Nikon camera, taking roll after roll of film, which she delighted in having developed, and taught herself how to paint with watercolors. When Blanche came back home from her travels abroad, she quit her work at the clerk's office, because she hated it, and took a job in the fabric store because it made her happy. She used her discount to purchase a bolt of fabric, printed gaily with bright yellow lemons. With it, she made herself a set of curtains to hang in the kitchen window and a matching apron. She tucked Marigny's recipe up into the back of her copy of *The Joy of Cooking*, and breathed a simple prayer to never need to use it again, to never need to call on the slow cooker for help in carrying a burden which had grown too heavy for her.

Blanche waited until Mardi Gras to use the Crock Pot again, making a crawfish and oyster stew she served alongside red beans and rice to the many new friends she invited to join her at the table. When Blanche cut into the King Cake, she shook off the remaining crumbs of the previous year and smiled. After all, difficult as it had been, it was the year her luck had changed for the better. Though the baby had been cut in half by the sharp tip of her knife, she took it as a symbol of more good fortune in the coming year. Under her lips, the mellow yeast of the pastry tasted like payback and freedom. Blanche licked the icing from her thumb, considering its sweetness.

## Sister Marigny's *Bon Rien* Gumbo, best served cold

➢ *First, make a roux. Add your troubles to the fat. Make it dark as blood from your broken heart*

➢ *One onion, chop it to bits and learn to love the sting of tears*

➢ *3 stalks celery, make a wish when you chop*

➢ *1 pepper for your trinity*

➢ *4 pieces garlic, sweet or bitter, depends on your treatment*

➢ *½ pound meat. Cut into cubes like bon rien cut your heart. Big enough to bite but not so big that you must chew.*

➢ *1 pound Andouille, ground for she who has taken his affections*

➢ *One fist of meat from crabs, keep their pinch*

➢ *Two fists of shrimp, with the shit torn away*

➢ *1 pound gumbo, taken to slices*

➢ *Cooked tomatoes, torn until you want no more*

➢ *1 tsp. of sugar, or more, if you are still bitter*

➢ *A handful of clean parsley, chopped into a fine fortune*

➢ *2 cups of drink, a toast*

➢ *Shake in Worstershire until you know you've had all that you wish in the pot*

➢ *Pepper sauce to bring a slap*

➢ *One pinch of salt, for your tears*

➢ *Two bay leaves and a sprig of thyme for the spice of bon rien*

➢ *One lemon, squeeze the juice for its pucker*

➢ *½ teaspoon cayenne, black pepper, and white pepper, hot as hell*

➢ *filé powder and green onions go on last for a happy life, when you have a bowl of hot rice waiting*

After the roux is done, cook your trinity with gumbo rounds until they are golden. Drop in the garlic last so the sweetness stays, and then set to the side. Brown meats, your *bon rien* will feel the heat and know that it is suppertime. When the meat is brown, put into the pot and set to medium. Leave the crab, shrimp and sausage to last. Add your drink, water, tomatoes and sugar, and season your meal to bring down the slap. Make a toast before you add in the drink, good health for you. When the meat splits under your fork, add the sausage, shrimp and crab. Know that your troubles are almost done and your belly will no more cry out in hunger. Take time to say goodnight while it cooks, may your rice be hot and fluffy for tomorrow. Squeeze the lemon, remove its seeds. Add the lemon juice to your stock, and then cook ten more minutes. Find the bay leaves and wish for justice as you pull them out. Add filé and green onion to your hot rice and set yourself down to the table for your meal. Tomorrow, eat a dish cold, and you will know that your meal has been blessed by righteousness.

# VOTER BASE
by Sarah Glenn

G ene Arnot sat in the bay window of his office, looking out over the bayous of Vermilion Bay. The sunset sky blazed pink and orange, framed by the twisted trunks of live oaks. Tall reeds stabbed up through the purple sheen of the water. Despite the idyllic scene, he fought a growing sense of dread. Gator Follette had called, wanting to see him. He hadn't heard from his father-in-law in years, perhaps even a decade.

His secretary, Matilde, had never met Gator. She'd been puzzled when Gene took the after-hours call. She was even more puzzled when he contacted his campaign manager to tell him that he would be late to the banquet. The mayor of Grenville didn't normally give such priority to a phone call from someone not in her files. Her face was full of questions, but he'd run her off. She was from Alexandria and didn't know everyone in the Old Families.

The room darkened, but he was reluctant to turn on the lamp. The pink of the sky softened and shifted to lavender as the sun dropped below the water. A faint tapping at the door, almost a scratch, disturbed the peace of dusk. He turned and rose. It was difficult to make out the face of the heavyset man who shuffled in, but he knew from the stance—and the sour smell which overwhelmed his secretary's potpourri—that it was Gator.

"It's been a long time, sir. I hope your urgent matter is something we can settle quickly. I have a speech to give in thirty minutes," Gene said, checking his Blackberry in a show of inconvenience. "I stayed here because it was you."

"Much obliged," the visitor said, sitting down on Gene's sofa. The ill-fitting orange baseball cap covered most of his head; Gator had finally shed the last of his hair.

"I'll get right to the point, since you seem to be so busy," Follette said. "Covins Homes filed to build along the waterline south of here. The Council—damned youngster—approved the zoning change. Are you really going to sign off on it?"

"I plan to." Harrison Covins had given generously to his state senate campaign. Gene was going to get out of this godforsaken swamp, move up in life. Move away from Grenville and its ever-present stench of frogs and fish. "Their request is a modest one, and the development will increase our tax base. That money could help Grenville renovate its schools, maybe even build a new library."

Gator's large hand crushed the arm of the couch, leaving a greenish smudge trail on the cream-colored fabric. "We like Grenville the way it is, Gene. It's quiet and peaceful here. Everyone goes about their business."

"I have to think about everyone, Gator, not just… the Families. Grenville needs this development. The citizens here want it."

"Not all of them," the old man snapped. His eyes reflected green in the fading light. "Covins may be your buddy now, but we have a previous claim on you. Don't forget that, *Mayor* Arnot."

"I haven't forgotten it. I'm still grateful, but the people of Grenville have a bigger claim. I'm sorry, but Covins is going to get their zoning change." He looked at his watch. "It's time for me to go. Are you going to leave...or do I need to call security?"

"No need." His visitor shuffled to his feet. "I have my own calls to make."

Most of the houses were dark when Gene headed for home. Dinner roiled in his stomach; by the time he'd arrived, they were out of chicken. All that was left? Shrimp étouffée. He'd eaten around the sickening bits of pale pink flesh, but its taint was making itself felt in his digestive tract.

The turnoff from Highway 82 quickly faded into the tall grasses despite the reflective markers he'd authorized the previous year. Fifteen minutes later, the driveway to his house peeked out from between two great live oaks. As he passed under a curtain of Spanish moss, Gene noticed a glow from behind the house. Gator's last words echoed in his ears.

He cut the headlights and rolled up to the carport, letting the motor run while he took his gun out of the glove box. After turning the engine off, he waited several moments, listening to the sounds of crickets and frogs, before unlocking the door. Then he eased the door release up slowly. Nothing moved towards him as he slid out of the car and crept along the side of the house. Above him, light reflected on tree limbs, rippling through magnolia leaves in a surreal fashion. Beyond them, he saw the twisted shapes of the mangroves shrouding Bayou Oublié. He kept one hand on the siding as he moved.

The smell, heavy and batrachian, hit him as he rounded the corner to the pool enclosure. There was a splash from inside, and Gene peered through the screen. A short stocky body crossed the water with powerful strokes. Gator stood near the diving board and grinned down at the swimmer. His gaze rose from the water and met Gene's through the mesh, teeth glowing soft green in the aquatic lights. He gestured to his son-in-law with one heavy arm.

Gene fumbled with the catch on the screen door, hands shaking, and entered the moist space. His Comptons skidded on the slick floor, mottled with slime. This wasn't what he had expected. As he approached the pool, he spotted a third figure lounging in a pool chair. He recognized the shape, and the memory of cold hands and wet, rubbery lips made his gorge rise.

"You're awful quiet for once. Thought I'd bring the family by," Gator said, "and let them see how you've been doing. The chemicals really aren't good for the boy, but a little bit won't hurt." The glittering eyes traveled down Gene's arm to the gun in his hand. "You thought we were burglars?" He laughed, an unpleasant croaking sound. "You could have shot your own wife and son."

Gene's eyes traveled back to the chair. Yes, it was Pearl. It had been some years, but he could still pick out the vestiges of her ravaged features. Gene had taken his first wrong step with Gator by telling him how lovely his little girl was. Gator's response: Gene was full of crap. She had never been an attractive woman; her eyes had always been bulgy and her chin nonexistent.

She'd worn a tiara at their wedding. It hadn't fit her well—it was slightly misshapen—but it bore large blue gems which he would discover later were sapphires. It was her grandmother's, and therefore she would not let him sell it. She wore the diadem now, and he saw it fit perfectly.

What a tremendous relief it had been when the sea called her away. He'd gotten on his knees and praised God that day. She, the bowlegged kid she'd borne, and Gator had all disappeared from his life… until today.

He forced himself to look at Pearl now. In the time since they'd parted, her forehead had sloped back and her skin had taken on an unhealthy blue-gray undertone. She stared at him with those protruding watery eyes, open far too wide to be normal. They didn't blink; he wondered if they still could.

"Hard to believe Gene Junior's gotten so big, isn't it?" Gator bent over the figure in the pool and rubbed the teenager's head. "It seems like only yesterday I was calling him my little fish taco. He's growing up on me. Come take a look."

He didn't want to obey, but morbid curiosity finally won. The boy reciprocated by swimming to poolside and staring up at him. Staring, with protuberant eyes like his mother's. The chin was too weak, the nose a little flat, but Gene could see some of himself there in the eyebrows, in the cheekbones, in the boy's pale thin hair. His gorge rose again, and it had nothing to do with the étouffée.

Gene put the gun away, inside his jacket. "Why did you bring them here?"

"To remind you of where you came from. You were a struggling young man too poor to attend college, much less pursue his interest in politics. We paid for that, Mayor. The gold of Y'nar-thlia, out there in the Gulf, paid for it because you married my little Pearl." He directed a hideous smile to her, made more horrible by the visible affection.

"I remember, sir. I'm still grateful. But you don't understand: Harrison Covins has been a major contributor to my current campaign. It's not just money; they have influence as well. Betraying them would be political suicide. It would ruin my chances to become anything but mayor of a small town."

"Not just any town. *Our* town." Gator took Gene's arm in a painful, moist grip and steered him outside into the darkness. "Mayor Arnot, it's not just your wife and son you must answer to."

The march across the back lawn, manicured to perfection, felt like forever to Gene, but not long enough. He found himself counting the travertine pavers that led to the edge of the water. He should have invested in the winding path the landscaper suggested.

◇ ◇ ◇ ◇

While stumbling in the dark, more painful images of the wedding rose unbidden in his mind. Half the pews had been loaded with his relatives, looking confusedly at the object of their golden boy's 'whirlwind romance', while only a quarter of the bride's side was populated. Not everyone could make it from the Mariana Trench, Gene would suppose later. When he lifted her veil, he could see the slightly protuberant eyes rimmed with makeup, which only accentuated the bulging.

His family didn't understand why he was marrying this girl; she wasn't very pretty. They had to admit she was more attractive than the rest of her family, though. His Uncle Remy would later refer to her as the girl from Toad Hall.

The wedding night had been the most disturbing. Her lips were so rubbery. Her tongue was cold, her body was cold, and she was even cold in places a woman shouldn't be cold. It was a wonder he could function at all that first time.

Only the thought of the money Gator had offered him kept him trying, kept him in the honeymoon suite, when every other part of him wanted to flee, run screaming into the night. Maybe God would be merciful and strike him dead before they reached the water. He wasn't.

The dock was broad and empty. Gene had sold the Stratos when Pearl left; he had no desire to leave dry land ever again. A meaty hand grabbed the back of his head and twisted it up, forcing him to stare out across Bayou Oublié. Dozens of dark bumps marred the moonlit surface of the water, moving closer to the land's edge. Those hadn't been frogs earlier.

Forms lurched out of the bayou, streaming water from their scales. Webbed feet broke free of cold mud with a sucking sound. The stink, a mixture of fish and reptile, rose from the bayou. He fought another wave of nausea, and stumbled as Gator released him.

*I must not panic. If I panic, I'm dead.*

They had all been people once, Gene told himself. Gator's people were infertile and had been forced to interbreed with humans for centuries. Most of them had been raised on land in human families, with human drives and interests. Even Pearl, repulsive as she was, had once laughed and chattered about TV shows and handsome country singers. He must have something in common with them. He could find it. Yes, he could.

They weren't monsters. They weren't monsters. If he thought they were monsters, they would rend his limbs from his body. No, they were his voters. His voter base. It was his job to appease them.

The crowd was uglier than usual, but Gene Arnot had faced ugly crowds before. The only difference was the price he would pay for failure. He cast about for an elevated place to stand, and spotted the stump of the live oak he'd had removed last summer. How appropriate.

Leaping atop it, he straightened to his full height and shoved his fear back down his gullet. Babies and angry constituents could both smell fear.

"I'm glad you've all come tonight," he said. "It'll save time. Let me explain to you what I have in mind." He scanned his audience. Slime dripped and gills flared, but he had their attention.

"For the past eight years, it has been my honor to serve as your mayor. You've all been wonderful to me, and I've done my best to fulfill your expectations."

Dead silence. He didn't even hear any insects.

"Gator Follette may have told you that I plan to allow Covins Homes to build along the western shore."

Angry cries and bleats ensued. The people on shore moved closer. Some clutched knives, others bared claws.

"Did he also tell you that I've filed to run for the State Senate?"

Apparently so… the throaty replies were interspersed with hisses.

"You're viewing this as something bad. I'm here to tell you why it's good for Grenville and good for you. Have you thought about the future of Vermilion Bay, and the Gulf in general?"

No answer, just gleaming eyes which reflected the security lights illuminating the back yard. There had to be at least a hundred of them. Gene turned to his son. The boy's eyes were curious, rather than angry.

"Junior, would you be kind enough to turn off those lights? I don't want to blind anyone." His son complied, mercifully dimming the faces of his growing audience. "There. I hope that's better."

"The Gulf," someone squawked.

It took him a moment to make out the words. The speaker's palate must have been entirely deformed. "Was that you, Mrs…. Desmarais? I'm sorry, it's a little harder for me to see now. Yes, the Gulf. Surely you've realized the oil companies are going to continue building platforms in the Gulf. Platforms extending deep into the ocean, damaging your homes. Drilling which disturbs your rest. More accidents, like the one with the Macondo well."

Gator cawed with laughter. "Is that all? Those platforms are nothing before our power... or have you forgotten about Katrina and Rita?"

"I haven't forgotten them. But," he paused for effect, "*they* have. New platforms have already gone up, and there is talk of erecting more of them. Even my father-in-law from the Sunshine State has surely heard the call. Oil from the Macondo spill still washes up on our shores, years later, but the mantra from Washington continues: Drill, drill, drill."

He paused, then placed a hand over his heart. "*I* plan to fight for your homes from Baton Rouge. Environmental protection will be a pillar of my policy."

"What good is one state senator?" another voice grunted. Beyond him were the sounds of more splashes and feet slogging through mud. Some of the larger shapes squatted on the lawn.

"It'd be one more voice than you have now. Or do you believe that Gillet is doing an effective job?" Gene knew he'd hit a nerve with that one; the hissing began anew. He raised a fist. "I intend to become a force to be reckoned with!" The croaks and grunts from the mass of shapes wasn't exactly approbation, but it wasn't directed at him anymore.

Gator waved his orange baseball cap to get everyone's attention. "He's still only one vote. There are thirty-eight others. These short-lived idiots only hear the call of fast money, not the greater voice of Father Dagon."

Damn it, Pearl's father had always hated him. "I don't intend to stop at the State Senate," he shouted to the crowd. "It's just a stepping-stone to greater things... like the governor's mansion!"

The clicking and ululations were definitely ones of approval. He had them; he knew it.

Gene turned to his rival, expecting to see impotent anger or disgust on that pulpous face. Instead, Gator had become perfectly composed. "I see you've set your sights high, Gene," his rival said more softly, but loud enough for his voice to carry. "But why did you betray us to Covins? If you care for the Families so, why are you letting them build on our pristine wetlands?"

Hah! Was that all the objection he could muster? "As I told you inside, Augustine"—Gene enjoyed seeing the spongy flesh twitch— "not accepting their bid would be political suicide. However, I believe it will turn to our advantage. There's been a problem with inbreeding for years in Grenville. This will bring new blood in—new people with money. You must admit that our fair town has struggled to pay its bills in these hard times. The new residents are professionals from Lafayette who want to raise families. Their children will play with ours, and their children will intermarry with ours. Eventually the houses will be theirs—new, sturdy houses, located conveniently near the water."

More clicks and excited croaks followed.

Gator's grumble had become a purr. "It seems that you have been thinking of our interests all along, Eugene. I don't know what I was thinking. I'm concerned, though. Have you spoken to the Board of Zoning recently?"

"Not in the last few days." No one built anything new within the city limits unless something else had fallen down. Why would they bother?

"I thought not. Jeanne Sergant tells me that your prospective breeding stock is interested in building a private school. Seems they don't think they should have to mix with the locals."

Painful coldness spread in Gene's stomach. "I see." Crap. The crowd was shifting from webbed foot to webbed foot, muttering, growling. Not good.

He straightened taller, raised his voice. "That's not going to happen. They can't shut us out. I won't let that happen."

"Really? And what, pray tell, will you do to stop it? The Council's already on their side."

Green reflective eyes were fixed on him, waiting for his response. He knew what to say, though. "They can't deny the son of the mayor, can they?"

Cheers broke out again. Gator's grin was wide and toothy. He patted the boy on the back. The boy gave the crowd a confused smile.

"Surely you wouldn't leave your son alone here, would you, Gene? He's nowhere near grown up."

"He has a mother," Gene countered. "I know the sea called to you, Pearl, but would you consider coming home... for the good of the town?"

He would be at the capital, he reminded himself. Far away from her and her cold embrace.

Pearl's eyes bugged more and a rime of watery film covered them. "I would be proud to."

"I think you should run for the School Board. You could open the door for other deserving youngsters."

"Wonderful!" Gator clapped his hands. "I didn't know you cared so deeply about us. It's not like you were born a member of the Families."

"But I am a member now. My blood is one with yours in my son's veins. To shut the Families out" — Gene thumped his chest "—is to shut *me* out."

Half of the crowd hurrahed; the other uttered bestial trills.

"You're the strongman we were looking for when we elected you, son. But tell me… how can you protect us all the way from Baton Rouge?"

"As I said before, I'll be that voice in the State Senate you need."

"It seems to me that your proper place is here. Pearl is a good woman, but these new neighbors are going to be a handful. She can't do it alone, especially with a hostile council. I think you should continue your good work here, to usher a new prosperous age into Grenville!"

Gene opened his mouth to object, but was drowned out by the crowd.

"We always plan for the long term. Gene Arnot for mayor again, and Gene Junior for State Senate when he grows up!"

"Arnot! Arnot! Arnot!" Clawed hands fist-pumped the air.

◊ ◊ ◊ ◊

When the rally ended, the celebration began. The Dubois brothers went to unlock their liquor store and brought back a truckload of beer and a case of champagne. Leroy Fournier and his boyfriend, the town caterers, rushed home to thaw out their special crawfish tartare and other delicacies. Celine Bertrand commandeered Gene's sound system and cranked up the zydeco.

Gene and Gator went back into the pool house to talk as the party commenced. Gator was triumphant.

"I knew you'd see things my way," he chortled, popping a piece of ceviche into his wide mouth. "And making my little girl happy was icing on the cake."

"But sir, I can't simply quit the race," Gene said. "I don't know all the regulations on campaign contributions, but Covins, at least, will want his money back. I don't have it anymore. It's all gone into the campaign."

Gator was all graciousness. "I'm certain that Y'nar-thlia could be persuaded to assist you with another loan. Consider it a down payment for Junior's campaign in a few years."

The door opened, and the pair was confronted by Pearl. Her globular eyes were rimmed in tears.

"I didn't realize how strongly you felt," she croaked. "I thought you were happy to see me leave. Now I know you were happy for *me*. Oh, darling…" she threw her thick arms around his neck and kissed him with those rubbery lips. "I'll never leave you again. We'll lead this town together."

"Together," he whispered, doing his best not to inhale.

"I think we should ask Daddy to babysit the rest of the night. I want to get to know you all over again. Besides—" she winked at Gator "— I think Junior needs a little brother or sister. Don't you think so, too?"

# DYING DAYS: APPLE BOTTOM
## By Armand Rosamilia

The Ku Klux Klan, in the form of sixteen hooded pot-bellied men waving American flags and spewing racial intolerance, stood on the Capitol Building steps and watched as the crowd grew.

"Nothing attracts a crowd like a crowd," Ellis Kingery said to the cute girl standing beside him.

"What?" she asked absently, her eyes watching the demonstration.

"I said... aww, forget it. My name is Ellis. What's your name?" He put on one of his big smiles. She was cute, a chubby girl with a big ol' booty and flopping boobs, maybe twenty-five. No more than thirty, Ellis reckoned. Her shorts were really tight across her apple bottom, and...

She was dating some black dude, who walked up and stared menacingly at Ellis, watching him check out his girlfriend's ass.

"Babe, you ready to go?" Black Dude asked Apple Bottom. He glanced at Ellis until Ellis found something else to look at.

"Give me a minute. I want to hear this bullshit."

"Exactly what it is. Why sit here and listen to their shit? Babe, they're telling you not to date a black man. As if it's any of their damn business."

Apple Bottom kept staring at the men on the Baton Rouge steps.

Ellis faded back a few people but made sure he angled

his body so he could still see her ass without her boyfriend any wiser. *Man, what a waste of a good ass. The things I could do with that…*

"You got a fucking problem, redneck?"

"No. Do you?" Ellis asked stupidly, knowing it was lame. But Black Dude had startled him. If he'd been paying more attention to the crowd and not her ass he would've seen Black Dude slip around and confront him. Now Ellis wanted to bolt, because the guy was huge. Probably a football or basketball player. A guy with a full scholarship to LSU, more than likely. Ellis had to work for a living. He couldn't afford college. Shit, he couldn't even afford to go to Tiger Stadium and see this guy play ball.

"If I see you staring at my girl's ass one more time I'm going to slap the taste from your mouth. Do you feel me?"

*I'd like to feel her ass cheeks*, Ellis thought but wisely kept his mouth shut. Mama always said he wasn't the sharpest Crayon in the box, but he knew better than to be a smartass and get a beat down. "No disrespect, bro."

"Bro? I ain't your fucking bro." Black Dude pointed at the Capitol Building. "Are you here, waiting for your daddy to get done talking shit, so you can go get chicken fingers after?"

Ellis was hungry. Raising Cane's chicken fingers would be really nice right now, if he had any money. He imagined dipping them in their sauce… "Shit, I don't know them crazy bastards. I'm just on my way to work. I saw all the people and decided to stop."

"You decided to stop and stare at my girl's ass."

Ellis put his hands up, looking around to see if anyone was going to jump in and break up a fight. If he could punch Black Dude in the face, then run and hope people would rush in to break it up, he'd have a fighting chance.

Black Dude put a hand up and Ellis flinched, which

made Black Dude grin and Ellis pissed he'd been messed with and shown he was scared. But not pissed enough to do something stupid.

"Is there a problem?" a police officer asked as he walked up, staring at both men.

Ellis sighed. The cop was black, too. If he sucker-punched Black Dude the black cop would beat his ass and call Ellis the racist, which was bullshit. He had nothing against minorities and especially the blacks. He'd hung out with a black guy in high school. Alright, he'd bought his weed from that black guy, but they talked. He didn't hate him or anything. "No problem here, officer."

Black Dude shook his head. "We were just going over some of the points brought up by his family onstage."

"That ain't funny," Ellis said.

The cop smiled.

*Great, they're going to drag me into a secluded parking lot or into the back of a squad car and beat my ass*, Ellis thought. *Because of my skin color. Ain't this a bitch?*

"Break it up. This garbage is almost done." The cop looked at his watch. "They have fifteen more minutes and then we can shut them down." As he was talking his radio kept buzzing on his shoulder, the sound turned down very low.

"Lots of action today," Black Dude said, kissing the cop's ass. Ellis wanted to run before they decided there was nothing better than beating up on a white boy.

"There's a disturbance near the campus, but I'm stuck here with the Clean Sheet Brigade," the cop said. He stopped and looked at both men. "Anyway, split up and go your own way."

Ellis heard what sounded like a gunshot. Where had it come from? Several people nearby were also looking around, so he hadn't imagined it. Even the cop walked away.

Black Dude turned and looked at Ellis to say something when they heard the next three shots in rapid succession.

Had the Ku Klux Klan been attacked? Some crazy black taking shots at the idiots in sheets? Ellis knew it couldn't be them, because the KKK was still on the steps talking shit into the mic. Whoever was shooting was in the crowd somewhere.

Ellis saw two cops running on the outskirts of the crowd, guns drawn and aimed at the sky as they moved. Something was going down.

Now, half of the crowd was watching behind them. Another group of people had been drawn to the rally, too.

*Nothing attracts a crowd like a crowd*, Ellis thought again. There were maybe a hundred people, all walking slowly… silently… bloody?

"What's the matter with them?" Black Dude asked.

"I'm not sure, but they look fucked up," Ellis said.

"Man, I wasn't talking to you. Shit."

Ellis started to say something smart when he saw a woman wearing a classy business suit but with blood dripping down her face, grab a man who was still watching the rally. The woman spun the poor guy around and clamped her bloody teeth onto his shoulder. He began to scream and now most everyone was turning to see what the commotion was about.

The black cop who'd been harassing Ellis turned up his radio and it was a wall of sound, officers yelling and dispatch screaming over them.

When another cop ran by, the black cop grabbed him by the arm. "What's going on? Are we under attack? Terrorists?"

The cop pulled away and shook his head. "People are biting other people… and worse," he said before running away. "I'm getting out of this mess."

"I'm going to agree with that guy," Ellis said. "Some crazy shit is going on. Look, that chick is biting someone now, too."

Black Dude looked at the black cop, maybe looking for support or for an order to do something, but the cop finally looked at both men and turned and ran towards the Capitol Building.

"We should follow him," Ellis said.

Black Dude frowned. "Screw that. I'm going to get my car and drive the hell out of this place."

"Cool. You got an Escalade?" Ellis asked.

"You racist white boy piece of shit." Black Dude turned and started running away. Ellis watched him go for a few steps before a man, his neck ripped and bloody, stepped into view, bloodshot eyes fixed on Ellis.

"Hey, uh, dude… wait up," Ellis yelled, pulled up his sagging pants, and chased after Black Dude. The guy wasn't very fast, though. *No way he's a starter on the LSU football team*, Ellis thought. *He's too small to be a lineman and not quick enough to be a safety or running back.*

An older man wearing a white cowboy hat and brandishing two old-looking pistols was shooting at people. As Ellis got closer he turned one of the guns on him.

"Don't shoot," Ellis yelled.

The man nodded and aimed away, firing. "Just keep breathing, kid. Don't get bitten. I've seen this before. It ain't gonna be pretty. Get to cover and hide."

Black Dude was up ahead, now in the parking lot and fumbling with his keys as he pulled them out of his pocket.

Ellis picked up the pace as the wall of bloody people closed in, like they were marching or something. He got to Black Dude just as a crazy woman was about to attack him from behind. Ellis shoulder-blocked the woman to the ground.

Black Dude, startled, dropped his keys. "Man, what are you doing?"

"Saving your bla...saving your ass," Ellis said. He watched as the woman tried to right herself, glaring at the two men. "We should leave."

"No shit. Help me find my keys," Black Dude said.

They both stopped looking when they realized his keys were under the woman, who was now crawling and gnashing her teeth.

"Bitch is gonna bite me," Ellis said. "This is all nuts. You think they're shooting a movie?"

"I think you're even dumber than you look. It's the apocalypse. The end of the damn world. Judgment Day, redneck." Black Dude kicked the woman in the face with his Crocs until he could get her moved enough to get his keys.

"Don't let her bite you." Ellis grinned. "Man, you're wearing Crocs. No wonder you couldn't run."

"They're really comfortable. And if they get wet... shit, why am I talking to you? Go away."

"No way. We're in this together. Besides..." Ellis looked around. "We're surrounded by these people, and they're going to rip us apart if we don't get out of here. I don't have a car. Where's yours?"

"Right here," Black Dude said.

Ellis laughed. "A green Ford Focus? Is this your white girlfriend's car?"

"Man, I'm about to knock you out. You racist hillbilly. This is my car."

The woman on the ground caught up and grabbed Ellis by the ankle. He stomped down on her head three times until she stopped, her eyes rolling back in her head.

A crowd of slow-walking people were approaching.

Black Dude opened his car door and sighed. "Damn it. Get in the car. Hurry up or I'm leaving you."

"Thanks," Ellis said and as soon as the lock popped he rushed into the car and put his seatbelt on. "I hope you're a good driver."

"I hope you shut up eventually."

Black Dude started the car just as two men slammed against his side window, startling him. He put the car in drive and got only a few feet before the parking lot was filled with people, all fixated on his car and the two passengers.

"Go around them," Ellis said.

"I can't."

"Then run them over if you have to," Ellis said.

People were walking into the car and a man fell onto the hood, crawling at Ellis as he reached up with one hand.

"This is not really happening," Black Dude said before stomping on the gas and cutting the wheel, throwing the man on the hood and knocking over two women in the way. But there were too many, and when he ran over another woman the back of the car slid to the right.

"I can't build up speed," Black Dude said.

"An escalade would've been perfect."

"Man, shut up."

He did a wide circle, thumping against people, until he cut the wheel back. "That cowboy is clearing a path."

The old man with the white hat had killed over a dozen of the crazies and was headed right toward them, shooting as he moved.

As they got closer, the cowboy shot the three crazies in front of them. There were many more pressed on either side, though, and the car shook even as Black Dude drove.

"Let me in," the cowboy yelled. "I'm running out of ammo."

"Don't let him in," Ellis said. "He doesn't look all that stable. It's a special kinda nuts to be shooting people in the head."

Black Dude stepped on the gas and plowed into more people, knocking them out of the way and running over some body parts. 'This is fucked up," he mumbled. "I'm killing people."

"They already look dead, in all fairness," Ellis said. He pointed. "If you can get through those cop cars we might have a chance."

"No way, I'll hit them."

"Or we stay here and die," Ellis said as a man missing an arm slammed against the passenger window.

"So damn dramatic, white boy," Black Dude said. But he aimed for the gap between two cop cars and went over the curb. The car jumped and slid to the right, the front wheels caught first on the curb and then on the median.

The Ford Focus slammed into the two cop cars on either side, wedging the car halfway through the gap.

Black Dude turned to Ellis. "Great call, dumbass." He tried his door but both sides were firmly between the cop cars. He started to roll down the window when bloody fingers pawed at him. He rolled the window back up.

"We're surrounded," Ellis said.

"No shit."

The car windows were being touched, bloody handprints left on the car.

"The doors won't open and even if they did, we'd never get more than a few feet. I'm not as fast as you, even though you seem slower than anyone I've ever seen play football," Ellis said.

"Football? Man, I'm a business major."

Ellis looked at the back seat. "If you had a blanket we could cover ourselves. Maybe they'd forget about us."

"I do have a blanket," Black Dude said as a woman fell onto the hood of the car and began crawling at them. "In the trunk."

"We could hide in the trunk," Ellis said.

"It's a hatchback," Black Dude said, but started climbing into the back seat.

"Where are you going?"

"To hide in the trunk under a blanket. You might be onto something." Black Dude swung over and around, ignoring the multitude of bodies pressed against the car. "I'm Brett, by the way."

"Ellis."

Brett (Ellis was still going to privately refer to him as Black Dude) pulled the backseat down and slipped into the trunk area, which didn't offer much room. Luckily there were only a few pieces of clothing and a large brown blanket in the space.

Ellis joined him awkwardly, curling up way too close. He could smell Black Dude's aftershave. "What are you wearing? It's not bad."

"I thought you were hitting on my girl. Were you asking her about me?"

"No way. I'm straight as a damn arrow," Ellis said defensively. "I was definitely hitting on your girlfriend."

"Watch it."

The people were pounding on the car but under the blanket Ellis felt safer than he had since this began.

"I hope she's alright," Brett said and the small area lit up as he began punching numbers on his cell phone.

"You calling her?"

"Shut up." The number rang three times and then went to voicemail. "This is Amber. I'm busy at the moment. Leave a message…"

"Her name is Amber?" Ellis blurted.

"You're lucky I can't move my arms too much or I'd punch you in the mouth. You are very disrespectful and it needs to end or I will end you," Brett said.

"I mean no disrespect. Sorry," Ellis said. He didn't want Black Dude to choke him to death in the trunk. "But… damn, she has a nice big ass on her. Just sayin'."

Black Dude sighed. Then Ellis heard him chuckle. "Yeah, she does have a great ass. I have to admit it."

Ellis smiled. "She has an apple bottom. Great shape to it, man. Congratulations."

"Thanks. She's really cool. I've never dated a girl like her. Usually, when I date a white or Puerto Rican chick, they want to act all ghetto. I was born in Slidell. My father is a doctor and my mother a lawyer," Bret said.

"If you're rich… why are you driving this piece of… a Ford Focus?"

"Because my parents taught me to earn everything. I worked summer jobs and after school during high school to buy a car and have spending money. My parents paid for LSU but I'll pay them back. It's what you do," Brett said.

"It's not what my family does. I had to drop out of school to get a job once my mom died. I walk to work, which is why I was even here today," Ellis said.

"You work at the sub shop around the corner, right? I go in there all the time."

"Yeah. The pay is shit and I stink like sliced meat at the end of my shift, but it's a job," Ellis said. "And I get to check out all the ladies who come this way after leaving the campus, too."

"Nice. Well, if we ever get out of this alive, I'll swing over and get a po' boy. That place does make a good po' boy," Brett said.

"And I'm sorry for saying shit about your girlfriend's amazing apple bottom ass cheeks."

"Now you're pushing it... hey, wait. Listen," Brett said.

"What? I don't hear anything."

"Exactly. The banging on the car stopped and so did the shooting and screaming. It's really quiet," Brett said.

"What do you think it means?"

"Maybe it's over. Maybe everyone is dead?"

"I hope it means the crowd moved away from this spot. Go check and see," Ellis said.

"Hell no. You go check. Pop into the backseat. You're smaller than me."

"No way. I'm staying right here under this blanket until I hear something to make me leave this hatchback. I'm just getting comfortable," Ellis said. "You go check. It's your car."

"This is why you're going to take a look. I'll throw you out," Brett said.

"You can try... ok, you could easily do it. I guess I'll go," Ellis said. He pushed against the backseat and let it slowly open, watching the windows on both sides. There was blood and what he hoped was only drool painting the glass, but nothing was pressed against the windows.

"What do you see?" Brett asked.

"A really expensive detailing bill, but nothing more so far. Give me a second, my legs are cramping." Ellis slipped into the backseat and looked around. The car was covered so much you couldn't see clearly out of any window, which he supposed was a good thing.

Brett awkwardly climbed out of the trunk as well and took out his car keys.

"What are you doing?"

"I have to turn the key so we can crack open a window and see what's going on. I'm not opening a door, are you?" Brett asked.

Ellis shook his head. "Just be quiet about it," he

whispered. He went to put his face to the glass to get a better view, but he'd seen enough horror movies to know as soon as the hero did it, a monster would slam against the glass and scare the shit out of everyone in the theater as well as the star of the film.

The window started to hum as Brett lowered it and Ellis was about to panic, the sound so loud in the quiet.

But there was nothing in the immediate area except body parts and so much blood he thought it was a bad movie set. *I need to stop watching so many horror flicks*, Ellis thought. He poked his head out of the window once it came all the way down and looked all around, making sure nothing was about to take a bite out of his head.

Brett joined him on his side of the car, putting his head out of the passenger side. "You think it's safe?"

"No. It's way too quiet," Ellis said. "Maybe if we can get around the corner to the sub shop we'll be safer. Plus, I'm really hungry. I could use a po' boy right about now."

"Yeah, me, too," Brett said.

Ellis began slipping his body out of the car window when he stopped. He'd noticed movement to his right and looked. "Holy shit, dude, look at the steps."

The front of the Capitol Building was packed with a mob, all trying to get into the building. The stage the KKK had used was destroyed, pieces of wood and equipment scattered on the ground where everyone had stood for the rally.

"They're the people biting and shit," Brett said.

"Zombies."

"Huh?"

Ellis nodded. Watching all those horror movies had come in handy. "Fucking zombies. They're going to bite people and turn them into zombies. We're screwed."

"I've never heard of zombies getting hard-ons and

raping people, though," Brett said.

Ellis nodded. "A buddy of mine who likes to read told me about this really cool zombie series he got into this year. In it, the zombies not only wanted to bite you, they wanted to sexually violate you. The guy is supposedly a great writer, too."

"It sounds stupid," Brett said. "I hope Amber isn't inside."

"You should hope she isn't part of the crowd," Ellis said. "That would really suck. And a waste of a great apple bottom. Um, sorry again."

"I need to save her," Brett said slowly.

"If you're planning on fighting through a horde of zombies, I'm going to be honest… I'm going to get some lunch. If you survive, come over and I'll make you a sandwich. Otherwise… you're on your own," Ellis said.

"I really love Amber. She's the best thing that ever happened to me."

"I'm sure she is. I've seen her. Dude, if I was tapping that big ass and I was in your shoes right now, it would be a very hard decision. Do you go in to save her and obviously die, or go and get something to eat and try to figure out a game plan that will make you look like the lone hero in this story? Decisions, decisions…" Ellis slipped out of the car and onto the police cruiser on his side, careful not to make too much noise and attract a zombie.

Brett got out and hopped down from the cop car hood and onto the bloody median, most of the grass pushed down and coated in red. "I know in my gut she's inside. If I walk away now I'll never be able to forgive myself."

"But you'll be alive to hate what you've done." Ellis stared at the group of zombies trying to push in the doors of the Capitol Building. "I'm going to guess there are fifty monsters between you and your apple bottom girl. You think you can get through them? I don't."

Brett took two steps toward the Capitol Building and stopped before glancing at Ellis.

◊ ◊ ◊ ◊

Ellis decided to make five po' boy's before everything went bad. Why waste good food? The power was already out and it wasn't like there was a line of customers at the door, waiting to order lunch. "Grab a plastic bag and fill it with chips, too."

Brett sighed and leaned against the counter. "I can make my own sandwich."

Ellis shook his head. "Customers aren't allowed on this side. If there are no rules, the world will end."

"Look outside. The world has already ended," Brett said. "And don't skimp on the roast beef, either. I want a real sandwich from this place for once."

"I'm going to make pretend I didn't hear that," Ellis said. "When we run out of meat I can get seafood. You like seafood? If not, more for me. I bet I can make us fifteen sandwiches for the road."

"Where do you think we're going?"

"Somewhere the zombies haven't attacked yet. I've always wanted to go to Georgia," Ellis said.

"For what?"

Ellis looked up from his work and grinned. "You ever see the ass on a chick from Atlanta?"

# CAJUN CRITTER
by Ethan Nahté

*June 25, 1957 - Bay of Campeche*

A large, tropical wave rolled across the southwestern water of the Gulf of Mexico. The storm developed so quickly it was never proclaimed a tropical storm. It was a tremendous monster that would become known as Hurricane Audrey, the first named hurricane of 1957. The eye and winds quickly grew in size and strength, the conditions favorable to feed the beast.

What meteorologists were unaware of was what lay within the storm… the source of the initial tidal wave dating five days back, beginning under the cloak of darkness on the morning of the 20th. The world governments didn't want another Roswell on their hands so they remained mute on the situation. The few men working that evening from the various branches agreed to acknowledge the craft as being a meteorite harmlessly crashing into the ocean. What they hadn't intended on was that vessel gliding beneath the ocean's surface, taking its own readings. What the vessel hadn't taken into account was that it was creating the perfect electrostatic charge within Mother Nature's mixing bowl.

From a nearby galaxy known as Klaskn T 'clh by its

inhabitants, near the rim of the Milky Way, a Rifmoftlitk explorer had voyaged. Her ship was now camouflaged within the storm as it swirled across the Gulf, her guidance systems and controls all but inoperable beneath her sucker pods of leathery, green and orange mottled flesh. Her ship was caught up in the swell it itself had created.

She had no way of telling time, but she knew she had been trapped within the storm for a very long period. The storm's strength had increased, its intensity and the barometric changes noticeable. Something large outside of the vortex was approaching or, to be more precise, the storm was approaching it, and *it* wasn't moving.

She could barely see out but she knew she needed to eject though it could mean her death. She had no idea if she could survive the atmosphere. All of her controls which would predicate her survival chances had gone awry as the electrostatic charge had increased, sending a surge through the entire ship. Regardless, she was certain the large, unmoving object was a disaster waiting to happen. With any luck, ejecting would get her above the storm and she would miss the object, or possibly be thrown completely free of the storm.

She looked out of the window once more. The metal giant was a structure of some sort. It had fire breathing from it and glowing orbs all about its body. She had no choice; it was now or never. She strapped herself in, then reached out with a winged forelimb, two sucker pods simultaneously pushing the ejector sequence. The hatch above her blew free and she was sucked away into the vortex of a Category 4 hurricane, the wind and water beating against her skin, nearly ripping it clean from her skeletal frame. She still was uncertain if she could breathe in this atmosphere. There was no air within the vacuum she was caught within. She distended her snout and lifted it an additional four feet, but it did little good.

The centrifugal force spun her to the top of the sixty-mile-wide eye. She looked below, watching as the storm devoured the oil rig, her vessel slamming into it, blowing it to pieces and tearing the metal from its moorings. Within seconds the stalwart giant was no more. She held on for life, wondering how long this journey would last.

*June 27, 1957 - Hwy. 61, near Maurepas*

The windshield wipers were on high, but the rain was beating against the glass of the new '57 Chevy Bel Air Sport Sedan so hard that Archie Grissom could barely see past the cherry red hood of his birthday present. At the moment he was almost wishing he had gotten the hard top. He wasn't going to let it deter him, though. They had left southern Baton Rouge an hour ago. Granted, they should've already been to their destination somewhere out in the swamps and sticks between Lake Maurepas and the Blind River, but this dadburned rain beat all.

"Archie, I don't know if this was such a good idea," Bigby Morris spoke up from the back seat. He was a bit of a nerd with his thick, black rimmed glasses and his hair greased back into a ducktail, trying to look a bit like Buddy Holly.

"Don't worry, Big. We'll get there, okay," Archie replied.

"But you said we've got to turn off 61. With all this rain, if the roads out there aren't paved, we'll be sunk up to our necks in gators."

"Ain't no gator gonna want your dorky ass no way, you little nimrod."

Bigby shot Sonny a dirty look. "Oh yeah? Well you can go kiss a mule, you dumb hick."

Sonny John Stovall turned around from the front seat, sitting shotgun, staring Bigby down. He tipped his cowboy hat back so Bigby had a better look at his dark, devilish eyes. Normally he'd be smoking a cigarette, but his smokes lay on the dash. He figured Archie wouldn't want smoking in his new ride.

"Boy, I may be a hick, but at least I don't listen to that long-haired shit."

"Hey, Elvis has been on the charts for ten weeks now with 'All Shook Up.' He played the Louisiana Hayride. He plays a mix of rock, country, blues, gospel…"

"Rock is a fad," Sonny interrupted.

"Ain't neither," Bigby argued. "It's done been around near a decade. You wait and see."

"Boys!" Archie yelled. "I'm trying to determine what's road, ditch, and river here. I don't need you quarreling like a couple of raccoons over a watermelon."

"Sorry, Archie," Bigby said rather sheepishly.

"Yeah, what he said," Sonny remarked as he turned back around. He reached into his pocket and pulled something small into the palm of his hand. He casually turned back to Bigby, extending his hand in a friendly manner. "Sorry about that, Big."

Bigby didn't trust Sonny, but he was willing to accept the apology, for Archie's sake if nothing else. He reached out and grabbed for Sonny's hand when something dropped onto his palm.

"Jumping Jehosephat! It's a spider! Awwwwwwwww!"

Bigby smacked at the plastic spider, screaming, pulling his feet into the air and scrambling away across the back seat.

Sonny was trying to talk between laughs. "Oh, good thing this car has such a large back seat. You should've seen your face," Sonny said, laughing and pointing at the frightened teen.

"You ass!" Bigby screamed, trying to hold back tears.

"Sonny, that's so not cool, man."

"Oh, come on, Archie. I can't help he's scared of spiders. I'm just funnin' him."

"Yeah, well I don't need him getting all freaked out in my car and scuffing the leather."

"Or pissing himself."

"Yeah, you're really funny, Sonny." Bigby was back to sitting normal, but as far away from the fake spider as possible. Sonny shook his head in dismay as he reached over the seat, searching for the spider. He finally found it, snapping it up and giving it a kiss before giving Bigby a wink.

"Seriously, guys, driving in this mess is bad enough without your shenanigans and arguing. This rain has been non-stop."

"Then why are we coming out here?" Sonny asked. "Ain't gonna be no crab or crawdad boil anyhow. They said that hurricane hit land today down around Cameron and is probably headed this way."

"If we don't get out here now we may not be able to get the moonshine for two or three weeks because the swamps and bayous will rise. So even if we don't have a boil for a couple of days, we may have one within the week," Archie said.

"Are you sure these guys will sell to us? I mean, none of us are eighteen yet."

"Jesus, Bigby," Sonny said with exasperation in his voice. "These guys are bootleggers and no telling what else. I don't think they're gonna exactly be checking our IDs at the door."

"Yeah, we just have to give the password," Archie added. "Hey, here's our turnoff."

Archie slowed to a stop, the Chevy's headlights slicing through the rain. The road was barely wider than a single lane and appeared to be pea gravel, the bayou swelling along each side. The cypress and tupelo trees rose hauntingly out of the murky blackness with outstretched skeletal limbs draped in Spanish moss. A formation of the trees and creeper vines stood guard, hovering close over the desolate road. An army of invading crawdads scrambling across the road seemed to be the only movement .

Sonny spoke up, "So how far we gotta go down this stretch to get to their cabin?" He asked as nonchalantly as possible.

"Lafitte said we go about three miles. Then we'll see a dead cypress," Archie replied.

Sonny looked at him in dismay. "You're shitting me? There must be a dead cypress for every twenty cypress out there, not to mention it's darker than a cow's bunghole on a moonless night out in this rain."

"Lafitte said this cypress stands out from all the others. After we turn, we go a couple hundred yards to a barbed wire fence. We walk from there," Archie said, mumbling the last part.

"This just keeps getting better and better," Sonny said, throwing his hands in the air

Bigby quietly sat in the back, his head down and doing his best to go unnoticed. He knew better than to be the object of Sonny's attention when his ire was up.

"Look, Sonny, you want something stronger than beer or Muscadine wine?" Archie asked.

"This shit better be good. And I better not go blind or I'll make you my slave till my dying days."

"Fine, I'll be your slave until your dying days."

"I mean it, dammit. You'll be feeding me my meals and

wiping my ass."

"Well don't be surprised to find arsenic in your first meal, you goat-humping bumpkin." Archie replied without a hint of a joke. Bigby, on the other hand, had to stifle his laughter.

The drive down the single lane was even slower. The rain had slacked off some, the trees blocked a portion of the downpour, cutting the intensity of the huge drops. Unfortunately, those same trees were also scraping the rag top of the convertible. Archie was praying he wouldn't get a tear in the material. He had barely had the car a month. At the halfway point, as the car rounded a slight curve, something large took off in front of the car.

"What was that?" Bigby asked, his heart thumping.

"I think it was a heron or a crane." Archie answered, hoping he was right.

"I knew they lived around water but I figured everything would be smart enough to take cover in this weather," Bigby replied

Sonny looked over his shoulder. "Look at us."

"Yeah, point taken," Bigby said.

"That's probably the only time you two have ever agreed on anything." Archie said.

They had been keeping track of mileage and not time, but it seemed to have taken an eternity to get to the dead cypress–and their contact hadn't lied–this dead cypress was like no other cypress or any other dead tree they had ever seen. The hulking tree was massive. It was hunched over like an old man with rheumatism, gnarled limbs going in one direction before switching in another direction. Five large, hollow holes loomed above like haunted orifices waiting to expel a demon, glowing eyes blinking in each of them. On different, thick limbs hung the remains of deteriorated ropes each fashioned into a noose. A tattered sign painted with the words "Revnooers Welkummed" with several bullet holes shot through it dangled from the center of the tree. Below were the remnants of some dead animal carcasses. Even in the rain, the stench of it was unbearable as the trio got out to survey the road they were supposed to turn down.

"That's nothing but mud, Arch," Sonny said. "Ain't no way we're getting out of there if you head down that."

"Tell you what, you two stand and make sure I don't get too deep or close to the water as I turn the car around. Then we'll walk it."

It took five minutes or so and a couple of close calls of nearly getting stuck in the mud, but Archie managed to get the car faced the other way. Their faces, hands and feet were soaked, but at least the rain was relatively warm and their slickers kept them somewhat dry. The wind picked up quite a bit and the rain stung as it smacked them in the face. Archie had brought a couple of flashlights with him. He carried one and handed the other one to Sonny.

The wind really began to howl; however a flapping noise could be heard as a force buffeted the trees. A loud crash followed. The sound of a large tree snapping in two and crashing into the swamp out in the distance brought everyone to a halt.

"What was that?" Archie asked.

"I ain't sure," Sonny replied.

"Probably just a downdraft or a microburst caught a dead tree in its path," Bigby replied, confident in his knowledge of science.

Sonny sneered but said nothing. That talk was above his head. He was a simple guy who enjoyed farming, Zydeco and country music, fighting, good food, good brew, and girls—not particularly in that order. He thought Archie was a pretty okay fellow, plus Archie's dad owned the bank which Sonny's dad had his loans through. He only put up with Bigby because Archie did for some reason.

◊ ◊ ◊ ◊

The Rifmoftlitk had ridden within the eye of the storm, nearing the coast of Texas and upon land as the cyclone pounded the shores of Louisiana. As the hurricane lost a little of its ferocity, the alien launched herself high into the air, spreading her wings and getting herself above the clouds. She glided for a long while, letting herself dry, riding the currents, but staying close to the mayhem below. As the sun descended and she began to tire, the Rifmoftlitk glided to the Earth, northeast of Audrey. She didn't know it was the path the hurricane would also follow.

As she sailed in below the clouds, the heat of the sun no longer provided thermals to help keep her aloft. The rain pounded down on the expanse of her sixty-foot wing membranes and the wind gales whipped from one direction only to spin and tear across the skies from the other direction a split second later. She found her flight in turmoil and lost altitude. As she attempted to recover she overcompensated as the wind shifted once more. Her wing membranes flared up, sending her tumbling backwards, out of control. Gravity took over and sent her twirling to the ground. She desperately threw out her forelimb and grasped a tupelo tree, wrapping the membrane and pods around it, sliding down the tree, shearing the branches clean. She threw out her other forelimb in desperation, grasping another tree twenty feet away to slow her descent. The upper portion was rotten, the force of her forelimb wrapping around it sent the old wood crashing into the blackness of Lake Maurepas.

She came to a halt just a few feet above the brackish

water; her limbs weary, her pods raw and sore. She tested the first tree she had grasped to see if it was sturdy enough to hold her. She released the second tree and put all of her weight on the first, digging all four feet into the bark to climb a little higher above the water. She wrapped her membranes around what was essentially a giant stick—now the limbs all ripped free. She was hungry, but she was too exhausted. She rested.

◊ ◊ ◊ ◊

The teenagers found the fence, along with the sign that said "No Trespassing. Survivors will be fed to the Kritters." To the right of the sign was a path, not much more than a rabbit trail, hidden behind a large oak. Six or seven minutes later they could hear the sounds of rain hitting a tin roof and an accordion and guitar off in the distance.

"Hey, you hear that?" Bigby asked.

"Sounds like my kinda people," Sonny said, starting to bypass Archie.

Archie threw his arm in front of his friend's chest. "Don't go running in there. We have to approach with caution and the password or we could end up with a few extra holes in us."

Archie and Sonny began walking forward once more.

"You think we should watch for traps?"

Archie and Sonny came to a sudden halt and shined their lights directly in front of their feet. Bigby had a point. They took their time, looking for trip wires, snares and bear traps but found nothing.

The moonshiners didn't need a trap to let them know anyone was approaching. Two dogs were putting up a fuss and the music came to a halt. As the trio came to the trailhead and into a bit of a clearing where a rickety log cabin sat on stilts four feet above the ground, one lone figure's silhouette could be seen standing in the doorway for a brief second before the .12 gauge blast blew a hunk of bark off the elm right above their heads.

All three boys hit the ground, face first into the mud, screaming not to be shot. Two other men came up on either side of them. Another came up the trail behind them. The man shooting at them from the cabin had been a diversion.

"You fellas got three seconds to start declarin' what y'all are out here about before I'z start fillin' youse full of lead," said a man with a thick Cajun accent. He had a .20 gauge double barrel pressed against Archie's skull.

Bigby raised his face from the mud and began stammering, "Dirty beans and rice and... mice... lice..."

The sounds of hammers cocking on shotguns dominated the storm.

"Shutup, Bigby!" Archie shouted. "Hold on, I'm looking for Jean Broussard."

"Who be lookin'?" asked the man who spoke earlier.

"Creole, etoufee, jambalaya rice—Monsieurrice—Monsieur Lafitte says you need to play nice," Archie said, conjuring up all the nerve he could muster.

"Lafitte, eh?" asked the man. "I am Broussard. And who are you wood rats?"

Archie rolled over and looked up, cautiously wiping some of the mud from his eyes and mouth. "Names aren't really that important. We were told we could buy some shine from you."

Sonny and Bigby were slowly wiping the mud from their faces. They looked up, Sonny's flashlight illuminating the image of Broussard's tanned, leathery skin. He had a long scar down the right side of his face which continued down his lean, powerful right arm and all the way to his knuckles. He looked down at them like a hawk sights a field mouse.

Broussard motioned with his weapon for them to get on their feet and march closer toward the cabin, stopping them just on the edge of the light shining through from the door. In the doorway stood a man, the one who had shot at them, with black hair and a thick, black mustache. He looked part Filipino and possibly Arcadian mix. He was holding two Catahoulas at bay.

"Zut! Matos, shut those damn dogs up!"

"Beau! Remy! Ta gueule!" Both dogs immediately quieted.

Broussard continued, "You boys turn off them flashlights. You think we make the white lightning here? We are only simple hunters and fishermen."

"Please, Mister… Monsieur Broussard. We've been on the road in this storm for over two hours, walked in this mess for another half hour, and your guy almost blew our heads off. We didn't risk coming out in a hurricane for nothing."

"Matos missed you on purpose. He was just getting your attention so we could get the drop on you."

"Helluva good job," Sonny interjected. "Come on, man. We could hear you playing before the dogs sent up the warning. Nothing better than some Zydeco and shine."

Broussard stepped over to Sonny and whipped out a Bowie knife, pressing it against Sonny's Adam's apple. "Boy, just cuz you wear the cowboy hat and look a little more country than these city boys don't mean youse like us, you get me, eh."

Sonny nodded only slightly. Broussard brought the blade down, a wicked smile crossing his face, the few teeth he had were rotten and his breath reeked.

"Now it zounds to me," Broussard continued, "like

y'all came a long way for nothing."

Archie slowly reached beneath his slicker and into his back pocket with one hand while holding his other hand up. He pulled out his wallet and waved it in front of Broussard, "We've got money."

"How much you think to pay?"

"Twenty for a gallon. We want to get a couple of gallons."

"Thirty for a gallon."

"Thirty?" Sonny shouted, stepping forward. A barrel quickly went up against his cheek. He stepped back.

"Fine, we can get one gallon. We don't have enough for two," Archie stated.

"How much you got?" asked an extremely ugly man in a very raspy voice. He was the man who had been towering behind them the entire time. He was obviously some sort of American Indian. His face was severely scarred, as if by cuts, but not from a straight edge of a knife. More like jagged bite wounds. When he opened his mouth it was obvious his teeth had all been filed.

The boys all just stared. This man was the scariest person they had ever seen.

"Don't be rude, boys, eh. Answer my friend, Gator Face," said Broussard with a hearty laugh.

Meekly, Archie said, "Uh, we, we got fifty."

"You sure about that?" Gator Face asked, putting his nose right up against Archie's nose.

Archie tried not to shit his pants. "I swear to you Mister Face, fifty is all we got. I can give it to you here or I can give it to you in there where it won't get wet or, if I can just grab my license you can keep the wallet. It's got to be worth another ten dollars or so. Genuine calf skin."

Gator laughed like a madman as he grasped the boy's shoulder and started forcing him towards the stairs of the cabin. Broussard motioned for the others to follow. The last man, a quiet old black man named Poker, followed up the rear.

As Archie's foot touched the first step, a great bolt of lightning illuminated the sky, and below the stairs, coming straight for him, was a black shadow.

"Holy shit, a bear!"

"Bah, that's just Honey. She'll only eat you if'n I tell her to eat you."

The boys could hear a chain rattle. They weren't sure how long or strong her chain was, but evidently she was at least under the illusion of being under some control.

"I've had her since she was a cub. She has only eaten one man from the I.R.S. and a couple of poachers." Broussard gave her a couple of more pats then motioned for everyone to go on up.

The cabin was what one would expect, an unkempt room filled with smoke and a musty smell. There was a solid, hand-carved table with chairs around it. There was a rocking chair and an old couch sitting around a potbelly stove that was burning and giving off a little heat despite it being summer. The room was lit by kerosene lanterns. There appeared to be a hallway and two doors that were probably bedrooms. The men must've bunked together.

"You can take off them fancy rain coats and drop 'em by the door," Broussard ordered. The trio did as they were told.

"Okay, boy, let's see your dough," said Gator.

Archie opened his wallet and pulled out the fifty dollars. He showed them the wallet was empty. Poker checked the pockets of the other two for wallets. He just grunted and shook his head.

Broussard smiled, "Well it looks like you boys was telling the truth. I like that. Tell you what, I'll give you two gallons since tonight has been such a bitch, eh."

"That would be great, Monsieur Broussard," Archie said with sincere modesty, not wanting to appear too eager.

"I mean, you boys have been through one helluva night. Gator, go get the jugs."

Gator left without a word.

"You don't keep it here?" Bigby asked, speaking for the first time since his bumbled attempt at the password.

All three men laughed. Matos cried out, "Oh, hell no!"

"Obviously you boys know nothing about the making of moonshine," said Broussard as he finished rolling something in a small paper on the table. He licked the paper, struck a match and lit it, taking a deep toke. The boys could tell it wasn't a cigarette. "If'n a still ever decides to go up, it makes one helluva hole in the ground, big, like dynamite."

"And you have more to worry about besides explosions, dogs, and black bears," exclaimed Matos in a joyous mood.

"We do?" all three asked.

"Sure. I mean, in the natural world you got snapping turtles which can get up to a hundred-and-fifty pounds and with one swift move they can break your leg between their jaws, wild pigs which can gore you and eat you alive, then gators that get up to fourteen feet or so and can chomp you up like that," he said, suddenly clapping his hands together like a thunderbolt, scaring them. "Then there are the smaller things such as the poisonous plants, spiders, and snakes. All sorts of nasties tend to come to the surface when it rains. They get flooded out of their homes. When that road floods, anything and everything crosses it."

Fear was evident upon the teenagers' faces. Matos was smiling, enjoying the effect his words were having upon them. "Then there's the supernatural."

"You can't mean all the voodoo, ghosts, and zombies we're always hearing about down in New Orleans?" Archie asked.

"Laugh if you will, but some of that stuff is real. Not to mention vampires, Baron Samedi and the Grunch."

"The what?" Sonny asked.

"Grunch," Matos continued. "They are little dwarf-like people who live on the outskirts of New Orleans, but they have moved more and more out into the swamps. They live in large groups and capture people to eat. That's why Gator looks the way he does. His people had a run in with the Grunch. Gator's kin began filing their own teeth down. When they capture one another it's eat or be eaten."

Bigby asked, "You mean that man, the one getting our moonshine, is a cannibal?"

"Only out of necessity. If you're a Grunch or, if he's starving. Or if he really doesn't like you and needs to hide the evidence," Matos said with a wry grin. "That's how he got his scars. He got attacked one night by five of the little buggers. They tried to eat him alive. He finally ripped one's throat out with his teeth then proceeded to capture the other four and boiled them in a pot.

"Of course he's not as bad as the KKK."

None of the boys commented on this. Sonny's dad was a member and the boys knew it."Yeah, ol' Poker over here didn't get his name from playing cards," Matos continued. "Poker, show them what civilized, white men like to do for fun?"

Poker looked at Matos. He shook his head, but Matos urged him on. Broussard just watched, checking the reaction of the boys, looking for tell-tale signs.

Poker finally gave in and dropped his pants. The boys didn't want to look at a naked man. They dropped their eyes to the floor. When Broussard insisted they look by cocking both barrels of his shotgun, they looked. Poker's genitals were a mangled, melted, indiscernible mess. It was grotesque. They weren't even sure how the man was able to carry out bodily functions.

"Go ahead and pull up your pants, Poker," Broussard ordered. "You see, a young, white girl, she claimed a black man tried to rape her. Poker looked like any other black man to her, but instead of hanging him, they decided to teach him a lesson. So they took him out to a field and tied him to a cross." Broussard grabbed the fire poker and opened the door to the potbelly stove, the coals to cook their meal that evening still glowed. He whistled while watching the tip get red then pulled the poker from the fire and approached the teens.

"They take the red hot stick from the fire," he continued, waving his own poker in front of the boy's crotches. "They slowly placed the hot tip against him over and over again, listening to him scream and pray… while he is tied to the cross. How ironic is that, eh? Then, after they have finished with him down there," he said, waving the poker a little closer to Bigby's crotch, watching sweat roll down the boy's pale face, "they tire of his screaming. They take the poker and they force it into his mouth. Poker, show them your tongue."

Poker opened his mouth and revealed a scarred and distorted mass of flesh behind two rows of forcibly broken teeth. It pained Archie just to look at it. Bigby was too busy paying attention to his own crotch to take much notice. Sonny was trying to stay cool. He knew this was a test. And that's when the still-glowing red tip came over to his crotch, then moved closer to his body as it sizzled up the buttons of his checkered shirt and sat just a hair's breadth from his lips. He could feel the sweat beading up on them and could tell they were beginning to blister.

"Now that happened many years ago and you boys would be but just babes. But your daddies might be havin' demselves some fun, eh. What say you, boy?" Broussard asked Sonny, looking him in the eye.

"No, Monsieur," Sonny replied. He wasn't sure if his daddy had anything to do with that particular event or not, but he was going to put it into his mind that his daddy hadn't.

Broussard eyed Sonny suspiciously for a few more seconds then brought the poker down. "Maybe he did, maybe he didn't. Hard to say, eh. But I think it stops here." With that he turned and replaced the poker back on the stand.

All three of them tried not to make it too obvious as they let out a breath of relief. They still weren't certain if they were getting out alive. Silently, they each thought to themselves to just stay as quiet as possible, get their jugs, and get out of this living hell. "Broussard, you haven't told them about the most famous monster of the swamps," Matos chirped up, enlivening the gathering once again.

"Oh, silly me. I forgot all about the Roux-Ga-Roux."

"Wait," said Bixby excitedly. "Isn't it sort of like a human with a wolf's head? A werewolf like the loup garou in France?"

"Oui! You are the smart one of the group even if you get nervous and piss yourself like a toy poodle."

"In all fairness, you did have guns pointed at our heads and had just blown a hole in a tree right above us."

"This is true, but still, that was all just a precaution. Mais, oui, le Roux-Ga-Roux may hunt you down, bite you and turn you into one, or kill you. Hell, you boys so young and cute he may just hunt you down and hump you doggie-style, eh." The moonshiners all laughed heartily for a few seconds.

A mighty roar exploded through the room. A terrifying figure bounded through the door wearing Gator's clothes with the head of a red wolf. The boys screamed. Archie tried to get behind the baying Catahoulas and Bigby ran down the hallway. Sonny was the only one to grab a weapon, the poker, and take a swing at the wolf's head. Broussard checked the swing, catching Sonny's arm and preventing him from making contact as the men all howled with delight.

Gator took off the wolf head. "Hey, country boy's got some balls. Good thing you stopped him or I may have had to have him for dinner."

Broussard released Sonny's arm. "Oui, Gator is not someone you want to make angry. Matos, shut them damn dogs up!"

Matos smacked each dog upside its head. The dogs each yelped then lay back down.

Another scream was heard as Bigby came running out of the shadows of the hallway, doing a manic dance and brushing away at his shoulders. Panic and fear filled his eyes.

"What the hell's gotten into him?" Matos asked.

"Spiders!" Bigby yelled. He came crashing into Sonny, who just shoved him off onto Archie.

Archie steadied his friend and looked him over. "You're clean, Bigby. I don't see any spiders on you."

"But there were webs and spiders back there."

"I don't doubt it, but you don't have any on you. You've killed them. Let's go." Archie looked Bigby in the eyes to make sure his friend understood. Bigby, still ashen-faced, gave him a slight nod and calmed himself to a degree.

"Got your jugs right here by the door," Gator said. "Just to prove to you there's nothing wrong with them…"

he took a swig from one jug while Poker took a swig from the other. They each passed their jug to either of the other two men in the room. The teens weren't keen on the idea of drinking after the scoundrels, but they weren't about to argue the point. Odds were the alcohol would kill any of the germs even if it wouldn't kill the imagery.

"Cool," Archie said as he and the others put their slickers back on. "You got the dough. We better hit the road before there's no road left. Still got a long trip back."

Matos handed his jug to Bigby, shoving the cork back in and slapping the boy on the back so hard his glasses almost flew off his face. Broussard corked his jug and slowly passed it to Sonny, not immediately releasing it. Sonny gave a slight tug then looked into Brossard's eyes.

"You remember what I said, eh."

Sonny silently nodded. Broussard released the jug and the boys made their way down the soaked steps, watching to make sure the bear didn't take them by surprise. They switched on their flashlights and found the trail.

◊ ◊ ◊ ◊

A bolt of lightning blasted a nearby tree, electrifying the water and lighting up the night. The Rifmoftlitk awoke, startled and panicked. What had been meant to be a simple, exploratory, scientific, fact-gathering mission had turned in to an abject failure which may result in her very own death. She could sense more changes in barometric pressure. Not only was the hurricane following this trajectory, but it was spawning more vicious, land-based funnels. She had no idea what tornadoes were, but she could detect the atmospheric changes.

She sniffed the air, the burning ozone and wood remains of the electrified tree strong upon the wind. She looked about as best she could, the whipping rain and debris in the darkness making it difficult. Her three pairs of eyes finally spotted a very small strip of surface that was different than the watery surface she was currently situated above

Weakened by the turmoil and lack of sustenance, she decided she would swing herself from tree to tree. Her wingspan and forelimbs could easily cover the expanse. She didn't need to expend energy until she had found nourishment. She wasn't certain what was edible; this would be trial and error.

◊ ◊ ◊ ◊

The muddy road became more of a slow trudge through the sludge. The boys had to help pull one another through, trading off holding the jugs. Their flashlights revealed a swarm of mosquitoes and homeless ants were crawling everywhere, thicker in number than the army of crawdads. They'd all be amazed if they didn't come down with pneumonia or malaria by the time this ordeal was all said and done.

Though it was difficult to see as a mild fog was settling in, Archie yelled over the storm, "There's the car. At least it hasn't washed away."

He opened the door, hesitating with all of the mud and muck on him, but he decided it didn't matter. He would give her a good cleaning as soon as the rain let up. He got in, the others followed suit.

The car started without hesitation, but when the headlights came on the teens noticed there wasn't much road left. It was barely wide enough for the inner walls of the tires to ride out of the water along the pea gravel. The remainder of the tire would be in the water, which meant

Archie would have to be extra careful because one little slip up would have them driving off into the swamp and quickly becoming gator bait.

The wind was also getting more voracious, slamming the car from all directions. The night sky was too dark to observe what the clouds were doing.

"I hope it doesn't start hailing," Bigby said, his fingers crossed.

"It won't," Archie answered. *I hope*, he thought. Winds from every direction with hail generally meant a tornado was on its way.

"Try the radio," Bigby suggested.

Sonny turned the knob so Archie could keep both hands and eyes on the road. All he got on the AM was static. "Too much interference." He switched it back off in disgust.

"I figured as much. Just hoping maybe we'd hear some news about the weather situation."

Sonny reached up on the dash and grabbed the pack of smokes. He tamped them against his hand and produced one. He pulled his Zippo and lit the cigarette, inhaling deeply.

"What the hell you doing?"

"Archie, this has been one helluva a night, and your car is a sodden mess anyhow. I'll come help you clean the damn thing but right now I need something to help me relax before I lose my dadgum mind."

Archie didn't say anything. He was pissed but he could understand. It didn't make it right, but he was in no mood to fight and try to drive, not until he heard the cork pop on the jug next to him.

"No you don't!"

Sonny flipped him the bird as he said, "Sit, twist and spin, man! I'm just having a couple of swigs then I'll put it up."

Archie shot him a dirty look and was about to launch into a tirade. He wasn't paying attention to the road or the large object slowly crossing it.

The car's left front tire rolled up and over the shell of the humongous snapping turtle. It bounced back down onto the frame, followed by the back tire ramming the shell. The Chevy careened off the road and into the brackish water, flipping partially onto its right side

Bigby had been straddling the hump in the center. The wreck had thrown him against the door, slamming his head into the window. The impact broke the frame of his glasses and cut him slightly, just above his right eye.

Archie had somehow managed to hang on to the wheel, keeping his feet pressed against the hump on the driver's side. Gravity was doing its best to drag him towards Sonny, but that was definitely not where he wanted to be. As a matter of fact, he wanted to be out of the car before it exploded because Sonny was screaming and on fire. He had no idea where the gallon jar of shine had gone -- probably the floorboard. It wouldn't take long before the white lightning would blow or trigger the second jar in the back seat by Bigby and send them all a mile high.

When the car had first hit the turtle, the moonshine had spilled all over the side of Sonny's face and down his shirt. The ashes from his cigarette had dropped into his lap, but nothing had immediately happened, until the car flipped onto its side. The cigarette slipped from his fingers and landed upon his neck, igniting the side of his face and shoulder.

If the car had rolled just a little more, Sonny would be submerged in water and the fire would've been doused, maybe never having occurred. Then again, Sonny would possibly be drowning, but that would be something Archie might be a little more prepared to handle. A blazing man screaming and flailing his arms while gravity was trying to force Archie on top of him was a different ballgame altogether. Archie couldn't even tell if water was in the car for Sonny to put his head in, or if Sonny could hear him or make sense of anything he said. The smoke and stench from burning flesh was overpowering. The oxygen seemed to evaporate from the enclosed space.

Archie tried to release the latch for the rag top, hoping he could get the top to go down and allow them to escape. The latch was jammed.

"Bigby, are you alive?"

"Yeah!"

"Try to crawl to the top and roll the window down! Crawl out!"

Archie was holding on to the arm rest with his left hand and had his feet braced against the floorboard as best he could while trying to roll down his window with his right hand. He managed to squirm out on top of the car. He saw that Bigby's window was mostly down. He reached through and helped pull him up, trying not to slip and kill himself on the wet metal. He could no longer hear Sonny screaming or feel him thrashing about. He figured his friend was dead, but they had no time to waste on sentiment.

◊ ◊ ◊ ◊

Not far from their location, the Rifmoftlitk perched above the road, spanning two trees. She could hear the screams and smell the smoke and flesh. It awakened something primeval. She could not see them yet, but she considered it prudent to be patient and observe. She noticed some of the swamp creatures also taking notice, their scaly snouts and eyes barely appearing above the water's surface. Then she heard the explosions and saw the multi-colored fireballs illuminate the bayou. It brought back horrible memories of war and turmoil as a child on her own planet.

◊ ◊ ◊ ◊

"We are in so much trouble," Bigby cried as they ran away from the remains of the car. The metal skeleton was fully ablaze, black smoke roiling into the torrential sky.

"Don't worry about that right now, Big. We've got to be more concerned with getting out of this swamp alive before the road is underwater. We've got to get to the main highway and hopefully hitch a ride to the nearest town." Archie reached in his pocket but knew before doing so that he didn't have the unwieldy flashlight in there. "Do you have a flashlight on you?"

"No, Sonny had the other light."

"This is going to be difficult with only bolts of lightning to guide us."

"Not to mention, I think I may have blood trickling into my eye. I don't think my lenses are broken, but the frame is."

Archie unbuckled his belt and looped it so the buckle held through the back loop of his jeans. "Instead of walking beside me with the water rising alongside the road, grab onto the end of my belt and follow behind me. Maybe we can both stay on the path better that way."

"Yeah, good idea," Bigby said, grabbing on. After a few moments he spoke up again, "Hey, Arch?"

"Yeah?"

"I always thought Sonny was a bastard, but I hated for him to go that way."

"I know, Big. I know." He couldn't bring himself to say anything else or tears would well up. He was having a difficult enough time trying to figure out where the road was. He was already running into overhanging branches and having to call out warnings to Bigby. He had more than a few cuts and scrapes before he decided he would keep his hands up in a defensive posture like a boxer in the ring.

Archie's progress was slow. Between partially dragging the weight of his buddy behind him, keeping his hands up, maintaining his concentration as the rain beat down on him and the relentlessly pounding wind in his face, Archie was wearing down. He had no idea how far they had come, but the fire could no longer be seen. He didn't know if it had succumbed or if they had walked far enough to be out of range.

Bigby wasn't faring as well. The knock to his head was worse than he thought and the swelling to his right temple and eye had increased. He was dragging his feet more and having a difficult time staying directly behind Archie. He staggered off to one side or the other before the slack in the belt would pull taut and he realized he was no longer behind Archie. At first his friend would comment in a friendly manner, then Archie just got to where he wouldn't comment at all. Bigby knew it wasn't because Archie was mad but because he, too, was exhausted.

Bigby stumbled once again. He heard Archie say something about an overhanging limb but couldn't make out the words. It didn't matter as Bigby realized his feet were in three inches of water. He staggered out of the swamp, stepping straight into a cypress branch covered in Spanish moss. Bigby's tired and delusional mind didn't register it as—moss—it was a spider's web.

He released the belt, throwing his hands to his face,

raking it to get it off, panicking before Archie was aware of what was happening. Bigby spun out of control, tripping over his own feet, pitching forward into the swamp. His body launched itself two yards out, thudding hard against a dead log, knocking the breath out of his lungs. It startled the cottonmouth which had curled up seeking a place to rest for a moment after nonstop swimming in the flooding bayou. A quick strike to Bigby's face resulted in a painful shriek.

"Bigby! Bigby!" Archie could barely make out his friend's form, or what he thought was Bigby, on a log. Maybe that was also a log. He called out for him for what had to have been another two or three minutes, but Bigby never replied. Instead, large splashes in the general area where Bigby had fallen were now being followed by hisses and growls. The water being smacked and slashed by heavy tails and snouts was unmistakable. Archie let out a scream of rage, the rain almost drowning him as he gave voice to the heavens, knowing the fate which had now befallen his easy-going friend who wanted nothing more than to enjoy the simple backbeats of rock 'n' roll.

Archie could hear some of the hissing getting closer. He couldn't quite see the gators, but he could make out hints of shadows moving closer. He knew the prehistoric beasts were coming up out of the swamp and if he didn't move he was going to be their next meal. The sound of the gators splashing into the water exploded within his ears. His feet slapping the mud as he semi-jogged echoed loudly within his head as he tried to stay on the darkened path. The beating of his heart within his eardrums competed with the rain beating down on him as the wind whistled Dixie. Archie was in a world of his own.

Unseen, the Rifmoftlitk, cloaked within the black of the night, watched silently from the trees. Its eyes followed

Archie, its snout sniffed the air, its taste sensors flicked about to find what they could discover. It was very interested in the screaming being as much as it was interested in the base creatures who ripped and devoured the other biped. The Rifmoftlitk noticed some of the stubby-legged beasts were even starting to make their way onto the solid path ahead of the lone biped, yet somehow the Rifmoftlitk knew the biped could not see the fate which awaited him.

Still weak and hungry, the Rifmoftlitk let her body dip down, a forelimb swooping low and three sucker pods easily attaching themselves to the broad body of a thrashing alligator. She wasn't sure what she was in for, so she had gone for one of the smaller ones to begin with, choosing one eight feet or so in length. The beast thrashed about, snapping and hissing, trying to whip her with its tail and dig into her with its claws, but to no avail. She reached out with her sensors, taking care to keep them away from the teeth. She had observed what those were capable of doing. She pushed on the hard, leathery skin, tasted the brackish water, sampling the salt and the muck. She pulled the creature nearer to her body's center where a wide maw opened up between her podded wings. Three rows of sharp teeth extended as she shoved the morsel in and chomped down. It was quite tasty if not a little tough. She quickly snatched up another nearly twice the size and a bit more of a fighter. Still, she hastily devoured it, for she could see that the biped was next on the menu.

She took flight as the wind's howling increased. Lightning crackled and thunder rolled. Archie could see from the radiance that three gators, mouths wide open, were on the road awaiting him while another was along the water's edge, ready to charge. People had the misconception gators moved slowly, but Archie knew that wasn't true. They could move quicker than a person when they wanted to. He'd even heard tales of them launching out of the water and pulling a full-sized buck or a bear into the swamp, rolling it several times as they killed their prey.

He stopped to look back over his shoulder, but all he saw was a mantle of darkness, not even the silhouette of the trees or the reflection of a ripple upon the water.

◊ ◊ ◊ ◊

*June, 28, 1957 - Farmhouse along Hwy. 61*

The state trooper watched as paramedics rolled the stretcher past, loading the young man into the ambulance. He turned to the farmer, his notepad in hand.

"So when you came out to assess the damage this morning, tell me again what you found?"

The sugarcane farmer, Henri Piedmont, pointed to a row of magnolia trees bordering his property. "The rain had finally let up a bit, so I came out to take a gander. My dogs was putting up a fuss and tore off across the field to them thar trees," he said, relaying the story in a slow fashion, unruffled as if he were talking about his crops. "So me and my two youngest go to see what's got them all up in a dander. And thar lay that young feller they just wheeled into the back of the ambulance."

"Did you touch him?" the trooper asked.

"No, sir, he was covered in them big circular bruises and draped in all kinds of stuff from the swamp. I figgered a tornado musta picked him up somewhere else and tossed him clean over to these parts. I told Leon to go tell his ma to fetch you fellers and an ambulance. I didn't know if the feller was alive or dead. You think he'll live?"

"Medics said he's been through some rough stuff but he should pull through. He's one of the lucky ones. We've got people dead all over the state from this storm. Once he comes to then maybe we'll find out more of the story and who he is and what happened."

"Not to mention the gators. Why, there were bits and pieces of gators hanging from a couple of the trees twenty feet up, eyeballs and guts all hanging down. Dadgum dogs from all over the countryside trying to play tug-o-war with gator. I don't know what's big enough or mean enough to eat a gator, much less hack it back up that high into a tree, but it's done got me and the missus plum scared, I tell ya."

The state trooper looked up in the tree where three other officers were taking photos and measurements. "Mr. Piedmont, I don't know what to tell you. But if you do see or hear anything, I suggest you lock your doors and load every weapon you've got."

In all honesty, he didn't think a squirrel gun was going to do it. He got into his patrol car and drove off, not realizing that the moss-covered cypress across the highway was mostly dead and what his mind automatically took as being part of the tree was the Rifmoftlitk, a curiously camouflaged onlooker. Maybe this scientific expedition would turn out okay after all once she could figure out a way back home to her children.

# BLACK MUD CURSE
by J. Jay Waller

"Y'all know this bayou is cursed." Becky directed the beam from her flashlight out across the overgrown bottomland at the foot of the hill below them. Beyond the shoulder-height weeds, a dark swath of Cyprus, Magnolia and Oak trees bordered both sides of the meandering channel. The half-moon hovered above heavy clouds building on the horizon. "Looks like a storm's coming. Sure y'all want be traipsing around down there at night?"

"You're not getting out of the bet that easy. It'll take more than rain or your granny's mud curse story to stop us. Right, Harold?" Joe turned and shined his light back up the trail. "Come on Fatboy. What's taking so long?"

"Is that the story about the old man who got eat up by some kind of beast?" Harold huffed as he clomped down the slope. Humidity plastered his thick black hair across his broad forehead.

"That's part of—"

"It's just more of the local drivel," Joe cut her off. "Apparently people settling this area way back before the Louisiana Purchase came across a widow woman living near the swamp. Some of the married men got caught visiting her, so they said she was a demon—"

"You're telling it wrong," Becky interrupted. "They

burned down her shack and chased after her, saying she was an evil spirit sent to tempt the souls of men. While trying to escape, she stumbled into a bog and sank. Before disappearing into the mud, she cursed the entire area and now she comes back on certain nights searching for the men who betrayed her."

Harold glanced from Becky to Joe. "Maybe we should come out tomorrow, during the day. We could skip school."

"Y'all bet me I wouldn't come out *tonight* and show you the graves I found." Becky headed down the last hill determined not to lose another bet to Joe. She shoved aside a low branch as frogs croaked mating calls and crickets chirped softly. Occasionally, the piercing chatter of a cicada would eclipse everything else, even drowning out the distant rumble of the B-52 bombers flying out of Barksdale Air Force Base. The evening breeze rustled through the pines, ushering in the musty aroma of mud and damp Spanish moss dangling from the nearby trees along the water's edge.

Following her, Joe shined the beam of his flashlight on Becky's backside where her faded cutoffs met her tanned thighs. He grinned at Harold, raising his eyebrows.

Becky looked over her shoulder. "Cut it out." She held her hand behind her, shielding her backside as she restrained a giggle. Turning, she looked up at them.

Joe slid the light up her body, pausing on the front of her pink T-shirt, and then bounced the beam back and forth between the rise of each breast.

"You're such a child." She folded her arms across her chest.

"Your mud monster story don't scare me none. If she shows up, all I gotta do is outrun Fatboy." Joe jerked his thumb toward Harold. "Just be faster than its next meal."

"Gee, thanks." Harold raised his hands in the air, the beam from his flashlight bouncing across the tree limbs above. "Let's go find those graves." He pushed past his friends.

Becky paused to watch him walk further down the hill, wondering what was bothering him now. He was stepping through the last of the trees when he suddenly stopped. His flashlight fell to the ground as he hopped and stumbled backward.

"Get it off me!" Harold squealed as he frantically brushed at his face, head and chest.

Becky shined her light on him. Gleaming threads stretched from the trunks of two trees toward Harold. She and Joe burst out laughing.

Harold continued to wipe the thick web out of his hair. "It's crawling on me. Kill it!"

Joe stepped over, making a cursory search for the large brown orbweaver spider. Becky tried to hold the light steady despite the giggles that rose up out of her.

Shrugging his shoulders, Joe stepped back. "There's nothing there."

Becky cleared her throat. "Good one, Pathfinder." She grabbed a stick off the ground and brushed away the spider silk which Harold had not broken. The orbweavers liked building their large webs between trees and had the bad habit of sitting in them right at face level. Months ago, she and Harold had spent an entire day walking through the woods killing the spiders by hitting them with a one-by-two board. It was like smacking a dangling packet of mayonnaise, spraying the leaves and pine needles with milky guts. They must have killed twenty or more. That was before Joe and his family had moved into the neighborhood. She stepped out of the trees and onto the narrow path through the tall grass.

"Come on, dork." Joe grabbed the flashlight off the ground and tossed it to Harold before following Becky. "There ain't no Civil War graves in the bottoms. It looks like a creek now, even though everyone still calls it a bayou, but back during the War it was all under water. I asked my dad and I checked on the Internet. I found a picture of an old handmade map showing that the swamp went all the way from Cyprus Bayou, up Red Chute past where Bodcau reservoir is now."

"You're wrong." Becky's tennis shoes crunched across the dried out clay as she shoved the weeds aside. "Captain Shreve blew up the log jam which caused this whole area to flood *before* the War. That's why they named Shreveport after him." She ran her fingers through her long dark hair as she pushed forward. For once she knew she was right. The graves were there and she was going to show him. She was tired of losing to Joe, like the time he had bet her five dollars he was better than her at folding a paper airplane using only their feet. He might have won that time, but not tonight.

"I don't know guys." Harold swatted at a mosquito while hurrying after them. "The bugs are getting really bad and it's going to rain. Let's go home. We can go to my house and have popcorn and…and my dad will tell us about the time he saw the ghost of the headless railroad man over in Forbing." He held his light like an old-style railroad lantern, waiving it back and forth above the ground. "The ghost hangs off the last car of the train as he rides up and down the tracks looking for his head. It got cut off in an accident."

"Yeah, right." Joe held an imaginary bottle up to his mouth and while stumbling around. "I heard a couple shots of bourbon helped your old man see the ghost."

Becky turned and punched him on the arm. "Don't be

such a jerk."

Joe glanced at the sky and then looked at her. "You don't believe in any of that mud monsters drivel and you know it. Otherwise, you wouldn't be out here."

"You calling my sainted granny a liar?" Becky poked her finger against Joe's chest, while fighting to keep her gaze steady. Even though she knew they were just stories, she'd never admit to him how many nights after hearing one of her grandmother's tales that she would lie awake in bed with the covers pulled over her head, too scared to sleep. Taking a deep breath to calm the pounding in her ears, she glanced at Harold and then back to Joe. "I've got nothing to be afraid of. The creature only goes after men who dare to wander into her bayou at night."

Becky pointed her flashlight at each boy as she embellished the story, trying to sound braver than she felt. "But don't worry, Granny says if the monster falls into the swamp, or gets caught in a heavy rainstorm, the water washes her back to plain old mud."

Joe laughed, the beam from his light flashing across the thick grass. "I gotta take a whiz," he announced. "I'm gonna run back to the trees unless someone wants to watch or maybe hold my…hand?"

"God, no." Becky turned away and covered her face. Why did he do things like that? He knew she wasn't that kind of girl. She let him kiss her, but that was all.

"I'll catch up." Joe disappeared into the night.

"Did you get the geometry homework done?" Harold asked.

"Humph." Becky turned and began pushing through the weeds.

"You can copy my answers if you want."

"Joe might need your help, but I don't. Math's my good subject."

"Oh yeah, I forgot. Is that a new thumb ring?"

"Yeah, Joe gave it to me yesterday," Becky replied before she could stop herself. She heard him sigh, but refused to look back at Harold. She knew that she'd see a hurt expression in his puppy dog eyes. She had told him several times she only liked him like a brother, but it was like he didn't hear her. "I think I'll get the matching necklace after I win this bet tonight."

"Was that over at the Bossier Mall—"

"Grarrrrrr!" Something growled low in the weeds and grabbed Harold's calf.

He screamed in a high-pitched, little-girl screech. Becky spun around; her eyes wide as her jaw dropped open. She tried to run, but her legs gave out. She collapsed onto the ground, her flashlight slamming into the dirt. Harold was frozen in place, his entire body shaking.

Joe stood up out of the thick grass, laughing while brushing the dirt from his hands and knees. "Did you think your old mud monster had come out to feed on your flesh?" He raised his hands into the air like claws and stretched his face into a mock snarl. "Better come check Harold, I think your baby might need changing." Joe laughed again.

Becky rose to her feet. A flash of heat surged up into her face. She should have known Joe would pull some kind of prank. He was the one who insisted they come out tonight to look at the graves, goading her until she agreed to the bet. He must have circled ahead and hidden in the grass, waiting for them to walk by. Her heart still thumping in her throat, she stomped toward Joe and swung flashlight at his head. He darted away, laughing harder.

"One of these days I'm gonna get you good!" Becky growled through clenched teeth. She inspected her darkened flashlight, holding it up and wiping the dirt off the lens. She flipped the switch several times. Nothing happened. "Great Joe, you broke it." She shook it hard. A sharp snap sounded and the lens, bulb, reflector and batteries flew off into the dark. Becky held the empty body of the light in her hand for several seconds and then tossed it away. "Gimme yours." Grabbing Harold's flashlight, she turned and headed down the trail.

"What did I do?" Harold held up his hands.

"What did I do?" Becky mimicked him with a high squeaky voice. "Blah, blah, blah." She moved her fingers and thumb open and closed like a talking mouth.

"Hold on," Joe called out. "I gotta find my light. I left it in the weeds."

"Tough shit, dumb ass." Becky continued on without stopping. She was in no mood to wait on him now. Her empty hand clenched and unclenched repeatedly as she fought through the thick grass. Joe would never let her hear the end of it. He'd tell everybody back in the neighborhood and at school how he had scared her so good she had actually fallen down. *Dammit!* How was she ever going to top that? The rest of the night, he'd be on guard. If only the legend were true, at least enough to scare the shit out of him. Then they'd see who was afraid to come out into the bayou at night.

"I can't find my light," Joe called out as he ran after them. "I guess we're down to one."

"The old graves are right over here." Becky moved out of the thinning grass toward a sprawling tangle of prickly vines. "I had my jeans and boots on earlier, so I was walking up in the berry patch. I think I was somewhere over this way." She stopped and looked around. The beam from her light slid over dark green pointed leaves and stringy runners covered with sharp stickers. "It's kind of hard to tell at night, everything looks so different." The darkness intensified as the heavy clouds spread over the last of the half moon.

"Sounds like an excuse to me. If you can't find the graves, you lose the bet." Joe began whistling.

"I can help you look," Harold offered.

Becky continued searching along the edge of the berry vines. "They should be right…eek!" she screamed, her feet suddenly breaking through the crusty surface and sinking into knee-deep mud. Her momentum carried her forward and she fell, her hands disappearing in the muck up to her elbows.

Harold gasped and backed up quickly. Tripping over his own feet, he fell to the ground. Joe rushed forward.

Becky wrenched herself upward, pulling her arms free. Turning at the waist slowly, she reached out to Joe as he crept forward cautiously. She grabbed the sleeves of his plaid shirt. He gripped her upper arms and pulled. Her legs came free with a loud sucking sound as she flopped onto the ground

"Are you okay?" Joe laughed as he helped her sit up, his hand in the middle of her back. He suddenly paused and then sniffed the air. "Whew, that stinks! It must be a rotten bog." He grimaced and then pulled off his plaid shirt. His white undershirt stood out in the darkness. "Here, use this to wipe off."

"I must have avoided it earlier because I was standing on the vines." Becky took the shirt and looked up at Joe. His eyes were full of concern as he searched her face. His parted lips reminded her of the kisses they had shared while sitting in the glider on her back porch. If only he was like that all the time. Warmth flushed up into her face. The wet mud tingled on her skin.

"Where's your flashlight?" Harold asked as he struggled to his feet. "Cottonmouths come out this time of night, you know. I don't wanna step on one."

Becky pointed at the dark spot on the ground where she had sunk into the mud. "I lost it in there." She looked back at Joe. He glanced toward Harold and then at her, the softness in his face was gone. "What?" she asked.

"Your shadow needs you." Joe stood and walked back toward the trail.

"What about the flashlight?" Harold whined.

"I ain't digging in the stinking mud just because Becky was stupid enough to fall in." Joe stopped, his face hidden in the darkness. "I hope you didn't get any of that shit on me. It'll stink for a month. Let's go." He moved off into the night. "And Becky...stay down wind. You stink worse than a slaughterhouse."

Becky sucked air through her clenched teeth, her body growing hotter despite the clinging mud. At least he could have stayed and helped her scrape off some of the grunge. She stood and began wiping her arms with Joe's shirt. No matter how much time she spent with him, if another boy was around and showed her the slightest bit of attention, Joe became a jealous ass.

A distant peal of thunder rumbled through the sky. A flash of lightning skittered across the thick clouds. Harold stepped toward her.

"I'm okay." She wiped a thick clump of mud off her thigh. Glancing up, she turned the shirt over to a dry spot and then wiped the front of her shin.

Harold stood there toying with the buttons on his shirt. Becky hoped he wouldn't take it off. He didn't have a T-shirt on underneath and she didn't want to see what the girls at school called his man-boobs.

A gust of wind brought the smell of rain. "We better get moving." Becky tossed Joe's grime-saturated shirt away. "I'll never be able to get all of this off of me until I get home. I'll probably have to wash down in the back yard with the hose."

Harold raced ahead of her. "Come on. Let's catch up with Joe."

"I'm coming, I'm…." Becky cut off the rest of her words. Every time Joe heard her say that, he had some juvenile joke about sex. Sometimes, she wondered if he ever thought of anything else. She wiped her dirty hands on her cutoffs and then brushed at a curl dangling over her eye, smearing mud on her face. Looking up, Harold and Joe had already disappeared into the night.

◊ ◊ ◊ ◊

Harold turned and cupped his hands to the sides of his mouth. "Becky!" He called out. "Becky!" He put his hand to his ear.

"Becky, Becky…where for art thou…." Joe said in a high, squeaky voice from somewhere up ahead.

"Come on Joe, wait up," Harold called out toward the darkness in front of him. "I think we should go back and find her. She could need help or something."

"That's exactly what she wants. She's laying a trap, just like I did. She's sneaking through the grass to scare me…to get even, for earlier."

"Becky! Becky!"

"You can stay here all night shouting until you're hoarse. I ain't waiting on you two dipshits."

◊ ◊ ◊ ◊

Becky heard Harold calling her name. She looked in the direction of his voice. The night seemed to be growing lighter even though it was still long before midnight and storm clouds completely obscured the moon and stars. The trees along the main channel were no longer dark masses. Now she could see details in the varying depths of shadows, some lighter, some still as dark as pitch. Her eyes must have finally adjusted to the night even though the light from the moon and the stars were now concealed.

Looking down, she was completely covered in filth. She took a deep breath. The humid air made her skin tingle as a warm sensation spread over her body. Her grime-soaked T-shirt clung to her like a second skin, the wet fabric showing every curve and detail. She could already hear Joe's comments about her high beams being on, and she could picture Harold ogling her breasts. Once she caught up with the boys, she'd have to walk the entire way home with her arms folded over her chest.

With every step, her clothes felt heavier, like a burden weighing her down. The material felt unnatural. Her skin stung wherever the cloth touched her, a little at first and then more with every passing moment. It had to be something interacting with the mud, maybe the dye or something in the detergent her mother used. Whatever it was, she couldn't endure it any longer. It felt like she fell into a fire ant nest.

She grabbed the bottom of her mud soaked T-shirt and peeled the stinging fabric away from her skin. Sliding it up and over her head, she dropped it at her feet. She unfastened the waistband of her cutoffs, pulled the zipper open and then pushed the shorts and her panties down her mud-covered legs. Kicking off her tennis shoes and pulling off her socks, she stepped free and stood on the ground, flexing her toes. The prior-day's warmth trapped in the clay seeped up through her soles of her feet.

Becky rubbed her hands over her flat stomach, the stinging sensation eased as warm mud spread across her skin and filled her navel. Her palms slid over her breasts and up her neck to her face. The pungent grime mixed with her own scent, filling her head with the rich smell of earth. Spreading her arms, she looked up into the dark sky. The rain was coming. It would scour the mud from her skin and her clothes. Then she would get dressed and walk home. Joe and Harold would be long gone by then; they'd never stay around in the rain. She sat down and closed her eyes. It was too bad she hadn't had a chance to get even with Joe.

Her thoughts drifted along with the sounds of the crickets and frogs as her breathing became deeper. Closing her eyes, the bitter peppery scent of the grass circled around her. It reminded her of the spicy smell of men dressed in dark clothes, their eyes smoldering with desire. Their lying mouths spouted out whispered promises which tickled her ears like a cool evening breeze. They wanted her to leave the bayou…leave her home…to stay with them. They tempted her with hungry mouths and eager bodies, only to feign indifference when confronted in the light of day by their accusing wives.

She took a deep breath. The air was heavy with the pungent aroma of flesh…the stench of men…men who had betrayed her. Their words echoed through the bottoms–rough and unpleasant like a barking dog. She stood up and headed toward the voices.

"Are you still back there, Fatboy, or did the mud puppy get you?" Joe shouted over his shoulder. A deep growl rattled the weeds behind him. The hair on the back of his head and neck stood on end. He crouched down, trying to hide. "You'll have to do better than that, Becky," he called out. "You'll never catch me off guard."

Muffled giggles floated out of the blackness.

Joe looked in the direction of the main channel. He knew if he got off the trail, it would be harder for Becky to find him. There was a fallen tree across the bayou, which would be his way out. Becky wouldn't chance it because she didn't know how to swim. All he had to do was get to the other side and then he could take the back way home. If he hurried, he could grab his digital camera and take some pictures of Becky, all covered in mud when she and Harold crossed the one-lane bridge into their neighborhood. He smiled and felt tightness in his jeans. Becky would look good all wet and muddy. The sound of someone shaking the grass up ahead made him turn.

"What the?" Harold's squeaky voice called out. " No! *No!*" A long shriek echoed through the bottoms.

Joe swallowed hard, his heart thudding in his ears, surprised at how realistic Howard's scream was. He must have teamed up with Becky to get even for scaring them both earlier. Sounds, like bones cracking, sent a shiver up his back. They were setting him up. That was the only explanation... unless. No. He shook his head. He was letting his imagination run away with him. It was only Harold and Becky breaking sticks. That's what it *had* to be.

An unpleasant but familiar odor drifted by on a gust of air. Joe couldn't place the smell at first. He took several deep breaths. It wasn't the rotten bog, but the odor was off somehow. He closed his eyes and sampled the air again. The memory of the whitetail deer he had killed and then butchered in his backyard sprang into his mind. It was the smell of blood.

Joe's eyes snapped open. His thick tongue stuck to the

roof of his dry mouth. He tried to swallow, but could not. There was no way it was blood. Not out here. He had to be mistaken. It was just his imagination, running wild in the dark with Becky's stupid mud monster story. He stepped off the trail and headed toward the log bridge, walking quickly, trying not to run.

Minutes later, Joe moved among the black trees along the banks of the bayou. Walking carefully from trunk to trunk while scanning the dark growth, he found the gap where the huge oak tree had fallen across the water. Crawling up onto the trunk, he stood up and moved out onto the log bridge, placing each footstep down, careful not to look toward the water below. A sound made him turn. Someone was coming through the grass just beyond the trees. He backed up a step. His heel caught on the bark, his ankle twisted and he tumbled off the log into the black stream with a loud splash.

Sputtering to the surface, Joe shook the water out of his hair as the languid current nudged him downstream. He looked back toward the log bridge. A dark shape separated from the shadows. He was sure it was Becky. The silhouette looked around for a few seconds and then darted away.

Joe swam to the far side of the channel. He could still climb the bank on the opposite side of the bayou and take the back way home. Pulling himself out of the water, a stabbing pain shot through his ankle. He fell back with a splash. He must have sprained it during the fall off the log. He smacked the surface of the water with his open hand. He'd be damned if he would ask Becky or fat Harold for help getting up the banks of the channel. No. There was a rope ladder just before the old one-lane bridge near his house where all the kids came down to sit in the shade and fish. He'd use that to climb out.

◊ ◊ ◊

A short time later, up ahead in the darkness, Joe could see the gap in the trees where the bridge crossed the bayou. Soon, he would be home and dry. A smattering of large raindrops hit the surface of the water like someone had tossed in a handful of pebbles. He paddled over to the edge and carefully climbed out of the water, keeping the weight off of his injured ankle. The banks were only about six feet high in this area, which would be much easier to climb. He found the rope ladder. A gush of rain suddenly dropped from the sky like someone had gutted a cloud. He reached for the first loop.

"Help me," came a female voice from under the bridge.

Joe's hand jerked back like he had been stung. He stumbled over his sore ankle and nearly fell down. "Shit, Becky," he gasped. "Dammit!" He put his hand over his heart. "You got me!" he shouted through the rain. "After all of that, you got me." He shielded his eyes with his hand as he tried to see into the shadows. "Where's Harold? Up there waiting to get even, too?" Joe gestured up the clay bank and then grabbed the rope.

"I need your help."

He stopped and looked around, trying to see if Harold was hiding in the shadows under the bridge. "Come on. No telling how much the water level will rise with this rain."

"Please. Don't leave me," she whispered, barely audible through the falling rain.

Joe smiled. "All right. How the hell did you get here so quickly? You must have run the whole way." He limped along the water's edge toward the bridge. "I guess we've got time. I could come under there and we could, uhm…have a little bit of fun first." Joe reached out his hand. "I'll bet you're kinda sexy when you're all wet and dirty."

A dark lanky arm swept out of the shadows and scratched something across his face, then vanished back into the gloom.

Joe gasped. "What the…" He stumbled back woodenly on his injured ankle, hands reaching toward the burning slashes on his cheeks and forehead. "Shit, Becky. That hurt. What'd you scratch me with?" He pulled bloodied fingers away, watching the dark fluid wash off in the rain. "This ain't funny no more. You could'a took out my eye." He grabbed the rope ladder with his left hand. Turning toward the shadows under the bridge, he pointed toward the water. "Stay down here. See if I care."

A mud-slick creature lunged forward. Its sharp teeth clamped down on his throat, cutting off Joe's scream. Gangly arms wrapped around his body, sharp claws digging into his back. The muscles in Joe's legs convulsed and kicked. His body arched, pulling him and his attacker backward. His feet slipped on the rain-slick clay. They tumbled, falling hard.

The beast's body bounced on top of Joe. He could feel its legs scrambling, feet scraping and clawing his shins though his jeans. Its jaws remained clenched on his throat. He couldn't breathe, but the stench of rotten mud filled his senses. Rain blurred his vision. He beat on the creature's back and head with his fists. He tried to twist free. A dark claw, silver ring encircling its thumb, reached through the rain and grabbed his face. Blackness squeezed his vision from the outside inward, leaving little flashes of light like distant lightning bugs. Joe's arms fell to the ground.

Moments later, the creature sat up on its haunches. Long mud-caked dreadlocks of hair hung over its yellow-rimmed eyes. It held up black talons which slowly dissolved into pink fingertips in the falling rain. Flesh appeared along its back, the curve of its shoulder and top of its thighs. Wrapping arms over its head, it tried to stand, but its rain-washed legs were numb. Its weakening arms soon dropped to its sides. Glancing upward into the deluge falling from the sky, streaks of mud running down its face, the creature toppled over.

Twisting streams of black mixed with crimson flowed into the rising bayou water as the downpour scoured away the rest of the creature. A short time later, Becky's naked body lay sprawled across Joe's corpse.

# THE RECYCLING OF THE SKIN
by Alexander S. Brown

D ouglas Reynolds feels agitated walking from the airport in Baton Rouge, LA. While pulling his wheel-studded luggage, his cellphone is wedged between ear and shoulder. Ignoring the mosquito circling his head, he listens to the voicemail left from his mother, Ileana. *Typical,* he figures, when she is nowhere to be seen.

"Dougie Darling," Ileana speaks in the recording, sounding like Katherine Hepburn in her later years, "I know I was supposed to pick you up from the airport but poor Lena, the woman I go to bingo with, was hospitalized today. I hope you don't mind taking a cab. If it's a bother, I'll reimburse you when you arrive. See you soon. Love you, darling."

Waiting on the sidewalk for a taxi, a wave of heat and humidity strikes, causing him to break a sweat. Removing his hand from the luggage, he swats at the mosquito, and misses. Squinting, due to the rays of a Louisiana sun, he ignores the insect dancing about him and puts on his sunglasses.

Within minutes of enduring the mosquito and the heat, a taxi is flagged and seized before anyone else can claim the luxury. Opening the taxi door, a blast of cold air hits him. After loading his luggage in the seat behind the taxi driver, he sits and slams the door. After sighing, he looks toward the driver. From what Douglas can see, he is a balding, overweight man in his mid-forties. The rearview mirror allows a glimpse of the driver's muddy irises, a few shades darker than his mocha skin. "Where ya goin', Podna?" He asks, his voice gruff and full of Creole culture.

"Rue Bourbon Crossing, please," requests Douglas, sounding frustrated for having to endure this hellish southern weather.

"Ah, Rue Bourbon, eh? Talk about blue blood," the cabbie said.

Although Douglas feels insulted by the comment, which came off sounding sarcastic, he takes the opportunity to brag. "I'm going there to see my mother. We have a family-owned company in Alaska." Keeping a bitter face, he hopes this makes the driver feel inferior.

"Yeah, what kinda business," asks the cabbie.

"Furs, we don't sell that cheap imitation crap. We sell the real deal. Maybe you have heard of us, Reynolds Fur?"

"Nope, haven't heard of ya," the cabbie admits.

"Yeah, you probably haven't. I doubt taxi wages would allow a man to buy his wife a fur."

This statement causes the driver to grow silent, the two men met eyes in the rearview mirror. The cabbie's eyes are full of resentment. Douglas smirks, the conversation has ended, and he can enjoy his air-conditioned ride without this Cajun rambling. Breaking eye contact, Douglas gazes out his side window, seeing the grungy city life.

Douglas has never been granted the opportunity to explore Baton Rouge before, and from what he can see of it, he wonders why his parents had fallen in love with the city. A year ago, before his father died of heart failure, his parents decided to take a final vacation in their seniority. Baton Rouge and New Orleans were the last two cities they visited. One of Douglas' final memories of his father, regards Ray explaining how beautiful the Rue Bourbon Crossing appeared. Ileana, shared his fancy. A month later, his father Ray died of a massive heart attack in his sleep. Seven months later, Ileana moved to Baton Rouge, which she explained held her most recent, dearest memories of Ray. For the last six months, she had been residing at the Rue Bourbon Crossing with a rent fee of $2,000 a month, utilities not included.

When the taxi approaches the historic complex, Douglas is astonished. He pays the driver, without tip. The cabbie mutters something Cajun under his breath, Douglas assumes whatever the man muttered is degrading. Despite this slur, nothing is instigated. After all, this cabbie will soon return to chauffeuring people around, while Douglas spends the next few days hob-knobbing and enjoying high balls.

Douglas collects his luggage then stands on the sidewalk, peering up at the strategically crafted architecture. To see the building in its entirety, he has to lean his head back at a neck-breaking bend. The building towers so great overhead, its peak blocks the sun like a vampire spreading its cape.

The length and width of this goliath building is the size of two football fields. Although his parents had found the residence warm and inviting, Douglas views the location just as brooding and gothic as New York's Dakota Apartments.

Trapped in its malevolent, cold shadow, his mouth hangs open. For some unknown reason, the scene sends a chill up his spine. It reminds him of the first time his father demonstrated how to skin an animal. The trick was to stun their prey, then skin it alive. Reason for this was because while the creature was alive, its body remained limber. This made it easier for the fur to be ripped away from its muscles. The first time he experienced this cruelty was when he was ten. The scream the fox had released as its flesh was yanked free was a nightmarish sound, which haunted him for years. Even now, the cry gets under his skin, but it is something he can live with considering the currency of furs.

Shaking off the chill, he enters the gothic styled architecture. Once setting foot into the empty lobby, he sees light suffers greatly, as the floor and its multiple halls are dimly lit with golden chandeliers. Looking down, he notices the floor is a mosaic of yellowed tile encrusted with a sepia stain. To the far left of the lobby is the elevator, appearing as antiqued and worn as the building.

After observing the surroundings one would expect on a ghost hunting program, he approaches the elevator doors and presses "up". Douglas stands for what seems like minutes, during which time he questions if it would have been faster to take the stairs. When his impatience reaches a level of tantrum throwing, the elevator dings and the doors open for him to enter.

Before stepping forward, he notices its cramped space, which can hold no more than five people. He sighs, entering the antique and presses number fifteen, the top floor. As the cubical is lifting up, an unpleasant squeak grinds from the elevator gears turning. The sound is enough to make his flesh crawl. The ride up feels unsteady and he fears this entrapment is on the verge of being out of order. Creeping upward to floor fifteen, Douglas is thankful he has never been claustrophobic.

When the elevator stops on the top level, Douglas steps out of the death trap. The floor upon this level also remains the stained mosaic tile. Posted before him, a plaque advertises the room numbers. In total, this floor maintains sixteen loft apartments. After observing the arrows which points where to go, he begins walking to the elevator's left. On both sides of the hall are doors placed spaciously, all of which probably housing lawyers, doctors, or other hot shots.

After rounding the corner at the end of this hall, his walk continues. The stretch before him is quiet and empty. He pauses before continuing and listens. When hearing nothing, he considers the apartments are sound-proofed, which is how his mother prefers living. She has always been one to hate noise of any type, as a matter of fact, she even hates music.

His walk continues then ends halfway down the hall, a door to his right advertises in gold, 15-J. At his feet, a doormat consisting of fake grass features a fake Magnolia on its upper right corner. Lifting up the matt, a brass key is accepted, used, and returned to its hiding spot.

When he faces the apartment, the living room quarters are flooded with natural light. The musty smell of tobacco lingers about the loft, indicating his mother has taken up smoking again. This is a habit she continuously picks up and drops whenever the mood hits. Ignoring the unpleasant smell, he steps inside the apartment, sits his luggage down, and locks himself in.

Scouting over the living room, the same old furniture that decorated her prior home is set in an inviting manner, it is almost too inviting. He assumes she hired a personal decorator, which makes sense due to her not having any decorating talents.

The furniture before him is a matching leather recliner and couch. On a rug, imported from God knows where, is an antiqued cherry wood table, offering a half empty crystal decanter, nearing this is a pack of cigarettes, ultra lights, unopened. In the recliner facing the front door is an overturned Anne Rice novel. Douglas never pegged Ileana as a fan of horror literature and assumes she has picked it up to become more familiar with Louisiana culture.

Meandering past the living room, and to the far left of the apartment, he enters what his gut indicates is the spare bedroom, to the right of this spare room threshold is the guest bathroom. To the right of that is the entrance to his mother's master bedroom. Flicking on the light switch, he is surprised to see the room is larger than expected. *Not bad,* he thinks.

Placing his luggage aside, he sits on his old queen-sized four poster bed and lays his cellphone beside him. He breathes deep then coughs. He detects the faint smell of rot, he grunts in disgust, telling himself the smell would be stronger if it wasn't for the cigarette smoke.

*If she expects me to sleep in this dump, she's going to have to deal with an open window or two,* he thinks. Not caring how hot it is outside, he stands from the mattress and opens the bedroom window. Upon doing this, wind enters, blowing the canary yellow curtains inward.

Leaning his head out, he inhales the fresh air then looks down at the people who are walking the sidewalk and the vehicles driving the streets. Shifting his attention up, he peers out over Baton Rouge and pauses, hoping to see something breathtaking, but sees nothing more than a grungy city baking under a blue sky.

He retracts through the window, the smell of decay still prominent but not as harsh. Forgetting his room and the smell he will have to tolerate, exploration of the suite begins. Located to the rear right of the apartment, and neighboring his mother's bedroom, is the kitchen and as expected it is spotless, but smaller than considered. All of the appliances are modern and he figures they are for show. His mother is the kind of woman who doesn't cook, unless she has to. She is the kind of woman who prefers eating out morning, noon, and evening.

Douglas turns to the refrigerator and opens its door, as expected it is empty besides an egg and a carton of milk. Opening the freezer, he sees a bottle of bourbon, a bottle of vodka, and a bottle of rum. *Man,* he thinks, *she's living it up after Pop died.* He can scold her on her vices but figures, what the Hell, she is in her 80's and if she wants to get drunk and smoke until her throat is sore, that is all her business.

Turning to the kitchen sink, he notices a clean whiskey glass. Considering the day he is enduring, he decides a hard beverage won't hurt. After opening the freezer, he selects a few ice cubes for whatever beverage the decanter contains in the living room.

Returning to the living quarters, which lacks both television and radio, he walks to the couch, sits, and uncorks the decanter. Once he removes the cork, he sniffs and discovers the alcohol is Scotch. This isn't his favorite poison, but it will work nonetheless.

Pouring himself a helping, he wonders when Ileana will be home. He looks at his watch and sees it is 3PM. *If she isn't home by dinner, I'll go out without her,* he reasons. Leaning back, he begins sipping the stout drink.

After acquiring the taste of what he always thought could best be described as liquefied burnt wood, he accepts a healthy swig of the Scotch. This causes his glass to empty more than half way. He tenses as the drink burns its way down his throat, then he drinks another generous helping, emptying the glass.

Douglas asks himself before continuing if he should stop drinking and he decides no, he deserves to get buzzed. After finishing his refill of Scotch, he begins experiencing a combination of being tipsy and jet lag.

Within the quarter hour, he tops off his refill, causing

the decanter to reach near empty. Leaning back with his last drink, for some unknown reason, a case of the willies overcome him. He could have wasted his relaxation time worrying about why he experienced this emotion, instead he discards this disturbance.

When polishing off his glass of Scotch, he figures a nap won't hurt. He looks at his watch and sees it is 4:30 PM. Since his mother hates driving in the dark, he is certain she will be home before 8:00 PM.

Placing the empty Scotch glass on one of the many coasters the coffee table offers, he feels a wave of light headedness hit him. *Whoa,* he thinks, *you're not twenty anymore, hell you're not even thirty anymore.*

Easing back into the cushions, he closes his eyes and dozes. What is intended as a light nap turns into five hours' worth of sleep. When his eyes open, he sees the apartment is dark with shadows from the fallen sun. Reaching to his left, he turns the lamp on beside the couch.

After rubbing his eyes with his thumb and index finger, he looks at his watch, reading 9:30 PM. This isn't like his mother at all. Reaching in his shirt pocket, he feels for his cellphone and remembers it is in the spare bedroom.

Standing in a stretch and yawning, he approaches the front door then flips on the overhead light, which is a smaller replica of the lobby chandeliers. The same dull intensity that lit the lower level bleeds over the room and reflects off the living room windows.

In that instant, he hears something outside scuffling, the ruckus comes from his open bedroom window. Although it sounds as if a flock of birds is disturbed, the sound belongs to something much more elaborate than a murder of crows or kit of pigeons. Although the scraping against the brick of the building causes him to jump, he walks curiously to the guest bedroom.

Upon reentering where he will sleep, the smell of rot diminishes. After flipping the light switch, he looks to his bed to find his cellphone missing. Confusion hits as he is certain the phone was discarded on the bedding. He looks to the floor, expecting to see where it fell from the mattress. When nothing is found, he resorts to crawling on his hands and knees to look beneath the bed. Still, the cellphone is not detected. *What the Hell,* he thinks, *I put the damned thing on the bed!*

Wind from the open window blows inward and chills his neck. He turns, at first dumbfounded, then he remembers the window has been open. Standing from where he crawled, he thinks Ileana has a landline. If he could find a phone, he could call his cell to discover where his property is hidden. Starting in the living room, he searches the apartment.

Failing to find a telephone in either the living area or kitchen, he enters the master bedroom, which is connected to the master bathroom. Before turning on the bedroom light, he notices the smell of decay increases. *Son of a bitch, what died in here?* he wonders, throwing a hand to cover his nose and mouth.

Despite the smell, he flips the light switch to his left. His eyes scout the room to find a queen size bed with mahogany tables sandwiching the headboard. On the side table closest to him, near an ashtray, digital clock, and lamp is a charging platform for a cordless landline. Unfortunately there is no phone. "Son of a bitch," he grumbles, wondering where the hell she keeps her phone.

Frustrated, he leaves the master bedroom and stomps across the living room, deciding the lobby will assist with a phone. Douglas reaches the front door and turns the knob. He is surprised when the knob refuses cooperation. *Dumb ass it's still locked*, he curses.

His fingers feel for the lock beneath the knob to find it has been broken off. For a moment, he looks down, thinking his sense of touch deceived him. He squints trying to see the lock, when his eyes refuse to adjust, he kneels down. Before another thought enters his mind, his mouth hangs open while inspecting the severed lock stub, which is too small to grasp.

"What the fuck?" He questions.

Douglas jumps to his feet and grips the knob with both hands. He turns with such force his face grows bright red and he breaks into a sweat. *I'm trapped,* he fears, *holy shit I'm trapped!* Instinct drives him to start beating on the door and yelling. After his hands grow sore from beating on the structure, he remembers these rooms are sound proof. He pauses, and wonders, *Are they really sound proof? Maybe everyone is dead?* The question is insane, however, ever since he arrived in this building he had not seen anyone else.

Attempting to keep a cool head, there is one last resort. Releasing the doorknob, he runs to the far right of the living room and opens the window. Gazing down into the street, he yells, "Help! I'm locked in!" When the pedestrians continue minding their own business, he considers the sounds of traffic, conversations, and loud music from the neighboring jazz club all cover his cry. After feeling like he has screamed himself hoarse, he gives up. Before retracting from the window, something large, at the right of the building, catches the corner of his eye.

Above the city lights but below the moonless sky, a blurred object on the ledge ducks out of sight, around a bricked column. This swift figure, whatever it could have been, is the size of a child nearing teenage years. "Hey! Hey!" He yells toward the direction in which the object is seen scuffling. Nothing moves or responds. He waits, staring, trying to allow his eyes to adjust to the darkness.

When nothing answers or moves, he questions if his eyes are playing tricks on him.

Uncertain of what he just witnessed his mind tries to fill in the blanks. Maybe a suicide jumper, or most likely an animal if it was anything -- he closes the window, and backs away, confused. After collecting himself, he reenters the spare bedroom. Not bothering to search under the bed any longer, he starts removing pillows from upon the mattress, hoping somehow his phone has worked its way beneath them.

Outside, a series of scuffling and scrabbling seizes his attention. Breaking himself free from the distraction, he returns to the floor, running his hands under the box springs once more. Pounding his fist against the wooden floor he exclaims, "I know I put that damned thing in here!"

Standing from where he searched, he looks to the window to see a gruesome thing glaring at him. He suffers a delayed reaction, which results in him jumping and screaming, "OH, SHIT!"

Between the waving canary curtains is a foul, scaly beast squatting on all fours in the windowsill. Its hands grip onto the window's ledge between its splayed bullfrog legs. Curled black nails at its fingers and toes tap at the flowered wallpaper while it stares. Its beady little eyes are the shape and color of black olives with red pupils.

Surrounding its alligator-turtle shaped face is a gray mane looking similar to moss. When its oversized mouth spits apart, strands of hair enter between its jaws. As it roars, its forked tongue flickers at him. Douglas panics upon seeing its teeth, which appear like shards of wood. It springs into the room and before its feet touch the floor, Douglas runs.

The swamp monster, with skin equivalent to a snake,

follows him. In a few swift movements, the reptilian hybrid is on his heels. Without the opportunity to enter the spare bathroom for shelter, Douglas' speed increases, allowing him time to enter the master bedroom, and lock the door.

Standing in bewilderment, he doesn't hear the thing beating the divider as expected. Instead there is silence. Douglas anticipates the moment the swamp mutation will enter this room, but it doesn't.

*That's what I saw while looking outside, it was that thing climbing the building like a lizard,* he fears. This swamp nightmare, whatever it is, has probably entered the apartment through the spare bedroom's open window. While he napped, it threw away the phones and broke the apartment door lock. *Why hadn't it killed me while I was sleeping,* he wondered, *perhaps it likes to hunt?* Douglas rushes to the bedroom window, making sure its latch is secure, which it wasn't.

When the lock fit into the groove, the swamp creature looks in from the outside. Despite the room being dark, Douglas is close enough to the window that the nightmare sees him. Backing away, he knows the bloodthirsty monster can break in whenever it likes. Douglas' back meets the wall nearing the door of the master bathroom. The thing taps on the glass as if testing its strength. Then the rotting smell which earlier agitated him returns, causing a dry heave. His eyes are clenched and watery due to his breath being stolen.

During Douglas' reaction, the monster smashes its fist against the window, causing shards and fragments of glass to clash against the floor. Douglas attempts to move to the room's exit but is prevented. The naked, muscular swamp thing flies through the air, and perches on the foot of the sleigh bed nearest him.

Its gray mane bristles as it roars, causing Douglas to scream. When the roar and scream dwindle together, the thing laughs, then it speaks, "Dougie Darling," its tone mimicking Ileana's vocals, "don't be scared. Come to Mommy."

Instead of approaching this monster who spoke like his mother, he retreats into the bathroom and locks the door. Light is applied and everything appears prim and proper, however, something is wrong. Now that he is confined in this room, he discovers this is where the smell of rot originated.

A jiggling begins at the door. Another dry heave sounds. "Dougie Darling, let Mother in," its voice calm and sweetening. The parroting voice makes his skin crawl. "Let me in!"

The freak-of-nature bashes into the door and breaks apart the lower hinge with a single thud. Douglas falls backwards into the tub and becomes entangled in the shower curtain. He struggles until discovering nothing restrains him.

His breath is caught until he looks up to see the horror dangling above. Draped over the towel rack is the naked skin of his mother, discolored with brown and purple bruising, indicating her body's deterioration. Like that of a skinned dear, the human pelt appears as if it has been carefully peeled away from the corpse.

The only parts of this skinned woman intact are her arms and legs, which reveals protruding bones. It appears as if the rest of the flesh has been used as a full body mask and its intact limbs intended for some sort of puppetry.

Another mighty slam causes the bathroom door to bust open and for Douglas' attention to be brought to the reptilian hybrid. The thing runs like an angered gorilla and with one leap, it lands on top of Douglas, who attempts to fight back. The swamp nightmare inserts a hooked nail below Douglas' Adam's apple and rips down to his groin.

Douglas screams as the monster slides its hands under his skin, loosening the flesh from his ribcage and muscles. Growing nauseated, Douglas feels fingers slide up his throat then into his face, loosening his skull from where his features are settled.

The creature begins sliding Douglas' upper body from its fleshy prison, causing his eyes to spread open in disbelief. This action causes air to sting his exposed nerve endings, making him release a never-ending scream.

Before the skinning concludes, the creature breaks Douglas' arms off at the elbows then continues slipping him from his entrapment. This procedure advances until the thing breaks Douglas' knee caps in half, allowing the lower parts of both legs to remain in the disguise.

Cautious not to damage the skin suit, the thing eases the remainder of Douglas' limbless body from where it has lived. At last, it sits with its legs extended. Its rear situated at the back of the tub and its feet crisscrossed.

With a mighty tug, it pulls Douglas' gory body into its lap. Douglas looks to the tub basin in disbelief, his skin is no longer a part of himself. Looking up from where his flesh lay crumpled, like a discarded work suit, he sees the oversized mouth of the swamp monster open. Douglas cries as his head enters the jaws of the creature. Before any plea can be vocalized, it bites into his brain, absorbing his thoughts.

With a splintery crunch, it dines. Within minutes it consumes Douglas' entire head. After eating, it steps into its new skin suit. Its hands and feet grab the broken bones in the arms and legs of the disguise, using them like a puppeteer.

Magically, the slit in the flesh from throat to crotch close. For minutes, the swamp beast squirms within the costume, until it becomes situated. Within seconds, the disguise makes what dwells within appear human. After showering, it walks to the spare bedroom then dresses itself and acquires Douglas' wallet.

It approaches the front door then opens it with a mighty twist. The apartment is forgotten as the trickster advances to the elevator, then into the lobby. Using Douglas' thoughts, the thing dials Roseanna, Douglas' ex-wife, on the lobby phone.

"Hello?" She asks.

"Hi, it's Douglas. I'm in Baton Rouge. Everything's fine, I lost my cell."

"Well, thanks for letting me know so our kids won't think you're ignoring them again."

"I wouldn't do that. You know how much I love Danielle and Quentin. I wanted to let you know I will be home this weekend and should be ready for them by five Friday night."

"Sounds good. They can't wait to see you."

"Tell them the feeling is mutual."

"Will do."

"Thanks, see you on Friday."

Once the call ends, the trickster ventures outside then blends into society. Later, it will return to the apartment to feast on scraps, just like it did to everyone in the entire apartment complex over the last year. In the coming week, this body will start to rot, but it will work well enough until father and children are reunited. Then like a million times prior, the trickster can live with the same freedom every other human being enjoys, until it requires new recycled flesh.

# RUNNER

by Henry P. Gravelle

*Bayou Sorrel*
*Iberville Parish, Louisiana*
Hour seven of Hurricane Katrina

Georgie Ducat guided his skiff through the darkness using the outboard motor as a rudder. Usually, under better circumstances, he would steer by oar; it was quieter when poaching gators but tonight the boat had become a rescue vehicle, his only hope.

Water sloshed around his ankles with floating pieces of torn netting, crushed beer cans, and shards of gator littering the floor of his poaching craft. The swamp had risen with the influx of water from fallen levees pouring into areas where tides had been denied access for so long and threatened to enter his modest cabin on the bayou's eastern bank. That's when he decided to leave for shelter.

He loaded two blankets and a case of Coors into the boat then ordered his common-law wife Paula in as well. They pushed off into the dank disturbed bayou just moments before the cabin submitted to the water's onslaught.

"Did 'ya take a light?" Paula yelled through the wind.

He twisted his head to hear as though catching her

words before Katrina whisked them away.

"Goddamn it!" He cursed realizing his error.

"No, don't ask god to damn anything," she yelled looking up to the treetops swishing frantically in the wind, "looks like he's pissed enough."

"Maybe he's not Cajun?" Georgie bellowed and ducked as a cypress branch whipped passed his head.

"Where're we going?" she screamed through the opening of the blanket placed over her head for protection. She tilted to hear an answer.

"Black Francine's."

Paula closed the blanket around her head and prayed she heard wrong. She opened it allowing rain and wind to thrash her face. "Black Francine's?"

"*Oui*," he shouted.

She sat upright causing the boat to come precariously close to capsizing. Georgie made a quick correction with the motor. "What are you doing? Sit still woman!"

Paula glared at him, "Have you lost your mind? Why are we going to the witch's shack?"

"*Sorciere* got plenty of money, money she won't need after tonight, baby doll," Georgie screamed through the blowing rain. He attempted to cover himself but could only grimace and take the beating the wind tossed against him.

Paula could always tell when he was playing smart or telling lies or just being a wise ass, yet tonight she couldn't be sure. "What you mean after tonight, Georgie. What're you gonna do?"

"I'm gonna get that witch's money."

"If you believe she's gonna let you just walk in and take her money you're a bigger fool than I thought."

"I'm not a fool, baby doll. I'm just tired of skinning gators. With her money we gonna buy a big house, maybe even a bigger boat," he said motioning to the one they were in.

She could hardly hear or see him but she could imagine the large grin across his face. He was serious and she knew it. "You gonna kill that woman, Georgie?"

He didn't answer, didn't have to. She knew he would. A roar of wind pushed through the bayou snapping cypress and gum trees like toothpicks. All around the boat, cracking timber and falling trees showed the power of Katrina's fury. One toppled into the water behind them sending a wave against the stern of the rowboat, covering Georgie with duckweed and algae.

"Son of a bitch!" he said trying to remove the vegetation in his lap with one hand and steer with the other. The blanket around his shoulders slipped off falling to the deepening puddle on the floor, "I've never seen such a storm."

"Maybe Black Francine knows you coming?" Paula yelled against a roar above which sounded like a freight train passing through the bayou.

"What you know 'bout her?" Georgie questioned, "She's just an ole woman."

"What everyone around here knows, Black Francine's in cahoots with the devil and practices voodoo. I heard she can see in the night and speak with animals too, 'specially gators."

Georgie glanced at Paula, the rain made him close one eye. "You think big gator gonna tell that witch I've been skinning his friends?" He chuckled.

Paula ignored him. "Folks say ole Black Francine been in the bayou for a damn long time, since she whored in Arcadia. Long time past."

"That's why she got so much money hidden away in that shack," Georgie said, "son of a bitch been here so long no one knows what she looks like. Maybe it's a lot of Cajun mumbo jumbo. In all my thirty years I've never see her, nothing but her run down shack."

"Nobody has ever seen her and lived, is what they say," Paula added.

"We'll know soon 'nough, baby doll," Georgie smiled looking over Paula's shoulder. She turned as the bow bumped against an aged dock, its timbers rotten. A vine covered shanty stood nestled between two large cypresses swirling in the wind like swaying giant sentinels.

"You wait here," Georgie said fastening the bow to one of the pilings. He then stepped carefully onto the rickety dock, "Make sure the boat doesn't slip away. I'll be right back."

Paula watched him bend into the wind trudging to the cabin where candlelight glowed from the single window. A shudder hanging by a hinge flapped with every gust, tapping against the rough planking of the ominous dwelling.

At the door Georgie removed a large bowie knife from his belt, one used to slit the bellies of gators, and pushed against the door. It swung open and he entered then closed it quickly. It was dark and quiet inside. Georgie squinted in the candlelight.

"What yo want of me, poacher?" a female voice startled him, seated just a few feet away on the opposite side of the candle.

"You know me?" Georgie remembered what Paula said about the witch talking to gators. He swallowed hard, "Don't rightly matter if you do or don't. I came here to relieve you of the money everyone knows you got somewhere in this shanty."

He spoke slowly allowing his eyes to grow accustomed to the meager light. The witch's form began to come into focus. Georgie inhaled a soft gasp at her features and thought to look away but was afraid not to keep an eye on her. Francine's weathered flesh showed the color of the bayou water. Her heritage was certainly not white, nor black, maybe Mulatto or Spanish, before time destroyed any distinction.

Tattered clothing drooped from a thin frame. A rag covered her head with strands of white hair touching the neck and ears. She smiled a toothless grin at Georgie, "I know more than you imagine, —poacher—your past, present and what's coming."

Francine ignored him while rocking slowly in the chair with a grin like the spider wore for the fly.

Georgie raised the knife for her to see. "Don't know why you smiling? I'm fixing to take your money no matter you be black, white or red skin. Now, be a lot easier if you'd point out the money 'fore I commence to slitting your belly and drop your innards right here on your own damn floor."

The candle flickered and went out from a gust surging through the walls. Georgie took a defensive stance with the knife, waving it back and forth, "Put that flame up, ole woman, so I can see you."

A fire burst to life from the hearth behind him sending Georgie across the room in confused surprise.

"Wonderment is all it is," Georgie said nervously, "you got yourself some spells, ole woman, but I got the knife and I'm still gonna take your money."

Francine stood; she saw the fear in his eyes, the quiver of the knife pointed at her and the uncertainty of his words. "I have nothing, poacher."

Thunder joined the chaos outside rumbling as a fierce gust lifted a section of the shanty's corrugated tin roof. It caused Georgie to take his eye off Francine for a second. When he looked back she held a burlap sack with her hand inside.

"Damn!" He shouted, pushing aside the table, lunging with the knife, flailing it against her clothes and flesh until she crumbled to the floor motionless. He wiped the blade on Francine's tattered dress then returned it to its sheath on his belt. The burlap sack lay next to Francine's body.

"What you got in there, ole woman? Gonna stick me with a big knife or maybe a gun?" He picked up the sack, a single gold coin dropped out. Georgie picked it up.

"I knew you had wealth in here," he said gleefully twirling it in his fingers, "Son of a bitch."

The door flew open and Paula ran in from the storm, almost falling over Francine. "Oh, no, Georgie, is she---?"

"Never mind, baby doll. Look here," he said holding up the coin, "there must be more of these round, help me look."

She stepped carefully over the body just as Francine's hand lunged and grasped Paula's boot.

"Georgie!"

Francine released her grip looking up at Paula, blood oozed from a throat wound. "You have coin, poacher, powerful coin. He come for it, you cannot escape from the demon with fury in its eyes. It will never stop, until you are destroyed."

"Who does it belong to?" Georgie demanded.

Francine grinned, "You'll see soon 'nough, poacher. You'll see evil and no one can help you, no one can see you, only the demon. You must find another to give the coin to, and they must run---"

Georgie held the coin close inspecting it. He found no mint markings, engraving or anything; a gold disc the size of a silver dollar.

"You must never stop, 'cause evil will catch you...and destroy you, unless---" Francine barely whispered.

"Unless what?" Paula said.

"You give it to someone who can see you...it is the only way to die peacefully---"

"This is bullshit. You're the one who's gonna die peacefully," Georgie placed his large hand over her mouth and pressed until no breath came from Francine.

"So much for the powerful witch, eh?"

"We have to go, Georgie. We'll never get out of here," Paula said.

He looked outside and saw the sheets of rain blowing sideways across the bayou. Large trees upended, tossed into the swirling turbulent water. Angry swells slapped at the swamps banks and exposed roots of cypress trees. Georgie knew if they didn't get to the roadway soon their chances of surviving were slim to none.

"Okay, we'll come back later. Come on baby girl, we go now."

"You think she put a spell on the coin?" Paula asked.

"You heard her, it belong to someone else," Georgie patted the knife in his belt. "Whoever it is, is gonna get skinned if he thinks he's getting that coin."

"She say it belong to the devil and ---"

"Never mind the ole woman's nonsense," he said placing the coin into his pocket, then took her arm leading her to the boat. They stepped over fallen branches and ducked whipping brush finally reaching the rotten pier. Georgie stopped short, Paula covered her mouth, "Oh, no."

The top of the outboard motor was all that showed above the water, the rest had sunk to the bayou's muddy bottom.

"What're we gonna do now?" Paula yelled.

Georgie scanned the area finding a path leading toward the road and away from the swamp. He leaned close to

Paula's ear, "Looks like she doesn't have a boat so we gonna follow this way outta here. Come on."

They stopped suddenly as a loud bellow echoed over the hurricane's wrath, a sound neither heard before nor could explain.

"What the hell is that?" Georgie said squinting deeper into the bayou.

"Georgie! Georgie!" Paula called out into the darkness surrounding them. She frantically ran in circles, tripping over brush and exposed roots. "Georgie!"

"I'm right here, baby doll, what wrong?"

He reached out to her but his hands went through her flesh like he had no substance. She looked into the swirling rain finding nothing but the hurricane's fury. She fell to her knees sobbing.

"I'm right here!" Georgie screamed in frustration into her ear. She was unresponsive. He realized she could not see him and they could not communicate, like the witch foretold.

Georgie took the coin from his pocket and ran back to the cabin, placing it on Francine's body. "Here you are ole witch, have it back."

Then he raced back to Paula, "I'm here, baby girl. I gave it back, it's all right now."

Paula looked confused, lost and frightened, "Georgie! Come back, Georgie, I don't know where I am. Help me...Georgie!"

Georgie was invisible and frightened of what the witch said. More so that the coin had returned, somehow back in his hand. He looked into the storm, past the shanty over the sloshing swamp and into the wind blown curtain of rain where he found a distorted shape standing by the bayou's edge; a shadow with fury in its eyes.

Georgie backed away, down the path, away from the

cabin and Paula. The approaching evil passed Paula following Georgie along the path, out of Bayou Sorrel.

Two days later
*Fifty miles away*

"Hear 'bout Ralphie?" the petite waitress asked the two young men eating their hamburgers. They continued, seemingly ignoring her. She stood over the table waiting for a response. Finally one came.

"I give up, Meg. What about Ralphie?" Tommy asked rolling his eyes.

"They found his Mustang in the marsh. They haven't been able to find hide nor hair of him."

The two boys stopped eating for a second then resumed with gusto. "Just shows he's a bad driver," Chuck stated through a mouthful of burger.

"I'm surprised at you two," Meg placed her hands on her hips as if scolding children, "Ralph is a friend of yours. If it was my friend I'd show a little more concern. They can't find him and think the current took him out into the river."

"And how did you come by all this information?" Tommy asked.

"My father came by earlier after searching the marsh."

"Nothing like having a deputy daddy," Chuck said, "you get all the local news first hand."

"That's not fair. My father asked if I saw Ralph because he cares and wondered if he came by."

Chuck looked at her as he dabbed his mouth with a napkin. When he finished he said, "Listen, Meg, it may not look it but we are concerned, you just have to understand Ralphie is constantly in some kind of trouble. You heard of Lady Luck? Ralphie is 'Mister No Luck'. Things happen to him all the time and if we got excited with every fender bender or stubbed toe he's involved in we'd be babysitting him twenty-four seven."

Meg sighed. "He's still your buddy and you should show more concern."

The two boys looked to one another. Chuck shrugged, "Okay, okay, we'll take a ride and see if we can help."

They left the diner and entered Chuck's Camaro, then sped off toward the last known place on earth where their friend was supposed to have been.

"What if Ralphie lent someone his car and doesn't even know it was in the marsh?" Tommy suggested.

Chuck shook his head, "Don't be an idiot. Ralphie wouldn't let anyone use his precious Mustang. Even if he did, where's the driver?"

The Camaro cruised easily along the two-lane roadway leading to marshlands flooded by the hurricane. It emptied into tidal basins connected to the Mississippi, not a half-mile away. When they crested a hill the sight of the emergency vehicles gave a pinch of seriousness to their friend's plight.

Ralphie's Mustang was twenty feet from the asphalt on its side, its undercarriage displayed to those on the embankment. Chuck parked. They got out, watching the search of the mud flats.

"Jesus, looks like Ralphie did it good this time," Tommy said.

"Sure 'nough," Chuck agreed with a shake of his head, "think they'll find the poor bastard?"

"He could be hurt, out there somewhere," Chuck nodded to the growing darkness, "and no one would find him 'til morning."

Tommy scanned the growing black void of the marsh. "So what do you want to do, go out there and help?"

"Nothing you boys can do," a voice sounded from behind. They turned to see Meg's father in his Deputy uniform, soiled from trudging into the muck of the marsh. He looked tired and drawn knowing it could just as well have been Meg in that half submerged car.

"We requested a Coast Guard chopper; they have searchlights to cover the area. I understand the concern for your friend, but you boys will only cause more problems if you go out there. Go on home and give us a call if he should show up."

"It's not like Ralph to just leave, he must be disoriented, or hurt," Chuck said.

"Or gone with the tide," Tommy whispered sadly.

Meg's dad lowered his head, "That's the consensus."

The Camaro parked behind Tommy's pickup at the rest area overlooking the canal where a tug pushed two barges carefully toward the Mississippi. Tommy and Chuck leaned against the truck each holding an empty Budweiser bottle.

"How long does someone have to be missing until he's declared dead?" Tommy asked taking two more beers from the cooler in the truck bed. He handed one to Chuck.

"He's been declared dead?" questioned Chuck.

"By, he, I assume you mean Ralph?"

"Yeah, Ralph."

"Just say his name; you don't have to beat around the bush with *he*."

"Kinda touchy today, Chucky?"

Chuck took a long swallow of the beer then wiped his lips on his wrist. He looked down the canal at a man fishing from the rock embankment and wished it was him.

"I haven't felt right since Ralphie disappeared; like there's something I should be doing. I dunno, I keep thinking about that damn marsh."

Tommy placed his hand on Chuck's shoulder. "It's

been a few days dude, with no sign of him, nothing in the marsh or basin. Face it, he's gone."

Tommy took a swig, swished the beer around in his mouth then swallowed. "I'm as sorry as you are. I liked the poor slob, really. You can't let it haunt you."

Chuck sighed, nodding in agreement, "Yeah, you're right but I still feel---"

Tommy interrupted, "Don't woulda, coulda, shoulda. It's not your fault, don't blame yourself. You had nothing to do with it."

"I'm not, I just don't feel myself. I feel like the time we inhaled those helium balloons."

"That was funny, man," Tommy laughed, "I almost pissed my pants when Ralphie tried to sing Folsom Prison, remember?"

Tommy took in a deep breath, squeaking out in a high-pitched voice mimicking Ralphie's performance on helium. *"I hear the train a coming---"*

Chuck ignored him, continuing on as though he was dissecting his strange new sensation. His mind spun with questions and theories about Ralph, none of which made Jack-shit sense to him.

"Maybe it's not my mind, maybe it's my soul?"

Tommy was in the middle of downing the rest of his beer and gagged on Chuck's revelation. Beer foamed from his nostrils, "Holy crap, Chucky. All that philosophy on two beers?"

"Yeah, holy crap. Every time I think of Ralphie I feel a pull, something tugging to go and find him, like he's waiting somewhere. A feeling like when you pass a crucifix and something inside tells you to make the sign of the cross; a command, from the soul."

"Aw, Chucky boy, the soul? Holy shit, buddy. This is getting out of control."

"I'm gonna go for a ride. I need some air."

"Air?" Tommy opened his arms to the wide open area, "How much more air you need, bro?"

Chuck sat behind the wheel of the Camaro, "I need to think."

"Think 'bout what? There's nothing you can do, don't you understand that? Come on, let's go downtown and find a few ladies."

"I'll see ya' later," Chuck pressed down on the accelerator.

Tommy shook his head as Chuck sped away. "Your soul? What are you smoking, dude?"

Dusk arrived, lingering behind the sunset over the western hills while Chuck drove absentmindedly, paying no attention to the road or where he was. His thoughts focused on the sensation directing him, taking him along the marsh road where Ralphie's car was found. Chuck's eyes were transfixed to the black ribbon of asphalt meandering the edge of the Atchafalaya River when a shape appeared before him. He swerved.

The Camaro's tires hit the dirt shoulder spewing rock and gravel spinning the car sideways. It stopped abruptly. Chuck peered through the subsiding dust at the object running towards him. It was Ralphie. His clothing torn, dried blood and mud covered his stocky All-Star high school, fullback body which appeared weak and dehydrated. His face was drawn and shallow with fear filled eyes, lips quivering, on the brink of tears.

"Can you see me? Can you see me?" He screamed, turning his head every which way, scanning the road and marsh.

Chuck got out just as Ralphie arrived beside the Camaro, "Ralphie! Where the hell have you been?"

"Jesus, God all mighty, thank you!" Ralphie clasped his

hands together and fell to his knees, leaning against the car.

Chuck knelt beside him, "What happened? We thought the river---"

"Look!" Ralphie cut him off.

"What?" Chuck asked.

Ralph tried to scan the deserted roadway in both directions but it was obvious his body was defeated. His eyes began to close, every breath labored. "Watch for it… the demon… it's coming."

Chuck looked up and down the road not knowing why or for what. "Demon? Let me get you to the hospital, you're delusional."

"No… no time. You gotta run… demon's close; wants coin."

"What the hell are you talking about?"

"Here…," Ralph opened his hand and revealed a gold coin. Chuck took it and ran his fingers over its smooth brilliance, "Where'd you find this?"

Ralphie struggled to speak. "I almost hit a guy who came outta' nowhere…car flipped, I was stuck…guy pulled me out; a Cajun. Said he'd been running for days…said a demon was after him 'cause he had that coin."

"Told me he stole it from some witch and she sent a demon to fetch it. I thought he was just another crazy-ass Cajun 'til I saw the shadow coming across the marsh. The Cajun told me to run and not stop 'cause it would catch up and kill me. I've been running since. No food, no rest, kept moving 'cause that thing keeps catching up," Ralphie coughed and wheezed until catching his breath. "I can't go on…only way to stop is pass on the coin."

Chuck looked at the coin and realized what Ralphie did, passed it on to him. He was skeptical but still gave a look up and down the roadway. "How come no one can see you?"

"It's the coin, has some kinda' power."

"But I saw you… you saw the Cajun?"

"I think it lets us see evil, and evil to find us," Ralphie looked confused, "I'm not evil am I, Chuck?"

Chuck looked at his friend, a church-going, God-fearing two-hundred pound high school football player, now reduced to an exhausted whimpering boy. Where was Ralph's evil? Chuck didn't know of any and wondered where his was.

"No, Ralph. You're not evil."

Ralph smiled at his friend. Pain etched his features bringing tears from his eyes. His body trembled as he struggled to force out a word.

"Run."

A rush of air left his throat and his eyes closed.

"Ralphie, Ralphie!" Chuck felt his pulse. Finding none, he stood over Ralph's body feeling the coin in his hand.

"Witch, demon…keep running? What happened to you, Ralphie?"

Chuck tossed the coin in the air and caught it with a snap of his fist and sighted the form at the crown of the roadway. It moved closer allowing Chuck to see the beastly head and fiery eyes, resembling something in horror shows at the Rialto or images depicting the devil. It neared with a rapid pace, not running, but moving with purpose and unrelenting speed.

Chuck dragged Ralph's body into the Camaro then he saw headlights appear behind the approaching demon. Chuck stood in the middle of the road ready to flag down the vehicle. The headlights illuminated the demon as vehicle and beast held a steady course toward Chuck.

Then the lights were directly behind the beast yet it did not falter nor did the vehicle as it drove through the demon, like a rock passing through a shadow.

Chuck recognized the truck and waved his arms frantically. "Tommy! Tommy, stop!"

The pickup screeched to a halt then backed up to the Camaro. Tommy got out and looked inside Chuck's car. "Holy crap, Ralphie! Where's Chuck?"

"Right here, Ralphie's dead, you gotta get me outta here," Chuck said as fast as he could. The shadow was cutting down the distance between them.

Tommy didn't answer feeling Ralphie for a pulse, "Goddamn, Ralphie, you're dead."

Tommy looked confused stepping back to his truck. "I gotta get the Sheriff."

"Take me with you!" Chuck yelled jumping into the truck as Tommy accelerated. Chuck's form passed through the truck and landed on the asphalt. He stood and threw the coin at the departing truck. It landed in the truck bed, bounced off one side then settling somewhere on the floor. Almost immediately Chuck felt something in his hand; the coin.

*Jesus, I can only get rid of it by finding someone who can see me?*

He quickly thought of running down the dark roadway with the prospect of running without stopping, without help, without rest.

*I can't be seen. I can't get help.*

The demon neared, its eyes glowed, talons flexed and a scaly mouth gleamed rows of brownish stained teeth. Chuck began to run after the fading taillights of Tommy's truck, as fast as he could at first, then seeing the demon well behind, he rested briefly.

His breathing was labored, his heart steady as he occasionally peered behind for the demon. Over his shoulder, swung a small weathered sign:

> Iberville Parish Church of…
> All God's Children Welcome
> Rev. Thomas Gilliam.

A church of what? Chuck wondered since that piece of the sign was broken off. He didn't care either, a church is a church, holy is holy and a sanctuary from his pursuer.

A heavy rumbling came from down the road where a semi rolled into view. Its lights illuminating everything in its path, including the demon. The big rig passed through the demon and sped past. Chuck ran to the front stoop of the cottage next to the church where a light burned in the window. He knocked frantically.

*Maybe they couldn't hear and see me?*

The familiar footsteps of the demon's cloven hoofs were at the edge of the picket fence surrounding the yard. Chuck banged furiously on the door, "Help! Help! Open the door, please!"

The door swung open. A man looked at Chuck with a confused disturbed glare. He wore a white shirt and jeans and was completely bald with green eyes that seemed to shift colors in the dim light of the doorway. His face was weather-beaten and drawn like shrimp fishermen of the Gulf. His hands were like ham hocks with huge digits attached. He pointed at the door with one.

"Please, son, the door withstood Katrina, I'd hate to see you take it off its hinges."

Chuck looked at the man in disbelief. Not only by his appearance but that he could see him. "You can see me?"

The man motioned for Chuck to enter, "Come on in, boy. 'Course I can see you. I'd look pretty foolish talking to nothing on my stoop. Here, sit over here," he pointed to a chair with one of his long fingers.

Chuck gave the room a quick glance. Beside his chair

was a small round table with a shaded lamp and a Bible on it. Next to it, a similar chair where the man placed himself. He lit a pipe filling the room with the scent of apple. "Now boy, what's all the excitement about?"

Chuck heard a footstep on the front porch. "Are you the Reverend?"

"That'd be me and this is my humble tabernacle, my esteemed righteous place of worship. And who might you be?" He asked leaning forward to get a better look.

Chuck swallowed before speaking. He could taste the pungent flavor of wet cinders, like a fire was just extinguished, mixed with the apple tobacco in Gilliam's pipe. This sanctuary was not feeling like a place of holy protection. Another creak was heard at the front stoop.

"I need your help, Reverend. I'm being chased by---" Chuck caught himself. How was he going to explain running from a shadow that wanted a gold coin stolen from a witch? Then he felt the coin inside his pocket. It was real.

"Reverend..." Chuck adjusted himself in his chair hopefully to convince the reverend of his sincerity, even though the man would certainly think him nuts, "I was given a coin by a friend---"

"That very nice," interrupted the Reverend, "and you come all the way out along this forsaken stretch of Parish roadway to share your good tidings with me; a donation to the church?" Thomas Gilliam smiled showing his stained and crooked teeth.

"No, Reverend. Please, hear me out."

Gilliam leaned back and drew on the pipe. A puff of aroma burst upward.

"My friend was given a coin by a man who said he stole it from a witch. The man told my friend a demon had been chasing him to get it back. He could not give it back or toss it away."

"No one can help him?" the Reverend asked interested so far in Chuck's tale.

"No, sir. The coin somehow makes you invisible. The demon can see you and you can see it, until it catches and kills you...unless you can pass it on."

"And you can only pass this coin on to someone who can see you?"

"Yes, sir, to someone who can---" Chuck stopped, then slowly stood watching the reverend enjoying his pipe. "How'd you know that?"

Thomas Gilliam nonchalantly removed the pipe from his mouth and stuck a pointed fingernail into the pipe bowl stirring the dying ash, then placed it back between his lips. He smiled. "You got my coin in your pocket, boy. And you're right, it lets you see evil. Tell me what you see?" Gilliam smiled wickedly.

Chuck stood, his eyes widened realizing he was in the presence of evil, maybe the devil himself. He stood, moving quickly to a nearby door. "You're no Reverend."

Gilliam held up a finger, a flame sprouted at the tip which he placed to the pipe then drew in smoke from the tobacco. Chuck felt the doorknob at his back and turned it. It was a closet and held a man's body which fell to the floor, a crucifix draped around his twisted neck.

"No, I'm not the Reverend," Gilliam said casually, "he is."

Chuck froze, trapped by the demon at the front door and whatever Gilliam was, in front of him. He watched the impostor morph into its unholy form; flesh to scales, warts and boils, red eyes and putrid breath from its throat. The beast stood bent from its height in the little cottage; blackened wings folded against its sides. It neared Chuck reaching with deformed fingers, long and cruel, eager to tear at human flesh. Chuck closed his eyes and screamed.

◊ ◊ ◊ ◊

Chuck opened his eyes slowly allowing the daylight to clear his vision. The ceiling, walls and sheets covering him were white. A woman beside his bed wore a stethoscope around her neck. She adjusted the IV attached to his left arm and noticed his open eyes.

"He's awake," she announced.

"Thank God almighty," Chuck heard the voice of his mother standing by the end of the bed with his father. He found his right arm inside a cast, gauze on his forehead and a firm brace held his neck.

Behind his parents, near the room's window, stood Tommy. Stains covered his clothing, his jeans torn and muddied; perspiration covered his flesh. His breathing hard and tired.

The nurse smiled, "I'll get the doctor."

Chuck felt the dryness in his throat when he tried to speak, the words creaked out, "what... happened?"

"It's all right, son," Dad said with a smile, "you don't have to talk right now."

Mom took hold of his hand, bringing slight pain to his arm. "You had an accident during the hurricane. But you're going to be fine, you're in the Medical Center in Plaquemine. You've been in a coma for three days. Do you remember anything?"

Chuck looked at her blankly while his mind slowly cleared from cloudy obscurities of the unconscious.

"No," he croaked.

Mom looked to Dad who hung his head. She looked back at Chuck. "On the marsh road. Ralphie and Tommy were with you. Ralphie was killed. I'm sorry, sweetheart."

Chuck couldn't believe what she said, nor recall an

accident claiming his friend's life. Tommy hung his head, also weeping. Chuck wanted to ask Tommy what happened, why did they have an accident, why was he in that condition?

He barely squeaked out his name, "Tommy---"

Dad answered, thinking his son asked about the other friend's welfare, "He's missing, son."

"Missing?" Chuck's gaze went to Tommy standing next to his mom.

"You can see me, bro?" Tommy asked.

"The Sheriff's department says the current must've pulled Tommy to the river, taken him clear to Orleans," Dad said.

"Missing?" Chuck repeated.

Tommy nervously nodded towards Chuck's parents, "They can't see me, bro. Don't you remember that Cajun come out 'o the marsh causing you to flip the Camaro?"

Tommy started to half smile and half cry filling Chuck in on the accident, "The dude was crazy, 'member? Ralphie was dead; you were banged up, the Cajun gave me a coin and told me to run 'cause a demon was coming for it. Well, turns out the dude's story was true. Damnedest thing I ever seen but this thing's been chasing me for three days. I'm spent, bro."

"I never had the coin?" Chuck said softly.

His parents looked confused at him then at each other.

"Relax, son" Dad said, "you've been through a lot."

Tommy stepped further into the corner of the room, leaning against the wall and sliding to the floor. "You've been in a coma, bro. I don't know why but you've been dreaming and trying to remember what really happened to us. You never had the coin… but somehow you saw the demon."

"Maybe I died…" Chuck squeaked out of his throat.

"You didn't die, son. Don't talk foolish," Chuck's mother said through tears.

"Maybe you did," Tommy said, his tone giving away his exhaustion. "And saw hell… and came back. You can't take the coin, you can't run. I don't know what I'm gonna do…?"

Chuck then understood it was a nightmare, visions running through his head confused by reality and fear. The door opened. Mom and Dad said hello to the doctor in unison. Chuck heard the doctor tell them how lucky their son was, considering his injuries; too bad about the other boys.

His face appeared over Chuck, gazing into his eyes; the bland scent of wet embers of apple tobacco filled his breath. Tommy sat on his haunches in the corner with his arms across his knees watching. Chuck could see Tommy's red-rimmed eyes from running and lack of rest. His gaze seemed miles away as though wondering how long he could run, how much longer he would have to.

"He needs rest, he's been through quite a shock," the doctor said, directing his mom and dad out of the room.

The doctor returned by Chuck's side injecting him with a drug taking effect immediately, warbling Chuck's vision and slowing the heart.

The doctor grinned showing stained canines. "Your friend can stay."

*He can see Tommy?*

Chuck's eyes opened wide, unable to act, only his mind, heart, breathing and eyes functioned. He cried silently in scream for Tommy, a scream unheard.

*Run!*

Chuck was unable to warn him of the demon doctor approaching for the coin. He could only see treetops outside the window, gently swaying like dancing Cajun women in the bayou.

# BAYOU BITES
by Jay Seate

The geographical distance between the back bayous of Louisiana to the bright lights and dark corners of New Orleans is short, but for the mind and soul, it can be a journey from one side of existence to another. So it was for Daniel La Beaux from Lafayette's Bend. Along with dozens of other settlements dating back to Napoleonic times, The Bend was one of the small, inconsequential places strung along the edges of the Louisiana Delta. A muggy little township, it lay like a washed-ashore oil drum along the road, straight from a Tennessee Williams tale. Green, humid, and hot, it smelled of crumbling blacktop, melting bubblegum, spilled grape soda, and dead carp; not bad if the place was all you knew. Daniel called it home because, until he was of age, he had no other choice.

Here was a civilization born of heat and damp, its heaviness imparted to speech, energy, and time. Bees droned drowsily in the wild honeysuckle. Little green lizards crisped their scales and scampered along the road. At night, the bayou came alive amidst the buzz of insects in the grass. The air was ripe with honeysuckle and the seminal scent of the swamp, the smells of green growth, varmints, and mud. Swamp gas skimmed off the water and floated through the jasmine like clouds of sweet perfume.

Fireflies darted in and out of view. Bats swooped, catching bugs and eating them. Small animals skittered through the brush. Night birds chirped.

So much life on the bayou, but Dan didn't know about real action until he wound up years later as a private investigator in New Orleans. It was from the edges of the Big Easy where a serenade led by cicadas and bullfrogs along the Mighty Mississippi reminded him of his past, his present accentuated by the plaintive sound of an occasional lonely foghorn somewhere upriver. The more recent sounds of the city reminded him not of where he'd sprung from, but rather of twisted hopes and broken dreams, a longing for something which seemed just out of reach.

On a recent steamy morning near the French Quarter, Dan parked his vehicle in front of a marble statue of a Confederate soldier covered with pigeon droppings. The canopy of sky was overcast with the usual high humidity, burning away the sordid dealings of the night. A covey of small children herded along by a gaunt nun passed by him on the sidewalk. She gave him a strained smile. The herd gave him pause. He reflected on the thin line between life and death, between these young innocents and the scenes he had witnessed as an investigator over the years. It was a flimsy divide between beauty and ugliness, between an innocent scene and a bloodbath.

Next, he came upon a wino leaning against a storefront while the smell of simmering shrimp hung in the air along with the soulful rhythm of a bluesy song. On the far side of the street, a Creole woman was setting out her cheap souvenirs and trinkets beneath the overhang of a second story gallery, her pipe clenched between her teeth. An old black man was already tap-dancing for a group of tourists. A wisp of steam rose from wet pavement evoking things that wouldn't stay buried, taking on an unnerving quality.

An old city with a past, with its two-hundred year history of blood, sweat, and tears—with its fortress ramparts and its slave markets. New cities weren't good for hiding secrets. They were cheap imitations, towns without souls. This was a town shrouded with superstition and only as safe as the strength of its levies. But the soul of the city-set-in-a-swamp—*Vieux Carre*—had a strong, resilient heartbeat.

The address Dan sought hid beyond a wrought-iron gate set in a garden wall. Fleur-de-lys ran across the top of the gate—a symbol linking the city to its French heritage. In New Orleans, there is always that peculiar, portentous quality of something otherworldly about—something carried on the breeze from the city's nooks and crannies, or from the above ground cemeteries, perhaps. But there is something passionate too. Beyond a wall armored with ivy and kudzu nestled a typical French-style courtyard draped with wisteria vines. Obligatory ornate grillwork ran along the second floor units. The courtyard was dappled with shadows from an ancient live oak that dripped with tattered banners of dusty gray Spanish moss. A wind-chime hung on a branch among the gray beards of moss. It tinkled in a faint breeze. *Ghost music.* "A serenade for the dead," the superstitious contingent of the city would have said.

The breeze brought with it the scent of magnolias. A brilliant glimpse of purple bougainvillea caught his eye. New Orleans could be such a strange and intoxicating place, just like the exotic mix of humanity which inhabited it. The elegant decadence of Halloween and Mardi Gras was always in the air to accompany those feelings of otherworldliness and passion. His nostrils filled with the second scent of blooming jasmine. The smell sweetened the air like overripe fruit—all these things reminders of why he stayed in this mosquito-laden part of the country.

He'd climbed out of the swamps and made something of himself, found an occupation which fit his inquisitive nature, even if his life as a PI had its negatives to accompany the positives. There were times when he abhorred what he was paid good money for—to dig up dirt on people who would prefer to keep their secrets buried. Blackmail, plain and simple, but what clients did with the information he gathered wasn't his call. He was just a guy who stuck the shovel beneath personas, turned up the worms then passed them on to third parties to deposit in the right places.

This time around his assignment had been to tail some rich-bitch wife from the Garden District, a neighbor of Anne Rice, in fact. La Beaux had candidly captured his current employer's wife on film. She liked to show up at galas, premiers, charity functions, but she also took pleasure in picking up bums off the street and rewarding them with a glance into a world they could never have imagined, experiencing brief but intense delusions of grandeur. That was her real charity work. No hunky health club employee or cute waiter to satisfy this affluent damsel. She preferred her pleasure down and dirty with some booze or drug infested low-life most people would cross the street to avoid.

He knocked and entered one of the courtyard's office doors that led to the man wanting proof of his wife's dalliances, a wealthy stock commodities husband, Joshua Bernard II. As Bernard studied the light-sensitive photos La Beaux had taken of his wife dragging some rummy into a fancy Canal Street hotel, his nostrils flared as if the smell from Estelle's companion emanated from the 8X10 glossies. "My wife, a woman of supposed class and breeding, seeking men off the street…the indignity of what might be taking place…"

La Beaux stood quietly, noticing Bernard's expensive designer suit with the pant cuffs breaking over just as expensive wingtips, allowing the big shot to contemplate he and his wife's future.

"I want something else from you, La Beaux. These photos beg for further investigation. I want you to playact. Make yourself known to her and see if she'll pick you up. I want to know exactly how far she goes with these skuzzballs."

"I don't think it takes much imagination to figure out what goes on behind closed doors," La Beaux replied, wanting nothing more than the money he'd been promised. "She's not running a mission."

"I've got to know to what level of degradation she has sunk."

La Beaux didn't like the sound of it, but when Bernard pulled a fistful of hundreds from a drawer and fanned them on the desktop before him, he reckoned he could stretch his talents to that of a street thespian.

"Double your fee for the pictures. Half now and half when you get with her and report back."

"Okay, Mr. Bernard, half now and half later, if she'll pick me up, that is."

Bernard chuckled in a way that only busy, superior people do. "I know you have the talent to imitate one of those cretins she's…taking up with."

"I'll do my best."

◊ ◊ ◊

La Beaux stopped shaving three days prior to Estelle Bernard's next opportunity to prowl. A few rumpled clothes and he looked as down and out as any bum along the river.

Like clockwork, Mrs. B hailed a taxi around 10 PM. La Beaux hailed another. His Indian cab driver made him flash some green before speeding off in pursuit of the first taxi. The cab followed her to an upscale restaurant/bar where La Beaux paid the cabbie and waited outside in the shadows for an hour and a half.

Finally, Estelle emerged alone, a little unsteady but still looking like at least half a million bucks. Her body had a way of sending off a signal and part of La Beaux's body got the message. She hailed a taxi and he prepared to do the same, but the lady's cab simply pulled down a half block and idled. La Beaux watched though a parade of passing vehicles. Estelle was watching the foot traffic apparently waiting to find someone to her liking, auditioning passersby.

Making his move, La Beaux dodged traffic, crossed the street, and sauntered up to the taxi's street-side passenger window. When he tapped on the glass, Estelle's head swiveled toward him just as the cabbie growled, "Get away from the lady, ya bum."

Estelle cracked her window an inch.

"I wouldn't do that, ma'am," the cabbie admonished.

"What is it?" she said to La Beaux.

"Wondered if a genteel lady such as yourself could spare a couple of bucks. I'm a little down on my luck at present."

She opened her dainty clutch bag and withdrew a ten-dollar bill. "Will this help?"

"You're very generous." La Beaux smiled. "Maybe someday I can do something for you?"

She shoved the bill through the narrow opening which connected her to the outside world where La Beaux's fingers awaited. "I doubt that," she said abruptly and rolled up the window.

La Beaux silently cursed himself for missing the opportunity. Perhaps he didn't appear down and out or filthy enough to satisfy her craving. There was nothing to do but walk away.

"Mister?" Mrs. B called.

La Beaux turned.

Estelle had rolled her window down, all the way this time, and motioned him back. "That was awfully rude of me. Let me give you a lift," she offered in her best Scarlet O'Hara southern drawl.

La Beaux's attitude changed as quickly as a glitzy marquee flashed from one color of light bulbs to another. He slowly walked around the rear of the cab, cracked open the door then hesitated.

"Get in. I won't bite. I know a place where you can have the good stuff to drink, unless you would rather blow your ten bucks on rot gut?"

Funny she would assume his vice was alcohol. He guessed she'd found booze to be the drug of choice among the street lice. Like Estelle's husband, he was becoming increasingly curious about how her walks on the wild side played out. La Beaux opened the car door and climbed in.

Mrs. B gave the driver an address. He stared through the rearview at the odd couple, but apparently had been driving long enough to witness about everything the backseat of a cab in New Orleans could offer.

They traveled in silence until Estelle asked his name.

"Pete," he answered.

"Well, Pete, this could be your lucky night. Ever spent time in a penthouse?"

La Beaux looked into her gray eyes and fought the urge to say, "Yeah, a time or two with babes just as hot as you," but instead said, "I don't mean to be disrespectful, but this is only a temporary situation with me. You don't have to do me any favors."

"I see. A noble man, temporarily on the skids." Her tone wasn't so much condescending as it was unconvinced. "I think you'll do just fine. I need a little help myself tonight."

La Beaux studied the woman's profile as it turned light then dark then light again as storefront lights swiftly crawled inside the cab and disappeared just as quickly. Playing along could be fun, but the money was more important than this skirt. He was supposed to report her predilections to the husband, not take a proactive part.

The taxi pulled in front of the highest office building in the city. "Come along," she told La Beaux. He obediently followed her past the doorman, whose palm she greased with a twenty. An elevator whisked them to the top floor. She unlocked a door and waved him through. "I promised a penthouse."

"You certainly did." He walked through the well-appointed space to the picture windows that extended the length of the room. The view revealed most of New Orleans's landmarks in all their multi-colored glory topped off by a crescent moon which floated between two tall buildings.

Suddenly Estelle was at La Beaux's side. "Breathtaking, isn't it? Makes you feel as if you own the whole city. Sustenance for the gods," she said as solemnly as if they had entered a church.

Below lay the circadian rhythm of glittering sprawl and people moving along the streets, a miniature etching in motion, bright, seductive, and full of both promise and sorrow. "The devils feast here also," La Beaux added, transfixed by the superficial beauty mixed with the ugly underbelly he knew to exist within his adopted city. Still looking at the panorama he asked, "So what am I doing here?"

"I think you know."

"An uptown girl like you? Why pick up a guy off the street like me?"

"Let's just say I like the earthy type. Let's say the earthier the better."

She stood close and smelled him. "You haven't been on the street long. Maybe you're telling the truth about not being a chronic loser."

He turned quickly and grabbed her shoulders. "Do you get your kicks from playing this little game of 'rich broad shows charity to some low-life bum'? I'll probably be happy to play along if you'll tell me what the game involves?"

"That's fair."

He released her and stepped back, realizing this had become more than a job. Although desperate to discover what made this particular variety of female tick, he was not about to lose sight of the payoff. The money was too good and Bernard was far too important to let his sudden lust for this *femme fatale* take him anywhere but out the door.

"Go to the bar and make us a drink, whatever you prefer. Let me step into the powder room and freshen up, then I'll show you what I like to do and how I like to do it."

"You want me to clean up a little?"

"You stay just like you are, but don't forget the drinks."

He had broken his own rule by not carrying the weapon he normally strapped to his right mid-calf, but the challenge of this caper seemed little more than staying dressed. Maybe she wanted to get off by licking the scent of the street off of him. He would let it go far enough to determine her proclivity before he made his apology, hit the road, and eventually reported to Joshua Bernard II as to what variety of kink his wifey liked to imbibe.

He carried the drinks to a coffee table and sprawled on one of the penthouse's sofas. He looked for the moon which had disappeared behind the top of a building with only its opposing tips visible on either side of the spire, like two sharp teeth, and waited with anticipation for the queen bee to reveal her true identity as Batgirl. "Sustenance for the gods, my ass," he said softly, a slight grin curving his lips. He reached for the solace of his scotch and took a long sip, enjoying the smooth burn in his throat and the spreading warmth alcohol provided.

Finally, the bathroom door creaked open. Estelle stood within. The trained lighting on the wallpaper bathed her with a soft golden backlight. La Beaux could see only that she stood naked, a silhouette of near perfection. She stepped over the threshold and came to him. The reflected light from other buildings painted her faultless torso in pinks, whites and blues.

Estelle picked up her drink and swallowed most of it. She towered over La Beaux, the intensity of her desire palpable. "Mmmm, a scotch man," she breathed.

La Beaux sat his tumbler down. His gaze was riveted on the smooth lines of the body—a body to die for, he thought. "What now?" he asked.

"Not much, just a kiss on the neck." She sat on his lap and nibbled around the scruffy stubble.

There had to be more to this than a slow burn leading to straight sex, La Beaux thought as she shifted, placing her knees on either side of his hips, straddling him, her generous lips planting kisses on his earlobe and neck.

"All right, sugar. I'm a little old for a hickey." La Beaux decided to get up from under her. But then, he saw something which froze him in place, something startling and unexpected. He closed his eyes tightly and opened them quickly to make sure he was not hallucinating.

Another silhouette stood between Estelle and the bathroom's glow. It glided toward the couple. La Beaux pushed against the woman draped over him, but she was like three hundred pounds of lead, an immovable object, attached to his neck like a gigantic leach.

Bernard II himself stood staring at the odd couple on the sofa. A warped, sneering smile not unlike his wife's, cracked his otherwise austere, businesslike countenance.

"Look who's here," he announced. "You see, La Beaux, when you're married to a she-devil like Estelle, you have to make certain concessions."

La Beaux again pushed against the taut body facing him, but he might as well have been pinned to the mat by a wrestler. He looked at Bernard, then back at Estelle who had, at least temporarily, come up for air. In spite of her sardonic smile, she looked different, her expression slowly changing into something unpleasant.

"What's the deal, Bernard?" La Beaux shouted. "Does she do things to men while you watch?"

"That's one way to put it, old chum. You have little choice but to go along with rather crude methods of entertainment when you live with a beautiful, insatiable blood-sucker."

La Beaux looked at Estelle again. He saw the elongated teeth beneath the wicked smile. Fear gripped him the way smog grips a city.

"I'm not so perverted, am I?" Estelle said with a pernicious pout. "I'm not going to have sex with you. I'm only going to suck a reasonable amount of blood. Not enough to kill you, just enough to give you the gift."

La Beaux tried to strike out with his fists but Estelle was too quick, a skilled defender, warding off the blow rendering it harmless. He instinctively reached for the weapon he'd never needed until now, yet knowing it wasn't there. A prayer sprang from the mind of the suddenly repentant man, a prayer that all of this was just a horrible dream or the result of some bad gumbo, but he knew it to be as real as the metal file cabinet in his office that held a few notes about his present client's wife, to be disposed of sooner than expected. The luminescent crescent on the canvas of night was now impaled by the skyscraper spire, captured by an uncaring, unforgiving city, as was he.

There was nothing left to do but scream. One long burst followed by a short one which came out as a pitiful cry.

"No use." Bernard smiled snidely. "Not up here above the city, above everyone and everything but us. Up here where the gods feast."

"Why me?" La Beaux wailed.

"Simple," Bernard continued. "She finds men who no one takes notice of to satisfy the inescapability of her hunger, the homeless, and the transient, those who fall through society's cracks. In your case, we needed someone who performs your kind of unscrupulous dirty work in the event anyone becomes suspicious about our nocturnal escapades."

La Beaux stared at Bernard.

"Oh, don't be so thick. That intuition or sixth sense some investigators possess I didn't sense in you and I was obviously correct. You didn't seem careful enough, a little sloppy; maybe you don't care for your work anymore. Maybe you're thinking about a return to whatever little jerkwater parish from whence you sprung. Whatever the case, we are your salvation. You'll be one of us now and you'll do anything to protect what we have, what we crave, including taking care of snoops if necessary. The thirst is all that will matter, and the desire to please. You have no one who is close. You won't miss the old way and no one will miss you."

"I lied. I do bite," Estelle told the helpless man pinned beneath her as she attached her face to his neck once again, this time in search of a large vein.

La Beaux flinched at the sharp sting of Estelle's penetrating fangs. He heard the gurgle of his blood entering her mouth and the half crunching, half smacking noise rose above her joyful, thankful moans. Tales of human night creatures had always been great campfire stories popular with both the Creoles and Cajuns, but he thought such things had been merely a creation of the superstition he'd left behind on his journey from the backwater bayous to the big city long ago.

"Just squeeze her breasts until she's finished," Bernard advised. "It will help give you a sense of familiarity and calm. Like mother's milk for the both of you."

La Beaux's strength and will to resist evaporated. He did what he was told as he gradually slid downward into whatever realm of existence these two beings might bring forth. Before his vision faded, the final scene transmitted to his brain was that of the huge fangs sprouting from Bernard's gums.

That little, rich chuckle again. "Not too much now, dear," Bernard II said to Mrs. Joshua Bernard II with the pure glee of anticipation. "Before he slips into the arms of Morpheus, save some for me."

Daniel La Beaux doesn't go out much anymore except on those special occasions when his new job requirements make it necessary. He now has meaning in his existence and a desperate goal. His PI business, money, and his old pursuits for pleasure have become irrelevant as others now pay his room and board. He waits only for the tap at his door which tells him one of Estelle's hookers has brought along a friend…someone to suck on, and it is his turn to feast as do the gods who own him. He is slave to these moments which satisfy a hunger more addictive than street drugs. The Bernards have cured La Beaux's self-pity by making him one of them. And now he is infected by the cure, locked in a colony of the damned.

There are those rare occasions when the creature at the door is none other than Estelle. He doesn't mind that she has taken to calling him La Blood or the dangerous new assignments he is sent on, for she is the one who made him what he is, the one whose breasts he delights in kneading while she takes more of his blood, the one who trapped him into becoming a part of her guilty pleasures, the one he exists to please. He would never question his *raison d'etra* in Louisiana, his sumptuous corner of the world.

# CHANGING FAVORS

by Margaret L. Colton

"C'mon darlin', don't be like that," Keith crooned. "Baby, you know this is a great opportunity for me. You know how I feel about you, but I can't pass this up." He tries giving me that grin which would normally melt my heart.

"Seriously? You love me so much you have to leave me?" I am torn between righteous indignation and crushing heartbreak.

"Katie, darlin', you know I meant every word I ever said, but this can't work now. I have to leave. I'll make tons of money on the oil rigs, but I won't be around. I want you to be happy. Go find someone else, settle down, have tons of kids." Keith shrugged. His eyes dart everywhere else but in my direction as he speaks. He runs his fingers through his hair like he's aggravated for having to explain trashing our life together. With each word he takes a step backward away from me. Obviously his mind was made up before now; bags were packed and he was leaving.

I stand there shaking, my life crumbling before me. My future torn apart. The visions of adorable children running around while I tended my garden next to the ornamental fence blur and fade. This man whom I had loved with all my heart, every fiber of my being for four years, is just leaving. He's telling me our life here in Baton Rouge has been just a temporary stop for him. He has plans. He has dreams. I thought they are the same as mine; he said they were the same. He promised me we would go down to New Orleans and marry at St. Louis Cathedral. He promised we would take my inheritance and move to a beautiful home in the Garden District. He said he would love me forever.

Instead he burned through a huge portion of my money, and is leaving me with broken dreams and a lie. I sacrificed so much for him; moving here to Baton Rouge away from my family, waiting patiently for the right time to get married, all the while building him up, supporting him, letting him make all the decisions and just loving him. I hate that the tears started. I didn't realize they were flowing, but there they are, the evidence soaking the front of my shirt.

"C'mon over here Katie-girl. Let's have a little fun for the last time." Keith smirks and lounges on the bed, patting the spot in front of him.

"You must be outta your damn mind if you think for one second I'm getting into that bed with you, Keith. Get out!" I snap. I feel it. All I want to do is set the bed on fire with him in it.

"Katie, baby, look we…"

"I said out. You know, I don't think you ever really loved me at all." I could feel my temper flaring. I don't want to sound like the desperate girlfriend, but I needed to know.

"I loved rolling in the sack with you baby. I care about you, but you know I ain't the marrying kind. All that wedding stuff scares the hell outta me. Settling down in a big fancy house? Not my thing. Go out and make yourself happy. Best of luck to you." Keith's nonchalant attitude shows as he grabs his duffel bag, his boots scraping along the hard-wood floor as he heads for the door.

"Oh, but you want me to be happy? You've strung me along for four years; making plans, all my hopes and dreams laid at your feet, all for what?"

"Look, honey, we had a good time and now it's over. Move on. I am. Maybe you'll cool down in eight months and I'll look you up when I'm on shore-leave…" Keith winks and strolls out of the door.

Standing there dumbfounded as the retorts fly through my brain, I'm mute and can only stare at the door. The anger shielding me a moment ago discarded, giving way to the real emotions crushing my being. The sudden achy heaviness in my chest takes my breath away. Sinking to the floor with my knees pulled to my forehead, I allow the sobbing to rack my body. I give in to the incredible pain tearing at me from the inside, robbing me of air and stopping my heart.

I don't know how long I lay there, but now it's dusk. My body is stiff and sore, my muscles like Jell-o from the emotional exhaustion. I need to get up, but my body is immobile, weighed down with emotions too hard to bear.

Moving through the living room toward the bathroom, I see the evidence of his deception. Pictures of us together are everywhere in the room; him with his dark hair and rugged good looks smiling that charming smile. His light blue, lying eyes shining as his arm draped around me.

Oh, and of course there I am. The contrasts strike me; my auburn hair to his dark coloring, I'm so petite and he's the hulking working man. I never looked like I belonged next to him. Sure I'm all smiles; I couldn't be happier. I was happy with the man of my dreams ready to dedicate my life to him forever. Every picture I'm the stupidly grinning one holding on to my man. What a fool.

I stumble into the bathroom to splash water on my face and catch a glimpse of myself in the mirror. My hair is a tangled mess. My eyes are now swollen and bloodshot while my face is tear-stained and blotchy. I am slim, but it seems like I am gaunt, pale, just a shadow of myself.

*Great, there's a way to find a man and move on. Someone please date the skeleton girl.*

"Move on" he said. Whatever. Like I can ever trust a guy again. The crying/sobbing/weeping must have helped because I'm starting to feel angry. What are the stages of grief again? I know anger is one and I feel it. I feel outraged. How dare he?

Just then my phone blows up. Of course Keith changed his Facebook status, and now all of my friends want to know what is going on. *Did I know? Did he cheat? What am I going to do now? Am I okay?* I don't know, am I okay? Will I ever be okay again? I sigh and spend the next three hours texting and talking on my phone.

I wake up a few hours later on the couch. I don't remember falling asleep, but I'm late for work. I run to the bathroom and shower. Putting the mascara on was a special kind of torture because my eyes are still so swollen. Screw it, I should just call in sick, but that responsible part of me said no, I don't have plans set up for a substitute teacher and my kids are counting on me. I finish smearing on the makeup, grab a bottle of water and run out the door.

My English Lit class is studying Shakespeare's *Twelfth Night.* I usually love getting into it with the kids, showing them the clever whimsy of his work, but today my heart is not in it. Twice today I hear, "Miss McAirn, are you ok?"

*No, kids, my heart has been ripped out and I spent yesterday crying in the fetal position.*

While the kids would understand my trauma and probably cry with me, I can just imagine the phone calls from the parents, not to mention the dressing down from my jerk principal.

My friends have a much better idea. We have spring break coming up in a few days and the end of Lent, so we will head down to New Orleans. Maybe wandering around and getting caught up in the New Orleans' vibe will help me 'move on'. Or at the very least, I will drink my way to oblivion down on Bourbon Street and forget all about Keith, the misery and heartache he's left in his wake. A couple of Hurricanes, a Hand-Grenade or two and some double-shot daiquiris should do the trick. No way could I stay sad in New Orleans, not with my friends around me and the party-vibe happening. Maybe just a few nights of carefree drinking will help quell the heartache and quench the fire of the blazing anger I'm feeling inside me towards Keith.

◊ ◊ ◊ ◊

My friend Darla with the minivan offered to drive. I just finished throwing stuff in a bag when I hear the horn outside my window. I grab my stuff and run for the door. Packing had been easy this time because I don't have to worry about impressing anyone. I just want to get away and feel better for a couple of days. Not that any would, but I pity the man who tries to talk to me this week—unless he's a bartender giving me booze—otherwise I'll just end up crying on his shoulder.

We check in to a couple of rooms at the Hotel St. Marie on Toulouse Street. It is our favorite hotel in the French Quarter with its old world charm and courtyard pool. Just far enough off of Bourbon Street to get away from the craziness but at only a half a block walk away, close enough to get a drink. A drink is what I am dying for after being cooped up in the van for close to two hours with my heart torn apart while my friends tried to cheer me up with chatter about nothing.

We throw our stuff in the drawers, change clothes and head to Lafitte's Blacksmith Shop at the far end of Bourbon, only a short five blocks away. The dark pirate-bar hangout is perfect for our first night in New Orleans. They have the best Hurricanes and I'm looking forward to the healing power of alcohol.

Dusk settled as the girls and I walk quickly down Bourbon towards Lafitte's. As we start to pass Marie Laveau's Voodoo Shop, a sharp chill runs through me, causing a shiver. The building is nothing special, small and run down, with broken shutters and a small air conditioning unit sticking out of a tiny window in the front. Neon lights don't glow around the shop to draw attention, instead there is just a small black and white sign over the first door. Strangely drawn to the shop, I slow down, glancing into the dark interior as I pass. The strange stories of Marie Laveau begin coming back to me.

Marie Laveau had been the famous Voodoo Queen of New Orleans even though she was a devout Catholic. Like so many other things in New Orleans, Marie Laveau was of two worlds and moved seamlessly through both. She never missed Mass, yet it was known she used her voodoo magic to help those in need. It is said her tomb could be found in St. Louis Cemetery No 1. If you know how to summon Marie she grants favors. Supposedly there were voodoo rituals performed at her tomb all the time to honor Marie Laveau and ask for favors. Maybe I should ask to get over Keith? I hug myself against the almost painful chill and move toward my friends, taking another hard look inside the voodoo shop through the second door.

"Ah cherie, c'mon in 'ere an let Marie help yah out."

The woman's heavy, Haitian-accented voice came from inside the voodoo shop, but I didn't see anyone.

"Excuse me?" I don't know what makes me stand there and answer instead of running to catch up to my friends. There is a tugging deep in my soul, a connection with whatever or whoever is in the shop. Something called out to my whole being, keeping me rooted to that spot, drawing my attention to nothing but the shop.

"Yah heard me right, cherie. I know yah secret pain. C'mon, baby, and let ol' Marie help." This time a short dark woman in a print dress and headscarf emerges from the shadows with a slight smile and outstretched hand.

"I...I...um...I'm supposed to..."

"I know, baby, but yah need some peace. Ain't gonna find it in dat bar." She waves her hand toward Laffite's and then extends her hand to me.

"Katie! What the hell? C'mon!" I hear Darla, our ringleader, shout over to me. They are almost half a block ahead of me.

Lafitte's is only two blocks from the voodoo shop, but the girls are anxious to get to the bar while it's still kind of early. If we wait much longer, there won't be any tables left.

"Yeah, I'll be a minute. Go ahead, grab a table, and order. I'm checking out this shop first." I hesitate but the draw of the woman and the shop is too strong to ignore.

"Hey, good idea! Get a voodoo doll of that asshole and we'll stick pins in his tiny prick all night! Whoo!" Darla and the girls turn and laugh as they continue down the sidewalk toward Lafitte's.

I turn after waving to the girls and move carefully toward the shop.

*What am I doing?* I don't believe in this stuff, and every time I've been by here it has felt like a tourist trap, not a place to gain help for a broken heart. Something deep inside me urges me into the shop. This compulsion narrows my focus to nothing else but going inside. Even though my mind was screaming to turn around and run toward my friends, my feet move me slowly inside. I need to be here.

"Sit dere, cherie." The woman points to the chair next to a table with an assortment of items like cards and... bones? They were misshapen, yellowed, and worn, yet slightly rounded and had some sort of carvings like ancient symbols on the different sides. No, they must be some kind of dice. They are probably antique dice made of animal bones or something.

"How can Marie Laveau help me?" I ask in a very small voice as the woman sat across the table from me.

Chuckling, the woman answers, "I'm Marie, suga, an I felt all dat pain from all da way in 'ere. Dat pain called out, sent a ripple right through 'ere. I knew we couldn't let such a pretty child suffer like dat. Now, let me see your hands, cherie."

I hold my palms out to her and she took them in her warm, callused hands for a moment as if she is weighing them. With an intense look to my face she lets go of my hands, and picks up a wooden cylinder with strange markings on it then places the bone-dice inside. I move my hands quickly as she scattered the pieces over the table.

"Mmm...hmmm...just what I thought. Yah got man trouble." She shook her head as she spoke and continued to sift through the bones on the table.

*Well of course she knew that. Half the block figured out I had man trouble from yelling back and forth to my friends.* My thoughts bring me back to reality and I begin to think I just need to go. *I'll find peace after a few Hurricanes...*

"No, no, cherie, this ain't ya normal man trouble. Dis one broke ya. Ya spirit is ruined. Ain't nothin' can help yah wit' that feelin' deep inside, but maybe a little bit o' vengeance will set tings right."

"What do you mean, like a voodoo doll or curse or something? I don't really believe in all that. No offense, but…"

"Suga, this ain't in my power to help with. Yah gotta go to Marie herself." The woman looks sad, or like she is holding something back.

"But I thought you were Marie? You said your name was Marie. I don't understand."

"Child, yah need Marie Laveau. Yah past my power to help. Da Queen herself got to help yah, baby." Marie sat back gazing intently, her warm brown eyes lit with a fire. I could almost see golden flames. She crossed her arms over her ample chest, nodding her head as she pursed her large lips in a determined line, like some sort of decision had been made. She was short and heavy, and exuding a power I could feel washing over me in that moment.

"I don't understand any of this. You said you were Marie and Marie could help me. Now you are telling me a Voodoo Queen, Marie Laveau, who lived over 150 years ago is the only one who can help me fix my broken heart? How? She's dead. How can she help me now?" I grip my hands together tightly, then lay my hands flat on the table as I fight for control of my emotions. "You must think I'm some gullible tourist. You see a sad face and decide to run some scam. Do you have some kit in here to mend my heart you are going to sell me next?" I jerk the chair backward from the table. "I'm not some wide-eyed tourist and I've been humiliated enough. Here let me pay you for your time so I can get back to my friends now." I fumble in my purse for my wallet.

"No cherie, no money. 'Ere's what yah do. Yah go down to St. Louis Cemetery. 'Ere's a map to Marie's tomb." She produces a faded slip of paper from her pocket, unfolding it to show me. Her eyes implore me to listen. "Yah go there, and on the right side mark three X's in red. An' then yah tell Marie yah troubles. Don't mark on da left, hear? Unless yah willin' to sacrifice. Yah ask Da Queen for help." She squeezes my hand before letting go and continues. "Now yah gotta bring an offering too, an' lay it at her tomb. She'll hear, and she'll answer yah quick. Jus' take this with yah an' when yah ready, you'll know what to do" The woman holds my arm and presses a slip of paper into my hand. She looks at me so earnestly I almost believe her.

"Um, okay, thank you. I'll consider it. Thank you." I hurry out of the shop, mumbling apologies as I bump into a group of ladies exploring the candles and giggling.

I practically run down the sidewalk the two blocks toward Lafitte's, scooting past the shuffling tourists in my way. It's darker out now, the air heavy and warm, but I still feel the remnants of the chill. I'm jumpy, almost agitated, and the slow-moving people are really aggravating me. I'm not usually impatient, but I'm in a hurry and I consider knocking them into the street. I grip the slip of paper tightly and move faster to my friends.

I arrive at Lafitte's. The sun has just set and the sky's quickly darkening, but the interior of the bar is really dark—it always is. With the help of the glow from the candles on the tables, I find my friends at a table toward the back room where the piano is located. Of course Darla found the best table possible, across from the restroom and under a window, not too far from the bar. They shift so I could be at the center of the table and there's a Hurricane waiting for me.

We sit at Lafitte's drinking, talking, and listening to the

piano. My friends are kind enough to commiserate with me by bashing Keith. I can't really join in. I just fake-smile and drink more. The heartache is back and I am on the verge of tears. Plus I'm distracted thinking about the woman from the voodoo shop, the intense way her eyes had been so sad, yet still bored into my soul. Is there really a way to feel better? I think back to the woman's silky voice, the cadence of her speech nearly hypnotic as she held out hope, yet confused me at the same time. Does she really want to help? My friends are disappointed I had not picked up a voodoo doll of Keith. Apparently they never liked him—he was a jerk, rude, and hit on most of them.

*Wait, what?* That got my attention quickly.

Darla spews out one of her encounters with Keith. "Oh yeah, at that party we had at my house a few months ago, Keith pulled me into a room and kissed me. Actually, honey, he was all over me. I told him no and he said you would never know. As flattering as that was, I would never do that to you." Darla's slurred accounting rings in my head as I look around the table. I realize several of my friends will not make eye contact with me.

*Wow really? My friends?* I start seeing images of Keith with my friends and I can feel the anger building again. *How many of them had he been with? How often?* "I don't understand. Keith did what?"

Around the table my friends confess that Keith had made passes at them. It never went anywhere with any of them, but only because they were my friends. He had kissed and grabbed them. Some of my friends slapped him, some told their boyfriends, but no one wanted to hurt me by telling me. My head spins wildly with these revelations, I need air. I got up, pushing my way through the crowds and stepping down to the sidewalk outside the bar. Shaken, reeling from what I had learned, I'm leaning against the lamppost, gulping in air. I look down at my hand with my now hazy vision and realize I am still clutching the slip of paper in my white-knuckled fist.

*Is the woman in the shop right? Could some long-dead voodoo queen really help me? Screw this, what do I have to lose?*

I stumble back to my friends and tell them I'm going back to the room. They say they will walk me back, but I refuse. We'd been here often enough that I know my way around and am going straight to the room. Dangerous, yes, but I don't want to ruin their 'fun'.

I do go to the room but only to change into comfy clothes and running shoes. On my way out I grab the ring Keith had given me and some bright red lipstick. I know right where I'm going—St. Louis Cemetery No 1. I hurry over the sidewalks and crossed Rampart then Basin, which is no easy feat with all the drunk drivers. My buzz has burned off in my anger and agitation, so now I only feel driven.

The cemetery closes to the public at 3pm, but unlike a lot of places, there are no metal spikes on the top of the walls. I go to the side off of St. Louis Street near the corner and use the rough bricks showing in the wall to scale the short distance. Then I hoist myself up to the top and jump down the 8 foot drop on the other side. It isn't a far jump but I do have to brace myself against a rough tomb as I land on it. Quickly I scramble off the tomb with a case of the willies because it's so creepy knowing there are so many bodies in the crypt under me. I scrape my hands a little, but nothing's going to stop me now.

I take the little slip of paper from my waistband and try to acclimate myself to the cemetery. I had been on tours here before, wandering and exploring around the cemetery, but now I have a destination I need to find and it's dark except for the very bright full moon. Even with that light I still need the light from my phone to help me navigate.

After twisting and turning around the cemetery I finally find it: Marie Laveau's tomb. It seems that others have been here as well. Red X's are on three sides of the tomb. Candles, flowers, Mardi Gras beads, shoes, and all kinds of trinkets are left as offerings at the entrance.

*How cliché am I?* Am I seriously considering asking a favor from a long dead Voodoo Queen? Yes, I'm angry and hurt, but I'll get over it, I don't know how though because it is crushing me. Oh hell, I'm here now so why not?

As I approach the tomb with my red lipstick in hand, my cell dies. It had been fully charged, but whatever. It takes me half a minute for my eyes to adjust and I realize the moon was so bright I can see without help from my useless phone's light. I step to the left side of the tomb, hoping if there were patrols in the cemetery the two tombs would shield me from being seen. Wait, hadn't the woman said the right side of the tomb unless I was willing to sacrifice? Sacrifice what? My freedom? I really don't want to get caught here. It's silly and I really don't think it matters. I'm staying where I have cover.

I use the lipstick to draw the three X's. The X's are about three inches big, touching and as neat as I can make them, drawing on plaster with lipstick. As I turn to head to the front of the tomb, I stumbled on a pillar candle left as an offering and my hand presses right on my X's.

*Damn!* Not only do I smear the X's but I get blood on the wall from my scrapes. I do not have anything to wipe it off with so I try my fingers, all that did was make more of a mess. I redraw the X's with my finger and then go over them with the lipstick. At this point it is a just a bloody mess and I decide to give up.

I pick my way carefully to the front of the tomb holding my bloody hand against the end of my t-shirt.

"Well Marie, like everything else, I screwed this up too. My boyfriend is a jerk, my dreams are trashed. Whatever. You can probably use this ring more than me." I drop the ring in the gravel by the entrance of the tomb among the other trinkets and start to walk away back toward the wall.

"Where you goin', child?" A honey-sweet voice purrs behind me.

*Damn I'm busted.* I twirl around with stupid excuses running through my head. I didn't want to spend the night in jail. But standing next to the tomb is not someone in uniform. She's a beautiful black woman with a flowing, beaded robe. She is almost translucent and her eyes are an intense shining brown. Or red? I blink but she's still there and I am rooted to the ground.

"I…I…Um…I'm sor… who are…" the words catch in my throat.

"I've been waiting for you. Come here let me see your hands." She has the same smile and outstretched hand as Marie in the voodoo shop had.

I take a step closer, my body trembling, torn between running away and obeying her. I hold out my hands, one scraped but okay, the other still bleeding a little from the cut. She doesn't touch me but her hands hover over mine, her eyes closed and it seems like she is whispering a chant or a prayer.

"You are hurtin', girl. I can feel your pain." She shakes her head slowly, eyes still closed. "You've been done wrong and your spirit is damaged." Opening her eyes she reaches out with her hand a breath away from my chest, over my heart. "Do you want help? Are you willing to sacrifice?" Her voice washes over me, chilling me to the bone, yet soothing me at the same time. I feel my head nod sadly in ascension, almost like I'm not in control, followed by her cooing, "I will help you."

Feeling woozy, my legs heavy, weak, I begin swaying in time to some unheard beat. Then her hand grasped my forehead like a vise-grip, like molten metal pouring on my face. I hear myself scream as my knees buckle. The last thing I remember is looking up through her fingers and seeing her wicked smile and glowing red eyes.

◊ ◊ ◊ ◊

"Wake up already Katie! C'mon! We are starving. Get up so we can get to the diner before the crowds."

My eyes open just slightly. Bright light burns into my corneas and I quickly shut them again. *Where am I? My friends are all around me? What's going on?* I try to open my eyes again and bring my hand up to shield them from the light. "What?" I manage to croak out.

"Ah, wow, she's hung over!" Darla informs the group as she laughs and pulls on my arm until I'm in a sitting position. "C'mon, some cheesy eggs will fix you right up. Well, that and a Bloody Mary or two. Up you go. We are leaving in five." She's chattering mindlessly as she pushes me toward the bathroom. Her voice grates on my nerves.

In the bathroom, I look at myself in the mirror. I look rough. My eyes are bloodshot and sunken in my head, my hands and knees are scraped and bruised. I'm wearing a blood-stained t-shirt for pjs.

*How did I get here?* The last thing I remember was Marie Laveau's hand on my head and falling to the ground in front of her. *How am I here now?* I search my brain for any clue, but nothing. A big blacked-out nothing. Even what I do remember is fuzzy. Maybe I dreamed it all up from my drunken stupor? I touch my forehead while staring into the mirror but nothing is there. I hear everyone moving around the room so I quickly shower and get dressed.

"Finally! Let's go!" Darla pulls me from the bathroom.

As we walk down the uneven sidewalks, I concentrate on not falling and trying to remember anything from last night.

"Katie, we should have walked you back to the room. I can't believe you fell. When we came in you were passed out and all scraped up. You were dead weight, not that you are fat at all, just difficult to move…" Darla's rambling answers at least some of my questions.

So, I fell going back to the room? That makes sense and is easy to do. I don't remember falling. I vaguely remember climbing the cemetery wall. The rest must have just been a dream from the combination of emotional upheaval, large quantities of booze, and my strange encounter from the voodoo shop. It's all easily explained, so why do I have this burning feeling in my chest? I feel so…different.

At the diner I get a Bloody Mary, steak and eggs. My steak is practically raw, which I never order like that, but today it's like a craving. I want bloody meat and can't explain it. Maybe I should go easier with the alcohol.

"Eww! Really Katie? That's just gross. Your steak is bleeding all over the plate!" God, Darla's voice is annoying me today. As she leans away I just want to stab her in the throat with the fork clutched tightly in my hand.

Where did that come from? Huh, I'm not usually violent. I must be hung over and crabby. I spend the rest of the meal in quiet contemplation. No one is really talking to me, probably giving me a wide berth because of my hangover and maybe the revelations from last night.

*Yeah, I remember that part. These skank bitches with Keith; I should rip their hair out then their eyes and…* Whoa! No! I love my friends. I would never hurt them. Why would I even think such a thing? I'm starting to freak myself out. Maybe

I should go sleep it off by myself.

We leave the diner and some of the girls want to shop and drink, I beg off to go back to the room and sleep. "I'll catch up to you all later. Have fun."

Back in the room I lie down and close my eyes, but every image just angers me. Keith kissing me. *Keith kissing Darla. His stupid, charming smile while we made wedding plans. Him telling me how much he loved me forever. His back as he walked out of the door. His face as he said he just wanted me to be happy...* I bolt straight up in the bed, panting, sweating, a burning sensation stuck in my throat like a scream trying to claw its way out.

I run to the bathroom, splashing water on my face, and snatch the Tums bottle and a glass of water. I take three Tums for the terrible heartburn and start drinking the water when I look up and see my reflection. The glass I held shatters as it drops from my hand to the sink. My eyes are not blue, but bleached out to silver, and bloodshot. I look like something from a horror movie. My hair is lighter too, not the usual auburn, it is a very light brown with streaks of gray? No, platinum. The streaks in my hair are practically white!

Oh my God! What to do? I start rummaging through my stuff. I don't even know what I'm looking for but I am frantic to find something, anything. I have to do something. Then I find my hat and large sunglasses. I hurry to cover my hair, slam the sunglasses on and run out of the door. I knew right where I was going. I practically ran down Bourbon Street to Marie Laveau's voodoo shop.

As I enter I look for Marie, but don't take off the glasses. It's dark in the room but I can see, though it seems everything is tinted a bit red.

"Can I help you" comes a deep, male voice from behind the counter.

"Ah, is Marie here today?" my voice is scratchy, barely above a whisper and there's a raging inferno in my throat.

"Ain't no Marie here." He shifts his footing and won't look at me as he wipes imaginary dust from the counter.

"Today or ever?" I demand. I am losing my patience quickly. I look at the clerk and think about ripping his throat out if I don't get the right answers soon.

"Don't yah go botherin' with him now. He's just bein' protective of me. C'mon back here an' let me get a look at yah." Marie steps from a backroom and hold the curtain open, motioning for me to come in.

"I have questions. What is happening to me? What have you done?" My questions tumble out as I take off my glasses and hat.

"I didn't do nothin', cherie. Queen Marie chose ta bless yah. Give yah the tools ta do what needs doin'."

"What? Blessed me? You mean cursed! Look at me! What is happening?" My voice rising from a rasp to a loud shriek. I want to hurt Marie. I want to scream. I want to scream—then I did. A blood-curling scream brings me to my knees, panting.

The man from the counter came running back, but Marie grabs him and motions for him to leave. He goes through another door across the room, shooting glances at me over his shoulder. I scare him. I scare me.

I look up at Marie from the floor as she speaks in a soft voice, slowly, like she is speaking to a child. "Yah becomin' a banshee, baby. By tonight yah be a full banshee."

"A what? What the hell are you talking about?" My rasping voice is back, but so is the burning ache in my throat.

*Banshee.* Of course I've heard of them in fairy tales from my grandmother. I'm Irish. What Irish kid hasn't heard of them? Fearful fairies, flying around screaming and foretelling violent death. I don't understand any of this or what this has to do with a Voodoo Queen or how this will help me.

"Look 'ere, cherie." Marie holds up a mirror. My hair is almost completely white now, with just a few streaks of brown. My skin is pale—almost translucent—and flawless. Silver eyes. My lips plumped and red. I look down at my hands and my skin is perfect—not a freckle anywhere—and my nails had grown out at least half an inch. I look up at Marie, confusion, fear, and anger warring within me.

"What is happening to me? What am I supposed to do?" I wail at Marie, barely able to get words past the burning in my throat. And something else weird—everything has an amber hue. It is like I am looking through filtered lenses, but I had taken my sunglasses off. I cover my face and began to sob. The sobbing became frantic and a bubble of sheer anger bursts somewhere inside me, consuming my whole being. I want to lash out and I don't care at whom or what. I fight myself for control...

"Yah come with me now an' I'll fix yah up best I can 'fore tonight." Marie beckons me to the back room where the man had disappeared earlier.

The room is small and sparse. There is a narrow bed with a wooden chest at the foot, a rocking chair, a dim floor lamp and table, and voodoo symbols covering the walls and ceiling. Trepidation causes me to pause crossing the threshold for a moment because the room seems like a cell.

Then I see chains in the corner. They are connected to a large metal ring set in what looks like a solid stone wall. I hesitate, but Marie gives me a push inside and tells me to sit on the bed. She rummages in the chest and pulls out a snowy white, filmy gown. It is so sheer I can practically see through it, and so incredibly soft. It weighs no more than air.

"Ya'll be wearin' this after yah rest for a bit, child. Lay down. I'll keep watch. Now lay down 'ere and I'll get yah something to drink." Marie reverently lays the gown next to me on the bed and leaves.

I sit for a moment not moving, my mind racing. *What do I do? How will I get answers?* But even in my confusion the fury is building inside of me. I do not understand that either. *Why am I so angry? All I want to do is hurt, destroy.* And the blaze in my throat is becoming unbearable. I am cold. So cold, like a bone-chilling freeze seeping into my every fiber. Shaking, I decide to get under the blanket.

Marie returns with the man from the counter close on her heels. He's holding a large, black goblet. Marie sits on the rocking chair while the man hesitantly approaches me. "Drink this, darlin', then sleep."

I seize the goblet and gulp down the contents. The drink is like syrup; sweet, thick, hot, coating my throat and calming the burn. I can speak again. "What the hell was that?" I practically scream as the man scampers from the room.

"Calm down now, baby. Feelin' better now?" Marie is practically purring and slowly rocking.

As the anger subsides I become weightless, and exhausted. My eyes can't stay open. My muscles won't respond as I sink into the oblivion of the mattress. I am helpless to do anything as Marie slips the blanket over me again as the room gets fuzzy. "My friends will wonder where I am. Maybe I should… should call or…" My consciousness fades; I am unable to move as I'm floating into darkness.

"Ain't nothin' more ta worry 'bout. Rest up now. There's a big night ahead." Marie is humming—or is it chanting—from the chair. I can no longer focus and my eyes would not stay open. All the fight fled me as I drift into oblivion.

◊ ◊ ◊ ◊

It is night. I sense it is night as I open my eyes in the little room. As I begin to focus everything still has that amber hue from before and yet is crystal clear. Blood pumps through my body, my muscles stretch with renewed strength, however the burning in my throat is back. I look down. Wait. I'm looking down on the bed! I look around. Marie is still in the rocking chair, smiling up at me, I want to rip the smile off of her face with my nails. I feel behind me and turn until my face presses against the ceiling.

*I have to be dreaming.*

"Exhale an' relax, cherie. Float on back down 'ere," Marie calls up to me.

I am too infuriated to relax. I blow hard on the ceiling and crash on the bed. "Dammit, woman, if you laugh I swear I'll rip your head off!" I hiss at Marie as she chuckles.

"No yah won't be hurtin' me, baby, or those chains over there come out. Now mind yah manners an' git yourself dressed." She picks up the dress and holds it out for me. I consider shredding it but she slowly shakes her head.

"Fine!" I snatch the gown from her.

"Won't be needin' any underthings wit' that dress, child."

*Whatever.* I rip off my clothes, strip down to nothing, but before I put on the dress I see myself. My skin is porcelain. Not a flaw anywhere. I look at my shin and the chicken pox scar is just gone. My entire body's smooth as silk, more like ceramic. I'm not cold either, or warm. I feel no temperature. I bring my hands into view. My fingers look more like claws, with long nails coming to sharp points. I rush putting the dress on, the distraction of my appearance forgotten as the unbearable volcanic heat in my throat draws all my attention. And an insistent raging pressure is growing inside of me, needing to lash out.

Marie turns me toward the mirror on the back of the door. That image cannot be me. This has to be some sort of trick. I give her an evil glare, but she points again to the mirror. The figure blinks when I do, reaches up to touch her stark, shiny white hair when I do. She opens her engorged red lips when I do, no sound coming out of either of us. Her bewildered, glowing, bloodshot silver eyes hold the same confusion, rage, and awe as mine. Her clawed hands run over the softness of the gown, caressing the perfectly formed, smooth body underneath the shear fabric, just as mine did. It is me, but not any form of me I could have imagined in my wildest dream.

I shriek, a horrible sound coming from the center of my being, erupting before I can stop it. It drains every ounce of strength I have and I fall back onto the bed, dazed. I hear Marie leave and come back a few minutes later with another goblet. I greedily reach for it, desperate for relief.

"There'll be no sleepin' this time." Marie titters as I drain the contents, as delicious as before and as the contents race through me, I gain better control of my emotions.

"Now, yah goin' go find da Voodoo Queen. She's got some chores for yah, honey." Marie steps out and motions for the counter man. "Take her to Da Queen, an' be quick."

I snap my head around to look at him. I see fear and lust in his eyes as he looks over me. He's mostly scared and that makes me smile. I don't know why, but I am pleased I can elicit fear from him just by glancing at him. Marie throws a dark cape with a hood over me, then I follow the man through another room and out of the back of the shop. We are in an alley and stay close to the walls. We don't say a word but I easily hear his heart beat pumping blood through his veins. He is truly scared of me. When we get to Basin Street he points between the buildings.

"You gonna float up there and over the street quick-like so no one sees you. Then you can float over the wall. Keep your cape on so you blend in with the sky." He whispers to me so rapidly I think I mishear him.

"You want me to fly? I don't fly. You must be crazy. How about if I rip your heart out instead then waltz over there and hand it to Marie Laveau?" I hiss at him, nearly blinded by my need to hurt him. My hands are shaking, in fact my whole body trembles with anticipation.

"No, please, Miss Katie. I'm on your side, just want to help you." He puts his hands up in front of him and pleads as he backs away.

I consider following him and tearing him apart but, suddenly I'm summoned to the cemetery. That same pull on my soul I had felt outside the voodoo shop is back times a million. I cannot ignore it, every muscle, every thought is compelled. I need to get to Marie Laveau. Nothing else matters but getting to her. I hold my breath and focus on the top of the building then I begin to rise. Weightless and in awe I reach the rooftop, I look across the street. I can see clearly even though it is dark. *How do I get across the huge street though? Up and down was one thing but over? I'm not freaking Superman.* The overwhelming fury rises in me again, tempered only by the need to get to the cemetery, to go to her. The pull is irresistible, urgent.

I decide to run and jump. I back up on the roof and

run as fast as I can, holding my breath and closing my eyes as I leap over the edge. The next thing I know I am soaring over the street so fast my brain has no time to process, and then land softly on the rooftop of the museum. Standing on the rooftop, I take a second to look back across the street. I had flown! My body just took over. As I floated down into the cemetery from the museum roof, I giggled with delight at the absolute freedom, like gravity doesn't apply to me. I am light and part of the air around me, only stronger. I only have to think about how I want to move and I am moving. I have no time to savor the joy of flying, after landing, the compulsion to make my way to Marie Laveau's tomb overwhelms me.

"Look at you, child! So beautiful! I knew you would be." Marie stands in front of her tomb with a wide smile on her face.

"You did this to me, you bitch! Undo it now before I rip you apart!" I screech at the top of my lungs, consumed with anger. I reach for the Voodoo Queen with my clawed hands when she raises her hand. My brain explodes in agonizing pain, like every blood vessel in my head has burst at once. I grab my head with both hands and wail, but there is no relief. I'm blind and my legs give out, dropping me to my knees before her.

"Control yourself now. You can't hurt me, and you've got things to do. I gave you what you wanted. Your spirit's not broken now. You're strong and beautiful and a force to be reckoned with." Marie lowers her hand and the pain subsides immediately as she continues to speak, my anger subdued for the moment as I rise from the ground.

"I don't understand any of this. They said I was a banshee?" My voice scratches past the burning in my throat.

"You are a banshee. I needed a new one and you are

perfect. You said you were willing to sacrifice. You summoned me from the left, not to ask a favor, but to volunteer." Marie waves her hand toward the left side of her tomb. "You will get your revenge on the one who wronged you and bring peace to other lovelorn souls who've been wronged. You feel it don't you?" She steps forward and cups my cheek tenderly before continuing. "The burning, the power, the anger at the injustice, and you want to make it right. You are a weapon against those who do wrong." Marie's voice is so compelling, so soothing. It all makes perfect sense. I'm in a trance, swaying as her voice flows over me. The raw power is bundled tightly inside of me, waiting for me to tap into it.

"What about my life? My friends?" I suddenly remembered who I was. How could I have forgotten? It must have been the transition time at the voodoo shop. I have been so focused on my change and the pull of Marie, I forgot who I was. Panic rose inside me, accompanied by the rage.

"Ah, well, there is always a sacrifice. Soon your old life won't matter. You have a higher purpose now and the sooner you start, the sooner you will forget the old and live for destiny." As she spoke her words, her voice soothed me like a balm on my heart. The panic fades, but the rage remains just under the surface.

"Do I have a choice?" I choke out a whisper, a slight bit of concern still on the edge of my consciousness.

"No, child, not anymore. It's time for you to serve now. You have to shrug off your mortal coil and petty life. Feel your power, let it flow through you. You know what you need to do first, don't you?" Marie smiles patiently as I concentrate

The burning in my throat is distracting, but the fury is boiling up in me. I embrace it, letting it flow through me, and one image comes to me: Keith. I want to destroy Keith. A blood-curling shriek flies out of my mouth before I can stop it.

"Yes my child, that's it. You see it, you feel it. This is what you are made for. Tell me, what will you do now?" Marie's questions came like a song, a chant as she sways back and forth with her arms spread wide, head back, eyes closed.

"I will find him and destroy him. He will pay…I…I feel him. I know where he is." The realization strikes me. I am awed. *How can I do this?* I am tuned in to him, completely focused.

"Go now. You'll know what to do. Come back to me when you finish." Marie's red eyes stare up at me. I am already floating above the tomb, cape discarded, glowing white against the night sky.

I concentrate on the rage flowing through me and the air flowing around me as I race through the night sky. Buildings fade to water, water becomes even bigger water. I cannot believe how fast I can move! Flying, I became one with the air able to move anyway I wish, yet drawn to my quarry.

I see the platform clearly in the night, even from such a far distance, and I smile wickedly. I see Keith leaning on a rail, smoking a cigarette while looking out over the water. I shriek, almost a hysterical laughing sound as I circle far off the platform. Keith drops his cigarette and looks around with a nervous jerk. I laugh to myself, feeling my power mix with my fury as I circle the platform, waiting for my opening. Anger pulsates within me, instinct leading me to what I need to do—what I want to do.

"Man, did you hear that?" Doug asks as he walks up to Keith. Both men look anxious.

"Yeah, Doug, probably some weird fish or something."

Keith shrugs and lights another cigarette, taking a long drag.

"I don't know, sounded like a screech owl to me." Doug answers, looking around nervously.

"What are you some kinda idiot? Look around. We're in the middle of the freakin' ocean. Owls can't fly out here, moron." Keith turns his back on Doug.

"Yeah okay Keith, whatever man. I'm goin' in." Doug turns and hurries off, obviously fearful, not waiting for a response from Keith.

"Good freakin' riddance," Keith mumbles.

"Always the charmer," I say, my voice a raspy whisper behind Keith.

He spins around and I watch as his eyes grow wide. I stand very still as his eyes graze over me from head to toe. I see the lust immediately burning in his greedy eyes. The sheer dress does nothing to hide my body and he obviously wants me because I can hear his heartbeat quicken slightly and his breath speed up. Then he blinks several times and shakes his head in disbelief.

"Katie? Is that you Katie? What happe...?" I am done hearing him speak, so I seize his throat. My nails drawing small trickles of blood.

I hear his heart pounding in fear this time, his lust forgotten as the terror seeps into his consciousness. His muscular arms and hands prove useless against my strength. I lift him off the ground with one hand as he struggles.

"Yes Keith, your Katie-girl. The woman you wanted to spend your life with, the one you loved more than your own life. I'm the new and improved version." I speak slowly as I run my hand over my new body. I know he can see right through the gown.

"Is this what you meant when you told me to 'move

on'?" I jeer at him then drop him to the walkway.

He tries to crawl away from me, one hand on his throat, the other grasping for anything to aid him. I let him struggle, flounder on the walkway, grabbing for the railing. I take a small step toward him, a vicious grin on my face. I lick the end of my finger where his blood is and smile at him. He becomes frantic to get away, his legs kicking in an almost blur trying to find footing and move from me at the same time.

He finally struggles upright holding tightly to the railing, but by then I have had enough of playing with him. The shriek that spews out of me came from the depth of my core. Keith covers his ears and falls to his knees. He tries to beg me to stop, but the words are simply soundless movements of his mouth. I shriek so long, like it will never end. Blood flows from Keith's eyes, nose, mouth, ears, it's like his blood is driven from his body. I stop shrieking and collapse to my knees in front of Keith, weakened from my efforts.

I take his head in my hands and look into his bloodied eyes. I lick the blood from his cheeks. It is sweet, warm, and soothes my throat. "Mmmm, you taste good." I rasp in his ear as I lick the blood from his jaw. His eyes widen with terror.

I smile a wicked smile at him then turn his head and bite into his neck, where my nails had drawn blood. I drink from his vein and the blood slides easily down my throat easing the inferno. I drain him until his heart stops beating, it is a spiritual moment for me, I'm dizzy and euphoric, but then I hear people running. I have to leave. I grab Keith's body as I rise up high above the platform. With my renewed strength he weighs nothing. I fly over the water and look down at Keith's lifeless body. "This was the only time I meant it when I said you tasted good." I laugh as I drop him in the Gulf. My laugh turns into a scream of triumph as I fly back to New Orleans. The same pull deep in my soul which brought me to Marie earlier that night now compels me to get back fast. My instincts tell me I am a creature of the night and I need to be out of the light. My skin crawls with anticipation of the light and I push myself faster to Marie and safety.

The sky is starting to lighten as I arrive back in St Louis Cemetery No 1. Marie Laveau came around the tomb to meet me, her red eyes glowing with excitement and pride.

"Child, you are wonderment! Look at you, better than I hoped for. You are a natural." She takes both of my hands in hers. "Now you go on back to the voodoo shop and rest. I'll send for you when it's time. You are going to be very busy soon." She embraced me.

My heart light, my soul free and complete, I now have a purpose. I turn to go, then whirl around and run over to the left side of Marie's tomb. I cut my palm with my nail then take the blood and circle the three X's I had drawn there earlier—the sign that my favor had been fulfilled. Shrieking, I float up into the thick New Orleans sky heading to the voodoo shop to await my next assignment.

# AUTHOR BIOGRAPHIES

## ALLIE MARINI BATTS

Allie Marini Batts holds degrees from Antioch University of Los Angeles & New College of Florida, meaning she can explain deconstructionism, but cannot perform simple math. Her work has been a finalist for Best of the Net & nominated for the Pushcart Prize. She is managing editor for the *NonBinary Review, Unbound Octavo*, & *Zoetic Press*, & has previously served on the masthead for *Lunch Ticket, Spry Literary Journal, The Weekenders Magazine, Mojave River Review & Press*, & *The Bookshelf Bombshells*. Allie is the author of *Unmade & Other Poems*, (Beautysleep Press, 2013) & *You Might Curse Before You Bless* (ELJ Publications, 2013). She has 5 collections forthcoming in 2015: *wingless, scorched & beautiful*, (Imaginary Friend Press), *Before Fire*, (ELJ Publications), *This Is How We End* (Bitterzoet), *Pictures From The Center Of The Universe* (Paper Nautilus, winner of the Vella Prize) & *Southern Cryptozoology: A Field Guide To Beasts Of The Southern Wild* (Hyacinth Girl Press.)

Allie rarely sleeps, and her mother has hypothesized that she is actually a robot fueled by Diet Coke & Sri Racha.

Find her on the web: facebook.com/AllieMariniBatts or @kiddeternity

## ALEXANDER S. BROWN

Alexander S. Brown is a Mississippi author who was published in 2008 with his first book Traumatized. Reviews for this short story collection were so favorable that it has been released as a special edition by Pro Se Press. Brown is currently one of the co-editors/coordinators with the *Southern Haunts Anthologies* published by Seventh Star Press. His horror novel *Syrenthia Falls* is represented by Dark Oak Press.

He is also the author of multiple young adult steampunk stories found in the *Dreams of Steam Anthologies*, *Capes and Clockwork Anthologies*, and the anthology *Clockwork Spells and Magical Bells*. His more extreme works can be found in the anthology *Luna's Children* published by Dark Oak Press.

Visit Smashwords.com, Amazon.com, and Barnesandnoble.com to download his monthly short stories known as Single Shots. These are represented by Pro Se Press and they are known as stories that will be featured in the upcoming book *The Night the Jack O'Lantern Went*.

## MARGARET L. COLTON

Margaret L. Colton is an avid history buff, especially in the areas of Medieval Europe, Ancient Greece and American History, she loves all things history. She has been imparting her historical knowledge on her students for the past 12 years, teaching not only historical subjects but psychology as well. She teaches in the same district she graduated from. Even though she has two Master's degrees in education, the writing community called to her.

Before beginning to write again after many years, she began editing and recently started ML Colton Editorial Services. Currently, she has a short story in *State of Horror: New Jersey, North Carolina, Louisiana* and others set to be published early next year. Besides dabbling with some short stories, she is the Editor-in-Chief at Charon Coin Press and has anthologies coming out early this year entitled *Paying the*

*Ferryman*, and *Carpe Noctem: Truly, Madly, Deeply.*

She has two beautiful daughters and a granddaughter who share her love of books and fun and some amazing friends around her. Even though she lives in Missouri and is a rabid Cardinals fan, she loves to travel to some of her favorite places like New Orleans, Florida and Hawaii.

Margaret L Colton can be reached at:

Facebook:

https://www.facebook.com/MLColtoneditservice

Email: MLColtoneditsvc@gmail.com

## SARAH GLENN

Sarah E. Glenn specializes in stories involving out-of-the-ordinary heroes and circumstances, usually with a sidecar of funny. She has a BS in journalism from the University of Kentucky, and has done graduate work in ancient languages, which helps her immensely with crossword puzzles. She belongs to the Short Mystery Fiction Society, the Historical Novel Society, and Sisters in Crime: the Speed City Indiana Chapter and the Guppies Chapter. She contributed *"New Age Old Story"* to *Fish Tales*, the first Guppy anthology.

Sarah developed strong ideals from her parents, a salesman turned missionary and a social worker. Due to their tutelage and that stint as a classical languages grad student, she's better read than her love of Kolchak, comic books, and fantasy role-playing games would suggest.

Sarah edited two different newsletters and was a first round judge in Futures Mysterious Anthology Magazine's 2003 "Slesar'sTwist Contest". More recently, she has been a judge for the 2011 and 2012 Derringers. She is now chief editor at *Mystery and Horror, LLC.*

# HENRY P. GRAVELLE

Henry P. Gravelle is the author of the *Doc Jacobi Western Adventures*, the *Buddy Sands Cases*, *The Bamboo Heart*, *Pug*, *The Fort Providence Watch*, *The Banshee*, *Apple Hill*, *Gunner's Rift*, *The Igloo Boys and Hobo* and two short story collections, *K9* and *Epitaph*.

He is also the screenwriter for several short films and a feature film to be produced in the near future.

Henry attended Northeastern University in Boston and currently resides along the south shore of Massachusetts.

www.henrygravelle.com

## AMANDA HARD

Amanda Hard is a former journalist and magazine editor who received her BFA in creative writing from the University of Evansville, in Evansville, Indiana. She is a member of the Horror Writers Association and her horror fiction has appeared in (or is forthcoming from) Ruthless Peoples Magazine, 22 More Quick Shivers from the Daily Nightmare, State of Horror: Louisiana, and State of Horror: Tennessee, both from Charon Coin Press. She lives with her husband and son in the cornfields of southern Indiana, where she practices necromancy and knits socks with deliberately placed holes.

## CHAD MCKEE

Chad McKee is a biologist who moonlights as a writer of fiction and poetry. His contributions can be found in the anthologies *Blood Rites*, *Best of House of Horror*, *Dark Visions*, and *D.O.A.: Extreme Horror Collection*, among others. He is an American Southerner who currently resides in Oxford,

England.

# ETHAN NAHTÉ

Ethan Nahté spent most of his youth writing fiction and performing music. He eventually received the National Quill & Scroll Award his senior year of high school. He took a break from fiction and performing, entering the fields of journalism and broadcast journalism where he slaved away for many years. The desire to write fiction struck him once more in 2004 when he wrote a story that won first place for the John L. Balderston award. He focused more on screenwriting after that, foregoing fiction once again for another five years, before returning and selling his first piece, a short story, to Yard Dog Press.

Since then Nahté has sold between one to two dozen stories, and even a poem or two, to various anthologies and e-zines. He still works in the journalism field, writing on a variety of subjects.

In addition to his short stories and screenplays, he is currently writing a novel and he has a new author site which is still in its early stages at http://www.NahteWords.com.

# ARMAND ROSAMILIA

Armand Rosamilia is a New Jersey boy currently living in sunny Florida, where he exacts revenge on his enemies and neighbors alike by writing them into his *Dying Days* zombie series. And not in good ways. He has over 120 releases to date, with more coming. He is also a radio and internet DJ and runs *Arm Cast: Dead Sexy Horror Podcast*, with interviews from the best authors, etc. in horror. He loves talking in third person. http://armandrosamilia.com

and armandrosamilia@gmail.com if you want to chat.

## JAY SEATE

No matter how Mr. Seate starts a story, it inevitably turns to the macabre. It may be told with hard core realism or erotic humor, but it gets his pulse racing enough to pull his corpse from the grave to write something new. He is especially keen on stories that transcend genre pigeonholing. His stories and memoirs appear in numerous magazines, newspapers, anthologies and webzines. Recent ones can be found at:
www.melange-books.com/authors/jtroyseate/jtroyseate.html
 and https://museituppublishing.com for those who like their tales intertwined with the paranormal. See it all at www.troyseateauthor.webs.com and on amazon.com. Blog: www.supernaturalsnackbar.wordpress.com.          Facebook author page: J. T. Seate. Jay Troy Seate on Twitter.

## TOMMY B. SMITH

Tommy B. Smith is a writer of dark fiction and the author of Poisonous and Pieces of Chaos. His work has appeared in numerous publications over the years to include Every Day Fiction, Night to Dawn, Black Petals, Blood Moon Rising, and a variety of other magazines and anthologies. He has previously worked with Morpheus Tales as editor of the magazine's Dark Sorcery and Urban Horror special issues. His presence infests Fort Smith, Arkansas, where he resides with his wife and cats. More information can be found on his website at http://www.tommybsmith.com.

## PAMELA TROY

Pamela Troy was born in New Orleans and grew up in southern and northern Louisiana. After graduating with an MFA from the University of North Carolina at Greensboro she moved to Pittsburgh, decided it was too cold, and moved on to the San Francisco Bay Area where she has lived for over twenty years. Her jobs have included bookseller, magazine production assistant, and telecom billing analyst. These days she works in the Events Department of the San Francisco Mechanics' Institute, the oldest library on the West Coast, and lives on Nob Hill with her husband and a large, angry orange cat. Her fiction has been published in *Space and Time*, *Crimson: an Online Horror Magazine*, *Night Terrors*, and TM Publishing's *Crimson Fog*.

## J. JAY WALLER

J. Jay Waller, his wife and dog (Izzy) live in Anchorage, Alaska. He enjoys writing fiction when he is not skiing, hiking, biking or enjoying the beautiful Alaska scenery. He also enjoys painting and working with digital photography. He has lived in North Carolina, Ohio, Panama, Louisiana, Arkansas, Texas, American Samoa, and Alaska. He has had short works previously published in *Alien Skin Magazine*, *Sideshow Fables*, *Butterfly Affect Anthology*, *Hungur Magazine*, *New Bedlam Project*, *Golden Visions Magazine*, *Rotting Tales*, *and Flash 713*. He is currently working on a suspense/horror novel that takes place in the Shreveport-Bossier City, Louisiana area.

## ABOUT THE EDITOR

Jerry Benns started writing when he was quite young. However, he began seriously writing in 2010 by launching his blog, TripThroughMyMind.com. Since then, he has expanded the site to include interviews with authors, book reviews, and sections to encourage building the writing community. Jerry's deep-seated enjoyment of reading and writing now has him embarking on the exciting journey of publishing by launching Charon Coin Press.

In 2014, after becoming the editor for the State of Horror anthology series, Jerry pursued the opportunity to purchase the series, and others, in order to release them under his new publishing company, Charon Coin Press. Jerry brings his experience from his previous marketing/branding company, as well 15 years of experience as a networker and project manager to Charon Coin Press.

Jerry continues to write short stories and his blog, in addition to working on an urban fantasy series. He also looks for ways to share the love of reading and books with the next generation.